TABLE OF CONTENTS

1	Death Warrants	1
2	Assassins at the Gate of Voxyri	13
3	Two Deputations Amuse Us	24
4	Rovard the Murvish, Sorcerer of Murcroinim	37
5	Justice	45
6	Yellow Sun, Silver Moon	52
7	Jilian	61
8	Kov Colun Mogper of Mursham	72
9	The Whip and the Claw	80
10	What Difference Does an Emperor Make?	85
11	Of Lahals After Battle	95
12	Jikaida over Vallia	104
13	A Bowman Topples a Blazing Brand	114
14	Lol Polisto ti Sygurd	124
15	I Postpone a Problem	143
16	The Carpeting of Ros the Claw	149
17	Disaster	162
18	We Gamble on Filbarrka's Zorcamen	169
19	Surprises in the Delphondian Campaign	179
20	The Battle of Kochwold	188
21	A Life for Vallia	207

List of Illustrations

"Entangled like wild beasts trapped in iron nets, the slaver choked." ii

"I felt the blast of psychic power." 35

"A mass of fleshy pseudopods writhed onto the trail." 128

"The beast hopped up out of the bog." 132

"I saw the bowmen swooping down and shooting into the ranks." 201

ON THE JIKAIDA CYCLE

A LIFE FOR KREGEN is the first volume of the Jikaida Cycle chronicling the history of Dray Prescot on the fascinating world of Kregen four hundred light years from Earth. Reared in the inhumanly harsh conditions of Nelson's Navy, he has been transported through the agencies of the Star Lords, the Everoinye, and the Savanti nal Aphrasöe to the terrible yet beautiful world of Kregen under Antares, where he has struggled through disaster and success to make a home.

He is a man above middle height, with brown hair and level brown eyes, brooding and dominating, with enormously broad shoulders and superbly powerful physique. There is about him an abrasive honesty and an indomitable courage. He moves like a savage hunting cat, quiet and deadly. He has acquired a number of titles and estates but now the people of the island empire of Vallia, which has been ripped into shreds by ambitious and mercenary invaders, have called on him to lead them to freedom as their emperor. Reluctant to accept the imperium, he shoulders the burden because, rightly or wrongly, he sees this as the lesser evil.

Dray Prescot is undeniably an enigmatic figure; but on the ferocious and lovely world of Kregen he has found headlong adventure, brilliant life and a deep and lasting love. Whatever lies in store for him—and we are fortunate that I have a fresh supply of the precious cassettes on which he records his narrative—life will continue to be a challenge under the streaming mingled lights of the Suns of Scorpio.

—*Alan Burt Akers*

"Entangled like a wild beast trapped in iron nets, the slaver choked."

A LIFE FOR KREGEN

by
Dray Prescot

as told to
ALAN BURT AKERS

*Illustrated by
Richard Hescox*

DAW BOOKS, INC.
DONALD A. WOLLHEIM, PUBLISHER

1301 Avenue of the Americas
New York, N.Y.   10019

Copyright ©, 1979, by Dray Prescot.

All Rights Reserved.

Cover art by Richard Hescox.

FIRST PRINTING, APRIL 1979

1 2 3 4 5 6 7 8 9

PRINTED IN U.S.A.

A LIFE FOR KREGEN

matter must be discussed."

It was not true, but it sounded genuine enough—and would be accepted as normal conduct.

Sir Norgoth shook his head.

"Ah no, You may be a king, as all men believe; but I know you would take this matter into your own hands."

Chapter One

Death Warrants

Signing death warrants is no decent occupation for a man. Yet there was no question in my mind that I, Dray Prescot, Lord of Strombor and Krozair of Zy, should delegate the wretched task.

The day had dawned bright and clear with the promise of a breeze to mellow the heat, and the drifting linking lights of the Suns of Scorpio bathed the early world through the windows in pastel tints of apple green and palest rose. By Zair! but this was a time to be alive. I breathed deeply and sat myself down at the balass desk and pulled the official forms nearer and forced myself to the job.

Nath Nazabhan, stony-faced, looked on. The small room was furnished with books and maps, chairs and the desk, and not much else. It was a room that suited me. But I had to sit there and scrawl Dray Prescot, Emperor of Vallia, in the abbreviated Kregish script, a mere DPEV, at the foot of each warrant, at the foot of what was a tree and a dangling rope and smashed neckbones. The reality sickened me.

"Thirteen this morning, majister."

"Aye, Nath. Thirteen miserable wights to be shuffled off."

"You have pity for them?"

"Perhaps. I can't afford pity for myself."

"Vallia would have been finished without you. As it is we've a task on our hands to tax my mythical namesake." Nath took up the first warrant as I pushed it across, signed. "The factions continue to squabble and the country is drenched in blood. The enemies of Vallia seem to grow stronger every day, by Vox, even though we hold the capital. Vondium is—"

"Vondium will stand!"

I looked up and I know my face held that leem-look of

1

primeval savagery that so displeases me and puts the frights up those unfortunate enough to be loo'ard. Nath fingered his chin and fell silent.

He wore a square-necked tunic of a soft pastel tint, girdled by a thin belt from which swung one of the long thin daggers of Vallia. He wore normal morning dress, as did I, and the spread fingers of his right hand groped for the hilt of an absent sword. My gaze shifted to the arms rack. No one on Kregen, that marvelous and mystical world of terror and beauty, strays far from a quick snatch at a weapon. It is not healthy.

"Yes, majister." Nath might be a fine limber young fighting man, commanding the Phalanx; he was a terror for strict discipline properly administered and maintained. Yet he could temper justice with mercy, as I well knew, understanding the ways of command. We had fought together to free Vallia from the enemies who had swarmed in to feast on a bleeding corpse, and his loyalty and devotion were unquestioned. The pen scratched as I signed, and then poised, the black ink glittering like an ebon diamond.

"Renko the Murais?" The name leaped out at me, written in that perfect script of Enevon Ob-Eye, my chief stylor. "I know a Renko the Murais. A tearaway, yes, very quick with an ax." I looked at the charge. "But not, I would have thought, the man to slay a Relt stylor."

"The charge was proved, majister."

Very stiff and formal, on a sudden, Nath Nazabhan.

"You are satisfied? Renko said nothing in his defense?"

"The case was tried by Tyr Jando ti Faleravensmot. A hard man, yes; but just."

I nodded. "You did not attend?"

"No, majister. The Second Jodhri was receiving new colors at the time, and I—"

"Yes. We were there together. The management of a city and what we have of an empire, quite apart from the army, takes up too much time." I shuffled the warrant aside. "Have in this Renko the Murais. I'll see him before I sign."

"It may not be the same man."

"Exactly my thought. But I must be sure."

"Quidang, majister!"

The papers lay on my desk and the tiny breeze whiffled in through the open casement and lifted the corners. I pondered. There just was not enough time. But—twelve men and the thirteenth might go free, if there had been a miscarriage of justice and Renko the Murais was the Renko I'd known in Valka. He'd been a Freedom Fighter then, when we'd cleared the island of Valka out and the people had fetched me to be their lord. Time would have to be found. I stared at Nath.

"Have Enevon send me in all the papers on these cases. Delay the executions," I said. "I would like to satisfy myself. . . ."

Without going on, I could see that Nath both fully understood why I did what I did, and despaired of me as an emperor who would have a fellow's head off in a trice.

The blurred shouts as orders were cracked out and repeated and the clink-clank of weapons drifted up from the court below where the guards worked at the drills that might keep them alive in battle. The flick-flick plant on the windowsill twined its long green tendrils hungrily, its orange cone-shaped flowers gaping emptily. Later on a dish of fat flies would have to be brought in to keep the flick-flick happy and lush.

"All the same, majister," said Nath, stroking his chin. "When you fight for your rights men must die. It is a law of nature. Death comes to us all—sooner or later—and—"

I smiled. I smiled at Nath Nazabhan and let the smile linger for a full heart-beat before my face resumed its usual craggy mask. I pushed the papers aside and picked up a fresh batch, details of weapons, stores, conditions of wagons. The paperwork was never-ending.

"You quote proverbs at me, Nath. Well, and so it may be true. But the state of the country demands we push out from Vondium and consolidate the midlands and the northeast. I do not know what rights there may be in this."

"You have been fetched to be Emperor of Vallia."

At my instinctive gesture of displeasure, he went doggedly on.

"Everyone shouts for you and they know why they shout. If we are to re-conquer Vallia—"

I glared up at him, sternly, and this time he paused. Then, without embarrassment, he said: "Yes, majister, I know your words. It is more liberation than conquest. But the facts remain and they cannot be altered. If our country is to find any peace at all we must unite ourselves under one flag. And that means the new flag of Vallia you have shown us."

"You have heard me speak of the Wizard of Loh called

Phu-Si-Yantong? Yes, well, he is a damned great villain filled with a maniacal desire to subdue and control and hold in his hand all the lands of Paz. It is an insane dream. But, in Vallia, where he has caused us so much trouble—what is the difference? Why should I take the throne and crown and not Yantong?"

Nath's gasp halted me. His face screwed up into the most ferocious scowl, like a chavonth about to charge.

"Because we've seen how the rast treats those he enslaves! By Vox, majister, as soon consign us all to Cottmer's Caverns as let that cramph Yantong rule us."

"So we consolidate what we have and then bring war and bloodshed and misery to the rest of the country—"

He shook his head, angry at the way I was treating him, for which I couldn't blame him. The truth was, and I think he saw a little of it, that I carried the blood-guilt badly.

"We can move with safety in the Imperial provinces surrounding Vondium. The northeast and all the Hawkwa country stands firm for Jak the Drang, Dray Prescot, as emperor. The midlands will rise for us. The northwest—we must deal with the arch-traitor Layco Jhansi and after that teach the Racters a lesson. They fight each other, for which Opaz be praised."

"The Blue Mountains," I said, mildly, "and the Black Mountains are nearer than Jhansi's province of Vennar."

He shook his head. "Only if we strike more westerly of north. And, majister, do not forget the Ochre Limits bar off Vennar and Falinur."

My glance favored the map hung on the wall. The colors mocked me. The mountain chains and rivers, the canals and forests, the badlands and the lush agricultural heartlands, all demanded attention. Movement of armies bedevils those who would bring overwhelming force to bear on their enemies.

"That is so, Nath. But the Blue Mountains—"

"The Empress, may Opaz shine the light of his countenance upon her, commands the hearts of all, and none more than those ruffians, the Blue Mountain Boys. I think whoever tried to subdue the Blue Mountains has rued the day."

Again, I smiled. Well, Delia and her Blue Mountain Boys are enough to make any old sweat perspire a trifle.

"I had thought we would use the Great River and hit the northwest by curving in from the east." My pointing finger described an arc in the air, extending those phantom lines of march on the map. "As we came in from the south. I had in mind a man to command that army."

He knew exactly what I meant. And, the stubborn old graint, ignored that with sublime self-confidence.

"Any man would be proud to be appointed Kapt and command any army you entrusted into his hands. And there are many men in the army worthy of the task." He looked at me, his eyebrows drawn down, almost challenging me. "As for me, majister, I command the Phalanx with your blessings and where you march there I march."

I grumped at this. "And have I not explained to you, Kyr Nath, that the Phalanx is not best suited to mountain work?"

"Layco Jhansi, who deserves to be shortened by a head, does not foment his insurrections in a mountainous country. The land up there is ideal for my Phalanx."

"And after you've seen off Jhansi, you'll go haring for those damned racters north of him? Yes, well, they all deserve to be made to see the error of their ways."

The papers before me now detailed the condition of the canal narrow boats I had ordered collected. From the famous canals of Vallia the vener were trudging in, hauling their boats, answering the call. The basins and pools of the capital were filling with the brilliantly painted boats. I needed a fleet, and the canalfolk, always proud and independent and disdainfully removed from the petty party politics of the island empire, had decided that for the sake of peace and prosperity and the movement of trade their star must be linked with the new emperor in Vondium. I was happy about that. I had good friends among the canalfolk. And they would be invaluable in the coming struggles.

The future loomed dark and ominous—as so often it does on Kregen, by Zair—and everyone who would stand with us and strike a blow for freedom, in the cant phrase, was welcome.

I say "in the cant phrase." But for the colossal task facing us more than cant would be needed. If we were to cleanse all Vallia, and the island was frighteningly large with many areas still virtually unpopulated, we must seek to make allies of all whom we could and only in the last resort take up arms against them. This was a view not highly regarded, I knew. But the new Dray Prescot saw the wisdom of it, even if my other persona, that wild leem Jak the Drang, was toughly contemptuous of shilly-shallying.

As though Jak the Drang flared up in me I pushed the papers away pettishly and stood up.

"By Vox! I need some fresh air."

Crossing to the arms rack I took down a solid leather belt with a fine rapier and main gauche already scabbarded, the lockets of plain bronze. The weapons were workmanlike, nothing fancy, with silver-wire wound hilts. A matched pair, they were balanced to perfection. Belting the gear on I half-turned to speak to Nath and saw a shadow move against the map. No shadow could be thrown there by the light from the window.

Nath leaped back and the slender dagger appeared in his fist. His face looked stricken.

"Daggers are useless here, Nath," I said, on a breath, quickly. "I think."

The shadow writhed and thickened and flowed, smoked coiling into the semblance of a man, a hunched man in a black cowl, the hood drawn forward so that only the deep furnace-glow of feral eyes showed, demoniac, peering.

Nath shuddered, a deep hollow revulsion of flesh. The dagger shook.

The thought flamed into my mind: "Thank Zair I had not marked the map with my intentions!"

The projected image of the sorcerer wavered, as though his powers fought to coalesce his immaterial substance within the imperial palace. The whole structure had been sealed by my own Wizard of Loh, Khe-Hi-Bjanching, against such lupul projections; but that had been some time ago. The sealings must be weakening with the passage of time. And Bjanching, along with my other old friends, had been hurled back to his home by the mightier sorcerous powers of Vanti, the guardian of the Sacred Pool of Baptism in far Aphrasöe.

We needed sorcerous help here. But Nath Nazabhan after that first stricken reaction responded as a warrior responds. A streak of light hurtled across the room. The dagger glittered as it flew from his hand. Straight through that insubstantial image it whisked, to clang and chime against the map, gouging out a chunk of Falinur, and so drop harmlessly to the floor.

"Devil's work!" burst out Nath, moving back, going for the arms rack, his fist already raking out for a fresh weapon.

"That will do no good." I stood quietly, feeling the blood in my veins, wondering what Phu-Si-Yantong intended now.

For, quite clearly, this lupul projection was Yantong. An evil emanation, certainly; and a dangerous one. He spied on us and he didn't give a single block of ice from Sicce if we knew or not.

The ruby eyes within the enveloping hood would strike a cold chill into the stoutest heart. Narrowly I surveyed this sorcerous apparition of a hated enemy. A cripple—that was the part Yantong had played during the only time I had met him. And it had not been face to face. Always, he kept himself hidden, shrouded. Perhaps he was in very truth a cripple. Maybe that might explain his crippled ambitions. The shadowy form moved of and within itself, as smoke coils upwards. The colors of the map showed through the image, fragmentarily, their brilliance dimmed.

As always and with everyone I attempt to see the best side. Always, the remembrance of the frog and the scorpion is with me, that a man no less than a scorpion must act to his nature. But, also, I do not forget that a man can judge the consequences, and although he might not fully comprehend all that will follow, must by the very nature of manhood understand that his actions will inevitably be followed by results. Yantong could not, I thought, be all evil. There had to be some streak of better feeling in him. So I looked at the hunched shadowed shape and I pondered.

Nath remained transfixed by the arms rack, held there, I fancied, no less by my words than by the apparition.

For six heartbeats Phu-Si-Yantong's lupul projection hovered in the room. I know, for I counted.

The spell broke as a trumpet pealed outside, high clarion notes against the blue. The outlines of the figure shimmered as though bathed in invisible heat. The hooded head turned. The glitter from those ruby eyes dimmed, sparking feebly, paled. As the form vanished the last of it to disappear was that pair of demoniac eyes.

I let out a breath.

Nath wiped the back of his hand across his forehead.

For a space neither of us spoke. We did not care to break the spiderweb of silence that fell after those silver trumpet notes.

Then I said, "By Vox! May Opaz rot the fellow. At least, he got nothing out of us."

A fraction unsteadily, Nath walked across to retrieve his dagger. He gestured with the blade.

"Falinur will never be the same."

I warmed to him. The experience through which he had just been would have left many a man gibbering.

"Seg wouldn't know whether to be glad or sorry."

"As to Seg Segutorio, the Kov of Falinur," said Nath, resheathing the dagger with a snick. "I know he was a blade comrade of yours; but he is peskily absent from his kovnate when we need all the friends we can muster."

It was not a rebuke. Merely a hard-headed comment.

I chose to say, with a little snap, "Seg is a blade comrade, not was."

Nath half lifted his chin; but he chose not to reply.

"Now, Nath, not a word of this to a living soul."

"Quidang, majister."

"Good. Yantong spies on us with an advantage. We must cloak our designs in shadow, sheath our plans in subterfuge. We hew to the plans I have mentioned—unless unforseen circumstances force us to alter them. If they do, we will."

The clepsydra on its own shelf told me that the hour was almost up and we were due on Voxyri Drinnik. A small ceremony was to be held there to mark the presentation of medals, bobs the swods in the ranks called them, like phalerae, and the importance of keeping the army happy outweighed much. The matter of Renko the Murais had been dealt with in court by one of the judges appointed to the task. It might be thought that presenting new colors to a Jodhri could not rank as importantly in a humanitarian scheme of government as being present in a court of justice. But a man has only so much time on Earth, or Kregen. No matter that because I had dipped in the Sacred Pool of Baptism I was assured of a thousand years of life, each day still contained only forty-eight burs. So we had been presenting standards when Renko had been sentenced. Now we must present bobs when we had promised. The apparition of Yantong must be pushed into its proper perspective.

And, anyway, what was there I could do about the Wizard of Loh? He worked through human tools. His minions sought to enslave the country. In our turn we must resist them.

Anything else was fantasy.

The days were filled with hard work. There was everything to do. The country was still in turmoil and no one talked of the Time of Troubles being over merely because Vondium was in our hands. Vondium, the proud city, was mostly ruins, with the grandiose rebuilding schemes of Yantong halted in mid-execution because I would not flog on the people to work as slaves, and, also, because they insisted on flocking to join the colors and form fresh regiments to help clear out the rest of the island.

Walking out into the mingled streaming suns shine of Antares, I hoisted up the rapier to sit more comfortably. The chances of assassins, stikitches, still being active and seeking my life, in the pay of any number of cramphs who would as lief snuff me out as they would snuff a last candle, remained high. A man must be ready always on Kregen to fight for his life, just as he is ready to sing or to drink, to eat or to laugh.

Many of my new comrades waited. Nath Nazabhan was a relatively new comrade, also, for we had been together since we had trained up the Phalanx in Therminsax ready for that great battle. My choice band waited for me. A right rough and tumble crowd, festooned with weapons, brilliant in a motley of uniforms, they greeted me with a roar. I bellowed back, most affably, banishing the dark schemes of Yantong from my mind. Together we rode for Voxyri Drinnik where the great victory had been gained that gave over Vondium to our hands.

The last of the Hamalese prisoners were being sent off back to their homes in Hamal. This had aroused great controversy and acrimony, men saying why did we not keep the rasts as slaves. I would not execute them, for I knew the Hamalians, knew their army, knew the swods in the ranks. I would not kill or enslave, and so they were sent home to Hamal. We still had a debt outstanding with the Empress Thyllis of Hamal, the despotic ruler of the greatest empire in the southern continent of Havilfar. Yantong had used her to further his own schemes; but Vallia had been invaded by Hamalese, there was the matter of the defective airboats, and, also, there was the island of Pandahem to be liberated.

Every way I turned there was work to my hand.

And, always, the greater menace of the Star Lords hovered over me. At a whim they could despatch me back to Earth, hurl me four hundred light years through the deeps of space, send me back to the planet of my birth and, perhaps, forget me and let me rot.

Fresh concepts about the Star Lords, the Everoinye, had

been plaguing me. I had begun to wonder if their designs were so baffling, after all, for certain events seemed to me to bear of only one interpretation. I will leave the reasoning by which I reached this surprising conclusion until later, contenting myself with the simple remark that, if there was good in every man, might there not be a greater good in the Everoinye, who were so much greater than men?

"Lahal, Majister!" bellowed Cleitar. He had once been Cleitar the Smith, and he bore his wicked war-hammer into action. But now he was generally called Cleitar the Standard, for he carried my own battle flag, that yellow cross on a scarlet field fighting men call Old Superb. He rode a zorca and his uniform was splendid.

I raised my hand in salute as we rode out. Vondium was a shadow of the great city it once had been. The other spirits in my choice band were mostly, at this time, from the provinces, for we had recruited there in our drive to the capital; but they were aware of the despoliation. We would rebuild; but our aim was to rebuild the heart of the country through the people and the agriculture and husbandry. Bricks and stones and mortar must follow that.

Volodu the Lungs, a leathery man if ever there was one whose appetite for ale could never, it seemed, be quenched, blew a stentorian blast on his immense trumpet. And that silver instrument was immense. With it Volodu had crushed in the head of a too froward Hamalese Hikdar, smashing through helmet and bone to the very brains beneath. The blast echoed through the streets and cleared a way for us as though we were a pompous procession of robed priests.

There was no need for lictors or any other street-clearing violence as the Emperor of Vallia rode out.

The ceremony passed off well, brilliant and dashing in the glitter of the Suns. I will not go into detail, save to say the old sweats took their medals with a swagger, and no doubt, like Vikatu the Dodger, would trade shamelessly on their prowess to dodge the column for a few sennights to come. And good luck to them. They had risked their lives and limbs in the battle line.

Like any good Kregen who tells the time of day by the state of his innards, I felt the time was ripe for a meal and so we wended our way back to the palace. I had barely crossed the first of the twin canals straddled by the Bridge of Voxyri with the confused onward shrilling of that great fight ringing in echoing remembrance in my head, and Naghan ti Lodkwara was as usual engaged in a slanging match with Targon the Tapster, when the shadows fleeted in.

A lancer, Naghan Cwonin, reined across. Dorgo the Clis shouted. Cleitar the Standard began to furl up the flag. Naghan ti Lodkwara and Targon the Tapster took mutual breaths and, instead of slanging each other, yelled the alarm.

The airboats floated down as though guided by rails.

There were six of them, and each one was of a capacity to hold a dozen fighting men.

So—we were in for a fight.

The devils had chosen their place well. The troops back on the Drinnik would never be over the Bridge in time to assist us. The streets were filled here with ordinary folk about their business trying to put Vondium back together again. Phu-Si-Yantong's spying mission must have told him what he wanted to know, and this was a direct result.

Shades of Rafik Avandil, Lion-man!

I ripped out the clanxer scabbarded to my zorca. He was a fine black, mettlesome, whom I called Snowy out of stupid humor as much as contrariness, and I'd ridden him because he needed the outing. The stables were not too well provided as yet, and discretion had to be used. But the men tumbling out of the airboats almost before they touched down were afoot, and so we, mounted on zorcas, were by that much better off.

Two fliers landed in our rear, cutting off a flight back the way we had come.

Cleitar had the flag furled and stowed away now, and his hammer glittered as he lifted it.

Nath Nazabhan drew his clanxer and called across to me, "Ride, majister—there is an alley mouth there—"

I looked at him.

"Well," he said, huffily, swirling the straight cut and thrust sword about, loosening up his muscles. "It was just an idea."

We numbered about twenty or so, bright rollicking companions of my choice band. We faced about four times our own numbers. Well. Yes, a situation in which I had found myself more than once, and usually through my own blockheadedness. I lifted in the stirrups. I'd gone out for a breath of fresh air. I was like, and my companions also, to taste blood as well as air. And the air we tasted might well be let in through our ribs.

"Straight through them!" I bellowed. "Slap bang and no tickles. No man stands for handstrokes. Ride like the agate-winged jutmen of Hodan-Set!"

We clapped in our heels and in a rampaging bunch roared into the forming ranks of our Chulik foemen.

Chapter Two

Assassins at the Gate of Voxyri

Oh, yes, they were Chuliks all right. Ferocious, yellow-skinned fighting men with ugly three-inch long tusks jutting cruelly up from the corners of their mouths. This bunch was as well-trained in the martial arts as any Chulik mercenary band on Kregen. Reared from their earliest infancy to the bearing of arms, trained to be cold and merciless killers, Chuliks can handle any variety of weaponry they need, and in that heartless and iron-hard discipline they had forgotten if ever they had known the softer virtues of humanity.

They are loyal mercenaries if they are paid and fed. They command higher fees than most, excepting Pachaks and Khibils and a few other, not many, of the vast variety of splendid humans on Kregen. They have always been and continue to be formidable opponents.

But my choice band recked nothing of that. Yelling and cursing they clapped in their heels and went racketing down.

The Chuliks with their oily yellow skins and long dangling pigtails from their shaven heads formed a line swiftly. Their faces remained blank and impassive. They knew exactly what they were doing and they did it well.

Their uniforms were simple tunics of brown cloth over which they wore armor of a scaled form, bronze-studded, highly barbaric and flaunting their power. Their helmets bore black and green feathers, but shorn short, workmanlike, a badge of identity clamping each tuft in place. Black and green. Well, they were colors I knew Yantong had used at least once, and so by their use now he seemed to be openly proclaiming his power and contempt for me.

Truth to tell, in that hectic moment as we belted along, I wondered if we would have done better for Cleitar to let Old Superb float free, a ringing challenge to the power confronting us. But that way lay the hubris, the megalomania, the self-importance I detest so much. I had sworn, as I was called to be Emperor of Vallia, that I would do a good sound workmanlike job. Pride is for the vainglorious, in excess, and its unbounded license has caused great sorrow in two worlds.

And then we were among them and Cleitar's hammer lifted dripping crimson, and so that answered that question.

At my back Korero the Shield bore a single targe, a small parade ornament, but with its yellow and scarlet traceries he fended a sweeping blow and lashed back with the blade gripped in his tail hand. Ferocious, Korero the Shield, a Kildoi whose four arms and handed tail both protect and devastate.

With a jolt and a crack we overbore the first line.

Chuliks sagged back—and when a Chulik sags he is either dead or dying.

The zorcas responded nobly as only those superb four-spindly-legged steeds can, all fire and spirit. Never meant for the charge, they flowed on and over in a fleetness of rhythm that bore us on and up. Like hunters at chase we cleared the first line and slammed into the second. But the Chuliks were ready, well-knowing the business of trackling a zorca-charge. Their weapons glittered. We sliced and drew our blades reeking in crimson as we leaped ahead. But the fray thickened and grew denser and Largo the Astorka was down, a spear through his throat. We yelled and swirled our blades and pressed on. But our progress slackened. The impetus of the charge dwindled.

The noise bellowed up, echoing in rolling confusion under the Gate of Voxyri. Volodu put three distinct dents into his massive silver trumpet, and each time burst out with genuine anguish at that desecration. But three Chuliks dropped as though the trumpet had been a poleaxe.

The third line of yellow-tuskers swayed, and men went down. But they held us. The zorcas drew back, pirouetting from a hedge of steel. Furiously I bellowed it out.

"Reform! Break out over the Bridge!"

We swung the zorcas about, their nimble hooves clicking on the cobbles where blood ran between the time-worn stones. The Chuliks back there were unlimbering crossbows, and this made me frown.

"Heads down!" I yelled and clapped in my heels and

Snowy surged on, picking up speed, elegantly avoiding tumbled bodies.

The bolts would have had us but for the Gate. The trajectory intersected the masonry and the bolts chinked and tumbled like chicks disturbed in the nest. In the next mur we were out in the sunshine again and bearing down on the men from the two guarding fliers. It was all nip and tuck. Korero surged ahead, despite my yell, and his little yellow and red shield whipped up.

I urged Snowy to greater efforts. In a bunch we crashed out and the Chuliks rose to meet us.

Naghan Cwonin's lance tip was a clotted red mass. He lowered that steel wedge of death and then he was hurled back off his saddle, trailing blood, yelling, a stux clear through him. The Chulik who had hurled that spear did not hurl another, for a streaking dagger crossed the narrowing space and chinked in most neatly over the brass-coiled rim of his corselet.

That Chulik bore a golden image of a grascent on his breast suspended by golden chains around his neck. The dagger protruded above the golden image of the risslaca for a heart beat, and then the Chulik walked forward, as a dead man walks, blindly, walked forward three paces, four, and almost a fifth before he tumbled under the hooves of the zorcas.

The weapons flamed. The Suns beat down. The dust lifted. And the blood spurted.

The pandemonium was, for a brief moment, akin to the last dying scenes in a sinking ship where the crew panic. Blades clashed. Korero's shield split asunder and he used the half in his hand to dash a Chulik away. But another leaped for him, his yellow tusks dripping, and my clanxer only just swept down in time in a precision-controlled arc that kissed death across a corded neck.

"My thanks, majister—"

"There's another devil, Korero—"

"Your back, Nath!"

"On, on!"

The shouts racketed as we forced our way on. And then we were through. Before us stretched the Bridge of Voxyri, and the open plain with the distant lines of men coming on swiftly. We could have ridden on. We might simply have nudged the zorcas to a further effort and ridden away.

But, as one man—as one man—we turned.

We turned back, raging, and tore once again into those murderous Chuliks and their yellow tusks and their ferocious military skills.

The mellow stone of the Bridge and the Gate, the coolness of blue shadows and the piercing brilliance of the suns light, the clatter of hooves, a distinctive, brittle, rousing sound, the pants of men in combat and the yells of the wounded, the stink of rawly spilled blood—yes, yes, it struck responsive chords in me. But until we were done with scenes of this ugliness Vallia would never be the peaceful country we all intended her to be.

Well—Nath Nazabhan and a few others might question that assumption—but it was what I intended.

The Chuliks saw their attack had failed. They had killed or wounded a number of us, and they had lost more men than they liked. With that quick appraisal of the situation that had earned them as much contempt—in this case misguided contempt—in the past as praise, they took their airboats aloft. The fliers lifted off, swiftly rising and turning to head toward the north.

North.

That made a kind of sense, although they might have been expected to head for the southwest, where no one seemed to know what was happening. Equally, they might have gone southeast, for the situation there was confused. The truth was they might have headed anywhere in Vallia, for we were ringed.

And, even so, this northward flight might be a mere subterfuge.

We were plagued by the lack of airboats. All the vollers had been confiscated by the victors, and we, late into the fray, had to make do with what sorry remnants we could scrape up. As for aerial patrols, they were carried out by a skeleton force that had no chance to halt any determined aerial attack.

Before the troops from the Drinnik reached us we were off our mounts and tending our wounded.

Those who had already started on their last journey to the Ice Floes of Sicce were Naghan Cwonin, Largo the Astorka, Nath the Flute, Aidan Narfolar ti Therduim, Roban Vander and Nath the Mak, sometimes known as Nath the Waso.

We had another five with wounds, great or small, from

which only one, Larghos Shinuim the Fortroi subsequently joined his comrades among the ice floes.

So we were cut down by a half.

Nath's face bore a grave look that I saw was compounded as much of worry as of grief and anger.

I attempted to rouse him.

"You, it was, Nath, who told me that all men must die in their time. Praise Opaz for those who survived."

"Wounded or slain," he said. "A half of us. Some will rally, of course. But it is not good enough."

I was not sure what he meant; but in the nature of the circumstances as the first of the men from the Drinnik reached us, I forebore to inquire. Had I done so I know now he would have given me no answer, or would have evaded the issue. What was planted in his mind then was subsequently made plain. And, I may add, to my own personal pleasure and profound gratitude to my comrades.

Looking up from the sprawled body of Nath the Flute, Dorgo the Clis contorted his scarred face into a grimace of anger. He was cut up by Nath's death, seeing they had been friends from boyhood, and however much of death a man sees in his life, the passing of a friend carries a heavier weight.

"Here they come," growled Dorgo, "making a right hullabaloo and late, too damned late, by Aduim's Belly."

"They ran as fast as they could, Dorgo," said Magin, who philosophically bound up a spear wound in his arm. His son, who had been unable to find the excitement he craved in his native Vallia and had gone to be a paktun, would have found all the nerve-tinglers he wanted now, in Vallia. And we could do with all those brave sprightly young men who had left sea-faring, trading Vallia to be mercenary swods overseas.

The men from the Drinnik came up, puffing a little, for they had run fast, as Magin said. They were Hakkodin, axe and halberd men who flanked the regimented files of the Phalanx, and they were raging that they were too late.

At their head came Barty Vessler, his shining, red, smooth, polished face a scarlet glow. No overemphasis can possibly convey the gorgeous color of Barty's face in these moments. He was infectiously impetuous as usual, and spluttering with mingled joy and rage.

"Jak," he bellowed. "Dray, I mean, majister! You might have been killed. Oh, my aching ribs. Oh for a zorca!"

Everyone laughed. There was no stopping that unleashing of pent-up emotion.

Gravely, I regarded him; gravely, for I was the only one not to laugh. Mean, tight-lipped, yes, if you will. But I looked with great favor on this young man, Barty Vessler, for all his incautious ways and feckless moments. And I knew well enough that if he'd had his zorca between his knees he'd have come bolting in from the rear upon the Chuliks and, for almost a certainty, got himself chopped for his chivalric notions.

His brown Vallian hair flopped wildly as he gesticulated. Young and filled with notions of honor, Barty Vessler, the Strom of Calimbrev, yet a fellow who saw the way that honor led him and unflinchingly followed it even if it led through Cottmer's Caverns.

Bells started up a-ringing and citizens came flocking down. The uproar was worse than the fight. I glanced at Nath and Barty and jerked my head. Volodu picked up the little sign and immediately slapped that silver trumpet to his lips.

Volodu the Lungs blew the Clear.

Well, the citizens wouldn't know the calls blown by the Phalanx, of course. But the silver notes cleared a way and having sorted out both the quick and the dead, and seen to the wounded, we trotted our zorcas on into the city. Barty took a spare mount and came with us, for he was of that choice band, without a single doubt.

Barty rode with Nath, and scraps of their conversation reached me. Barty was saying: ". . . quite agree with you, Nath. It just is not good enough."

And Nath, gravely, answering: "Time something positive was done about it, and done quick, by Vox."

They were up to some deviltry, I fancied, and left them to it. I needed a drink of tea, and that was doing something positive, and the quicker the sooner. So we trotted through ruined Vondium the Proud, and the people gave us a cheer as we passed, and so we crossed the wide kyro before the imperial palace, and passed through the gates where the guards slapped their three-grained staffs across, most smartly, and we let the hostlers take the zorcas in an inner court where purple flowers hung down in a scented profusion. The zorcas had done well, and we patted them affectionately as they were led off.

"Let us meet in the Sapphire Reception Room," I called to

them as they prepared to trudge off to their quarters. "That is informal enough and yet formal for what we must decide."

I met their puzzled looks with a benign disregard that made them all the more curious.

Barty and Nath exchanged quick, puzzled looks.

But I shouldered off and into the inner apartments of the palace, looking for a rapid bath to wash off the muck and blood, and then for the tea and a repast that would keep the leems of hunger at bay for a bur or so. It was still too early for wine.

The Sapphire Reception Room and most of the wing which housed that informal chamber for semi-formal gatherings had been spared the fire that had gutted a very great deal of the old palace. Yantong had rebuilt much; but the place sagged as though tired, towers and spires toppled inwards and walls slaked along the entrenchments, so that the skyline that had once lifted so arrogantly now looked like a haphazard collection of tooth-stumped jaws. The imperial palace of Vondium looked rather like a tent with the central pole chopped down. Some essential work still went on so as to house conveniently the people involved in the type of government I intended—if that is not too strong a word for the still bumbling ideas I entertained on running the country—and carpenters and masons and brickies gave a pleasing air of busy activity. No one was slave. The reverberations of that stringent policy to which, despite all opposition, I clung, had made, was making, and would continue to make life unpleasant in silly and petty ways as much as large and ponderable fashions.

A party brought in the uniforms and equipment of the dead Chuliks. They had taken their wounded with them. As I say, Chuliks are fighting men.

Giving instructions for the lot to be dumped in the Sapphire Reception Room and for tea in immense quantities to be prepared I carried on into the small suite we had managed to make habitable. The rooms were not large; but they possessed walls and ceilings, and the water still ran, pumped up by windmills hastily erected on the roof. If you looked out of the north window you saw the charred stump of the old Wersting Tower where they used to keep kennelled those fearsome hunting animals. Already green growing shoots clambered across the blackened crevices and specks of brilliant color lightened with blooms the sere gauntness of the wrack.

Delia was not to be found in the outer rooms, and her handmaidens told me she was in the bedroom. Like me, Delia kept only a very few personal servants, and if I do not mention them overmuch it is because they were so good that they had become a part of our life. Floria and Rosala tended Delia, and they were girls formed for the delight of the gods, smiling, bright of eye, brilliant of lip, with natures that decked the world in sunshine. No obstacle would be placed in their path when, as is the way of the world, they would wish to marry the young men of their choice. The same openness applied to Emder, a quiet-spoken, gentle, dextrous and extraordinarily competent man who looked after most of my material wants. If you wish to call him a valet, the description matches perhaps half of his duties. He was a treasure and I valued him as a friend.

"Bedroom?" I said. Then, already stripping off the bloodstained clothing: "The empress is not ill?"

"Oh, no, majis," they chorused, and laughed.

Only in the most deeply felt personal relations could the diminutive majis be substituted for majister. Nath Nazabhan would not allow himself the usage, although the offer had been made.

"Well, then, you pretty shishis—out with it!"

Emder, smiling, gathering the clothing, slinging my crusted clanxer harness over his shoulder, said, "The empress has never been better, praise Opaz. The bath is drawn—"

One of my own rules is that because so many times I have presented myself to Delia in a shocking state, hairy, filthy, bleeding, almost done-for, whenever it is possible for me to bathe and change and look at least halfway respectable I will do so. I took the bath first before discovering what the laughter and the little mystery was all about.

Feeling refreshed and still toweling my hair I went through to the bedroom. A pang struck me as no familiar and horrific form arose to check on everyone daring to enter the room where Delia, the Empress of Vallia, took her ease. Melow the Supple, that horrendous and sweet-natured Manhound, had been sorcerously sent back to her native Faol and my eldest son Drak was off there now, trying to find her, and with her her son Kardo. By Krun! A few Manhounds in our ranks would do wonders for the discomfiture of those who opposed us.

Inside the doorway with my bare feet sinking into Walfarg

weave rugs the towel dangled over into my face. I could see nothing and gave the towel a swipe out of the way as I walked on. When the yellow toweling whisked away I stood gaping more than a trifle foolishly at Delia.

She looked like a twisted bundle tied up ready for the laundry.

Instinctively, for this was Kregen, I leaped forward and even half-naked straight from the bath a dagger dangled at my side. This I drew.

Delia laughed.

"You silly old fossil. Just stand still and let me get out of this slowly and properly."

"By Zair—"

"Wait."

I waited.

She sat on the rug with her right leg bent over her left, the left foot tucked in and pointed and her left arm stretched down her right foot from knee to ankle. Her upper body twisted right around from the waist, although she sat firmly on the floor, until I thought she could look back over her own shoulders. Her right arm was bent behind her back. And that rounded right knee was jammed tightly up under her left armpit. She looked—well, she looked marvelous, of course, all tied up like that of her own volition—but the power and serenity flowing from her took my breath away.

Carefully, moving with a grace that caught at my throat, she unwound herself.

At last she lay back, her arms at her side, and for all anyone would know she might be laid out ready for her last journey to the Kregen equivalent of the Valley of the Kings.

Then, with a smile, a small, cheeky smile, she sat up and said, "I'm ravenous!"

"There is tea in the Sapphire Reception Room. Shouldn't you wear a leotard for that kind of thing?"

"In my own bedroom? With only a grizzly old graint of a husband to blunder in?"

"Well, you run perilous risks—"

"Not now—I don't. I am for tea and miscile and palines—"

"What was that?"

She told me the Kregish for the Spinal Twist, the equivalent to the Sanskrit Ardha-matsyendrasana.

"That's all a part of the Disciplines of the Sisters of the

Rose? We have similar although far less seductive exercises in the Krozairs."

"Hardly exercises, Dray. A way of tuning in with Opaz, I think; a way of getting through material worlds to what really matters beyond them."

"I know."

Shaking my head at the marvel of Delia I saw about getting dressed. A simple tunic sufficed me, and Delia wore a soft laypom-colored tunic girded with a narrow belt fashioned from interlinked silver flowers. We both swung daggers from the belts. She looked gorgeous. The dress in its magical way set off the glory of her face and those brown eyes that could be so melting or so imperious, and added a special luster to the chestnut tints in her brown hair. Fit, she looked, radiant. As they say on Kregen, she had the yrium for an empress.

We went together through the hastily refurbished corridors and past blackened and windowless openings in the walls to the Sapphire Reception Room. My people were already there, changed and foaming for the meal. They waited for us, as was decent; but we were not late. We might have been, had Delia not been of so determined a nature.

In the absence of any properly organized palace retinue and court dignitaries, the rump made do as best they could. A major-domo—old Garfon the Staff—hobbled up to me, for he had taken an arrow in his heel and it was slow to heal, and banged the balass, golden-banded staff down on the flags by the door. I stopped his yell at once. If the people in there didn't yet know me, then, by Vox, I was in the wrong business. And, yet, they could know only the outward me, the Dray Prescot who banged and barged about and thumped skulls and got things done. They could know nothing of the Dray Prescot who for long hours agonized over what to do for the best, and hoped he could do it, and trembled in doubt.

"A strange happenstance, majister," Old Garfon the Staff boomed. He was a mite put out, as all major-domos are, that he hadn't got around to bellowing out titles. "Two embassies await audience and crave your indulgence."

"Spit it out, Garfon, for my mouth is like the Ochre Limits."

"They await audience in the Second Enrobing Chamber—that was spared except for the northeast corner of the roof—and, well, majister, it is indeed passing strange."

Delia put her hand on my arm. So I just said, "Well?"

"One embassy is from the Racters."

"Those cramphs. Well, they deal legally, or, at least, most of the time. Go on."

"The other is from Layco Jhansi."

A gasp broke from my people who listened.

My brows drew down.

"A deputation from the most powerful political party in Vallia—or, at least, the party that was the most powerful. And a deputation from the old emperor's chief pallan, who betrayed him and tried to assassinate him. This is, good Garfon, exceedingly interesting."

"It does not take a wizard to divine what they want," said Delia.

Barty Vessler bubbled over, half-laughing, half-enraged at what he saw as the effrontery of it.

"Each is prepared to offer you an alliance, majister. That is the gist of it. One against the other, I'll warrant."

"Aye," I said. "Each offers alliance, for they are at each other's throats up there in the northwest."

Delia laughed, a pure tinkle of sound.

I nodded.

"And, seeing they are like savage leems, one with the other, you have put both deputations, Garfon the Staff, both of them together in the same chamber."

Chapter Three

Two Deputations Amuse Us

The aftermath of that damned vision of the Wizard of Loh, Phu-Si-Yantong, clung unpleasantly. I would not forget what he had attempted against me during the Battle of Voxyri when he had sent me a personal and hideous vision of Delia betrayed by the arch-seducer, Quergey the Murgey. That plot had failed and in nerving me to take a fateful decision had brought Vondium into our hands. That was the battle in which the Phalanx had finally decided it could go up against any kind of army and win, without doubt, against my stern admonishments.

So my anger was still fizzing and undirected, for Yantong could be anywhere in Paz, manipulating his puppets at a distance. I could, for the moment, do nothing against him.

So it behooved me to contain and control anger against the masters of these two deputations. They deserved anger—and the people of Vallia opposed to them would call it righteous anger—but I tried to look into the future. Alliances must be formed, in order to bring to a rapid close the agony that ripped Vallia apart.

Garfon the Staff went scurrying off to separate the two deputations. He went with Barty's raucous comment that he might find the Second Enrobing Chamber a sea of blood if he did not hurry.

One or two voices raised at that, commenting that the event might be a Good Thing, that it would rid the world of a few more rasts.

"Palines," said Delia, with firm practicality, offering me the dish heaped with the succulent yellow berries.

Scooping a handful I cocked an eye at Nath Nazabhan, as, cup in hand, he sauntered across. "Neither of them, majister, for my money."

I chewed. "If we do not have to fight one or t'other, that will free half of our hands."

Korero laughed.

"Mayhap. But an alliance with a traitor or a bunch of political chauvinists is not to my liking." Nath was serious.

"Nor mine, by Vox!" said Barty.

"If you were drowning and an unpleasant villain saw fit to stretch out a hand to save you, would you refuse?"

"That's different!" And: "That's not fair!"

"Nevertheless, we are like to drown under the weight of the military and aerial force the Hamalese and the insurrectionists can bring against us. We hold Vondium, parts of the midlands, and the northeast. The northwest, at the least, is held by Vallians. All the rest—"

"Quite! All the rest is enslaved by this bastard Wizard of Loh, or his minions, or by damned revolutionaries!" Barty was most wroth. His face shone like that famous polished red apple set out at the forefront of the grocer's stall. His brown Vallian eyes popped. He would have gone on, but Delia said, "Barty." He shut his mouth as a trout shuts on a fly.

"I repeat. At the least, these are Vallians."

Now I said this with some malice. I had sojourned long in Hamal, and knew its ways and people passing well. I had good friends there—admittedly, friends who did not know I was at the time Prince Majister of Vallia. Hamal as the hated enemy had wronged Vallia, that was generally acknowledged. But the Empress Thyllis must answer for much of those crimes. Once this mess was sorted out we must march in friendship with Hamal. Common sanity indicated that. So by stressing the very Vallianness of the compact offered, I sought to open their eyes. Once they agreed, then I could spring the snapper. . . .

Old Archolax the Bones, spare, wiry, dressed somberly in dark gray with a golden and scarron chain about him, spoke up. His face bore deep lines from nose to mouth, and his air of gravitas was heightened by the emphasis of his diction. He had been newly appointed Pallan of the Treasury—for Lykon Crimahan was still away fighting for his estates of Forli and the money situation needed immediate attention—and he took his position seriously.

"If they offer an alliance through their embassies, majister, they are in need of assistance, one against the other. It would be well to seek to know to what degree and amount they are willing to pay for such an alliance. Opaz knows, the treasury is bone dry."

"A shrewd thought, Archolax."

"Anyway," said Barty, a little mollified and once again able to meet Delia's eye. "Let them wait a while." He handed me a plate heaped with sandwiches and with a cup perched on the side. We habitually stood to talk and eat during these sessions, although comfortable seats, brought from all over the ruins of the palace, were available.

I started to eat, and, wolfing down a bamber sandwich, said, "I'll keep 'em waiting just as long as protocol demands."

In the event I gulped down the rest of the meal and wiped my hands on a yellow cloth and went away to the Second Enrobing Chamber, determined to let chance arrange which embassy I saw first. Garfon the Staff had left that from the Racters there, and had shown that from Layco Jhansi to the Samphron Hall's anteroom. The Samphron Hall no longer existed, being a mere maze of foundations, and the anteroom still persisted in smelling of smoke.

The party from the Racters numbered four, and they were led by a man I knew, Strom Luthien.

His thin shrewd face with the bright sharp eyes and the permanently hungry expression did not betray his thoughts as I entered. Guards stood at the door. I wore a rapier, picked up from Emder on the way. We regarded each other for a space.

Finally, with an ironical bow, he said: "Majister." With a sweep of his hand he indicated his companions and named them. Each one wore the black and white favors of the Racters, flaunting those colors here in Vondium from whence all the known Racters had fled.

Luthien was a Strom—that is roughly equivalent to an Earthly count—by title alone, for he no longer owned lands. He was the perfect agent for the Racters, and knew it and acted the part well. His insolence was veiled just enough so that no offense might be taken—at least, not by me, who was not an emperor in the mold of emperors of the past.

The offer was as we had expected. Alliance between our two forces first against Layco Jhansi, and then against the Hamalese and the mercenaries and all the other vermin who had flooded into Vallia to pillage. He made no mention of the embassy from Jhansi. I forebore to bring up what was clearly a prickly subject. I kept a graven and serious look on my face—not a difficult task, by Krun!—and heard him out.

The clothes these four Racters wore were the usual decent Vallian buff coats and breeches. Their wide Vallian hats with the black and white feathers lay on a side table. They bore no arms. My guards would have seen to that, and relieved them of their rapiers and main gauches long before they were conducted here. I studied the clothes and discreet insignia. Nothing out of the way there.

Memory of the golden image of the grascent, that leaping scaled risslaca with the powerful hind legs and wedge-shaped head of destruction, worn by the Chulik who had attempted to slay us under the Gate of Voxyri, made me wonder if Phu-Si-Yantong had infiltrated the ranks of the Racters. It was most unlikely that he had not. But he would scarcely parade that kind of hidden exercise of power openly.

When that particular Wizard of Loh struck he struck from the shadows.

Well, of course, they all do. But Yantong's menace held a special brand of cunning and absolute conviction of superiority. I still fancied I could find something in him of admiration to ordinary folk; but I had to acknowledge that it would be damned hard to unearth.

"What answer shall we carry back, majister?"

I let them hang a space before I replied.

"I must ponder on this," I said, at last, keeping a straight face. "It is not a light matter."

"It touches the well-being of all Vallia."

"That is sooth. Tell me, from whom do you come?"

"We represent the Racters."

"That I know. But who sent you? Who is still alive who commands your allegiance among the black and whites?"

"Those whom you met in Natyzha Famphreon's garden, and others. We are a strong and virile party, and—"

"Spare me the boasting. Layco Jhansi will no doubt say the same of his powers."

"That cramph!" burst out Strom Luthien. His narrow face betrayed all the bile in him. "He should be strung up by the heels and left to rot."

"Tell me, Strom Luthien. What does Natyzha Famphreon say to the new emperor? Or did she not give you a private message?"

Luthien allowed his thin dark moustache to lift at one corner. "Aye, she did. I give it to you under the code of heraldry."

I nodded. "Speak."

"When a leem leads a ponsho flock, the chavonths gather. But it is the Werstings who take the flesh."

I did not laugh. The brazen old hussy! At least, she recognized that I was in sober truth comparable to a leem, a powerful and elemental force of destruction imprisoned in human guise and apostrophized as a leem, an eight-legged hunting beast of superabundant energy and incredible ferocity. She knew I was not the fake, the pseudo Hyr-Jikai, the publicity-created Prince of Power without a shred of Jikai about him that so many people in Vallia and other parts still believed me to be.

And, as you will readily perceive, that did not verge on megalomania, on overweening pride, or on puffed-up vanity. No, by Krun! It was all those horrendous things rolled into one and spread out, like a mirror of truth, for me to stare at my own dark reflection and recoil from—if I still had the morality.

But, I sensed dimly that I must distinguish between the sins of evil self-importance and a too-crazed ego-mania, and a sober understanding that to do the things I had set my hand to would demand, must demand, a man prepared to accept the darker destinies of humanity as well as the lighter.

These thoughts were not pleasant, and Strom Luthien moved back a pace, his hand falling to the empty scabbard. He no doubt thought my displeasure had been occasioned by the words of Natysha he had relayed. Well, he was wrong. But I did not disillusion him.

"Those are the words of San Blarnoi, I believe." I said in that old nutmeg-grating voice. "Very well. Whatever I may decide about this offer of an alliance, there remains this. You may carry back to your masters this word: 'A man pleads with his wife to do something and she refuses on the ground he is giving her orders.'" I glared hotly at the Racters. "You may tell all the Racters that the new emperor in Vondium is the emperor. There is no other. All their puppets have tangled strings. And there are regiments of fighting men with shears to untangle them—finally."

Strom Luthien knew me of old. I do not think he had heard me talk like this before. He had not witnessed the gradual emergence of Jak the Drang.

And, I admit, and with perhaps not enough shame, that I welcomed the chance to let the Racters know the true position.

Luthien swallowed down and got out a few words.

"We will carry your message—majister."

There was no sarcasm in that last word.

I nodded and left them. Before I could face the embassy from Layco Jhansi—and he deserved to swing high, as my men said—I went along to our private rooms. Delia was not there, for which I was thankful. I bathed my face and then found a cup of water and drank that, and spat, and so pulling my tunic straight, marched off for the anteroom to the Samphron Hall.

This Layco Jhansi.... His province was Vennar, immediately to the east of the Black Mountains, a land that gave him an ample income, being lush and fertile in areas which afforded good husbandry and barren in others, where mining brought silver and alkwoin and other valuable minerals to swell his coffers. His colors were Ochre and Silver. He had been the old emperor's chief pallan, his strong right hand, and he had betrayed that trust. He had set Ashti Melekhi to poison the emperor and when that plot had been foiled had seized his chance in the Time of Troubles and struck for the power himself. He had taken over Falinur. He was, without a doubt, still a most powerful foeman. I wondered whom he had sent to talk business with me.

The ashy taste of smoke still clung about the anteroom as I nodded to the guards at the doors and went in.

Jhansi had sent five people to attempt to persuade me to ally with him.

I knew only one, Ralton Dwa-Erentor, the second son of a minor noble, who might style himself Tyr because his father's rank and his own title did not come directly from the hands of the emperor. Had the emperor bestowed the title, Dwa-Erentor would have been Kyr Ralton. I nodded to him, as politeness dictated, for he had proved himself a keen racing man, riding sleeths, a dinosaur-like saddle animal I do not much care for, and I fancied he hewed to Jhansi's party because of his father.

The leader of the deputation rose from the chair to greet me. He rose slowly. I allowed this. I would be patient, understanding, and I would not lose my temper. So I, Dray Prescot, decided.

Ha!

This ambassador introduced himself as Malervo Norgoth, a man whose immediately striking feature was the thinness of his legs and the bulk of his body, which overlapped him on all sides like a loosely-tied haywain. His face bore traces of makeup. I eyed him as he spoke; but he piped up with a bold front, confident that what he had to say was of the utmost importance. Well, it was to him and his master, no doubt.

He wore hard-wearing traveling clothes of buff and gray, and, like his companions, his weapons had been removed. He was a Tarek—a rank of the minor nobility—no doubt created by Kov Layco Jhansi. He was a man whose own importance expanded or receded with the company he kept. And, it was perfectly plain from his bumptious manner, he regarded me as a fake-emperor and someone in whose company he might expand wonderfully.

As he made me the expected offer, I sudied his companions. They seemed to me a bizarre lot. One of them, a very tall Rapa whose vulturine head was adorned with green and yellow feathers, and whose clothes hinted at armor beneath, grasped a long steel chain of polished links. The collar was empty, a round of bronze-studded steel. I wondered what manner of feral beast normally occupied that hoop of metal. The ring appeared large enough for a chavonth; probably it was a wersting, half-tamed and savage given half a chance. I doubted it would be a strigicaw.

The fourth personage was a woman, and, to be frank, she was one of the ugliest women I have ever seen. I felt quite sorry for her, for her personal appearance was clean and decent, good clothes, freshly cleansed face, tidy hair and impeccable fingernails. But the cast of her features resembled so much the stern-end of a swordship that I fancied she bore a deep-seated wounded pride under her harsh exterior.

And the last of this deputation—the first, given their respective powers—stood looking at me from under wild tangled brows. His eyes were Vallian brown. But his face was the face of an ascetic, marked by lines of self-inflicted punishment, grooved with masochistic fervor. He wore a hitched-up robe of skins, pelts out. His head was crowned by a rawly yellow skull, the skull of a leem, as I judged, and ornaments and bangles dangled and clanked as he moved. His left hand grasped a morntarch, the crook garnished with brilliants and the shaft embellished with wrapped skins and the legs of small animals and a couple of rast skulls. The smell wafting from this sorcerer, Rovard the Murvish, assured him a wide berth, and the woman kept herself at the far end of the line from him. I wrinkled up my nostrils at his stink; but I gave no sign of the affront I felt he gave me, here in the imperial palace of Vondium. By Vox! I'd been flung down here before the throne in a much worse condition and stinking far higher. He shook the clattering morntarch, softly, as though to remind me of his powers.

Yet, despite those vaunted powers—and how real they were I did not fully know—which he shared as an initiate in the Brotherhood of the Sorcerers of Murcroinim, he wore a gaudy gold and emerald belt from which swung empty scabbards.

Malervo Norgoth, the ambassador, was winding up the preliminary terms of his offer.

Listening, I tried to understand why Jhansi would have sent these particular people and what they could bring to the deputation. Jhansi was a rogue, well enough, and had proved it; but he was shrewd. He liked to work through other people and, as in the case of Ashti Melekhi, when they failed him he would unhesitatingly destroy them.

"Falinur," I interrupted. "How stands Falinur in this?"

Norgoth smirked, very supercilious. "The Falinurese stand with Kov Layco."

That seemed likely. The two provinces marched, the east of Vennar and the west of Falinur sharing a common boundary. The Falinurese had detested their new kov, my staunch comrade, Seg Segutorio, because for one reason he had tried to stamp out slavery. The people of Falinur would have been happy to throw in their lot with Jhansi. Well, that plot had failed and the attempt to seize power by force in the descent on the capital had gone awry when Phu-Si-Yantong's puppets had appeared on the scene. But the current situation was new and I had to learn what I could. So we talked for a space and then I told them I would consider the matter, as I had told the embassy from the Racters.

Norgoth shook his head.

"That is not good enough! We must carry an answer back today—within the bur, for you have kept us waiting long enough as it is."

I stared at him.

He stood his ground, whereat I was pleased, for that meant

I was keeping my temper and my face must appear bland and indifferent.

"There are people—nobles and pallans—with whom the matter must be discussed."

This was not true; but it sounded genuine enough and would be accepted as normal conduct.

Again Norgoth shook his head.

"Not so. You may be a nithing, as all men believe; but I do know you would take this matter into your own hands."

"Believe it. And reck that when I say I will think on this and tell you my answer, that is what I mean."

The woman opened her mouth to speak, and Ralton Dwa-Erentor, that canny sleeth racer, butted in swiftly. He clearly wished to pacify the rising passions here.

"Surely, Tarek Malervo—two burs will not make all that difference?"

Ralton glanced at me as he spoke, so that I understood his genuine desire to help. But his words were wholly wrong.

"Two burs!" shouted Norgoth. "Two burs! We must have the answer, here and now."

And, of course, Ralton Dwa-Erentor should have seen that I, had I been your ordinary run of emperors, would never have stood still for any kind of time limit. Two burs or instantly. But he tried to help, and that forgave him much. A fleeting thought of Thelda, Seg's wife, the lady kovneva, crossed my mind. She was always trying to help and making a mess of things. She'd been sorcerously flung back to her home in Evir, far in the north of Vallia, and what had happened to her since then Opaz alone knew. I fancied that Seg had gone looking for her. That would explain his absence even though he had been sent off to his home in Erthyrdrin at the northern tip of Loh.

By Zair! What I wouldn't give to have Seg and Inch and Balass and Turko and Oby and all the others with me, here and now, ready to face the perils that lay ahead!

And my family, scattered every which way, each one busy about his or her pursuits—I would really have to talk seriously to Delia and see about rounding them up. Although that would not be the way I'd phrase it, by Vox.

So I looked at Norgoth, this Tarek Malervo Norgoth, and I felt the old blood thumping and I gripped my fists together into the small of my back and ground my jaws down, tightly, so as to keep the proceedings on a halfway decent level of civilized transaction. But it was hard, by Zair, it was hard.

At last I unclenched those old rat-traps of mine and managed to say in a quiet voice: "Here and now, Norgoth? Then you must expect the answer to be no, surely?"

"Aye! That we do expect. I have said so all along."

"But I have not!" burst out Ralton Dwa-Erentor. His young face looked sullen, determined, as though he had built up a charge and now it was coming spilling out. The sullenness was very close to mutiny. "We must stand with honest Vallians against the Racters and the bastards from Hamal and their Opaz-forsaken cramphs of mercenaries."

They tell me that friends and friendship are becoming dirty words in this wonderful new civilization we are building here on Earth. That may be, and may be for the worse. But as I stood watching Ralton as he spoke so vehemently, I felt that in other circumstances we could have been friends. The determination in him to say out what he believed in, against the feelings of the ambassador, warmed me.

I bent my brows on Malervo Norgoth.

"Why does Layco Jhansi choose you to lead the deputation, if you seek only rejection as an answer?"

Ralton fired up at this; but the woman turned her battleship-old-head and he simmered down. But he glowered most handsomely.

"We knew the Racters were sending. That, alone, seemed good enough reason." The contempt in Norgoth stung.

Everyone spied on everyone else. Of course. That was just another of the pretty little ways of life an honest old sea dog had to understand. And, in all this, just how much was the devil's work of Phu-Si-Yantong?

"I still see no value in this mission from Jhansi."

"Will you or will you not stand with us against the Racters?"

"I have said, I will ponder this and give you my answer presently."

A rattle from the sorcerer drew my attention away from Norgoth.

A blank and horrifying whiteness shrouded his eyes so they looked like corpse-eyes, glaring sightlessly upon me. Foam speckled his lips and dripped in white-tinged green streamers upon the unkempt beard. He trembled. He shook as a tree shakes in the tempest. The hard bean-rattle of his morntarch clicked and clattered like the claws of rats. His right arm lifted and extended horizontally. The clenched fist uncurled and the long brown fingernails, rimmed in grime, spread and the forefinger pointed at my breast.

His panting filled the anteroom with opaque beats of sound.

"Now you will see why!" shouted Norgoth. His thin legs carried that gross body sideways, away from the sorcerer, and his face betrayed a glee made manifest in his delight at my coming destruction.

I felt the blast of psychic power.

I felt it. Like a wall of rushing air as one puts one's head over the shield in a flier. Like the blow from an axe against the brim of the helmet. Like the nuzzling embrace of a graint as that great beast seeks to crush ribs and pelvis and skull. All of these sensations flared in the scything attack. I staggered. I took a step backwards.

Norgoth yelled again, urging his sorcerer, this Rovard the Murvish, to greater effort, demanding that he render me incapable and in his power.

So they did not wish to kill me. They had deeper designs. Their object was to place me in hypnosis, a saturated psychic state in which I would obey every command they chose to give me, in which I would be their puppet.

Well, I have been the puppet of the Star Lords, aye, and of the Savanti, too. I have been used by Wizards of Loh in ways that are passing strange, and have fought. And I have been the recipient of favors from Zena Iztar, that superhuman woman who from time to time had appeared to me, exhorting me to courage and to perseverance, and who had enabled the genuine formation of a devoted Order of Brothers, the Kroveres of Iztar. She it was who had extended some measure of protection over me, spreading her aegis. And even the Star Lords had descended from their aloof mistiness to afford me a defense against Phu-Si-Yantong. So I staggered back and then recovered and glared at the sorcerer with a malice that rose fiery and lurid from the depths of my spirit.

Well, poor fool, Dray Prescot. Instantly Rovard the Murvish spun his magical apparatus into wilder swings and sweeps and the reek of him puffed loathsomely into the anteroom. But I stood there, defying him. Poor fool indeed!

For, of course, I should have appeared to succumb. I should have pretended to fall under the hypnotic sway. In a

A Life for Kregen 35

"I felt the blast of phychic power."

deceit like that I could have carried off easily enough, I fancy, lay the way to learn much.

But I did not. I do not think it was pride, pride that showed itself in my unsought ability to withstand his sorcery. For I have little truck with pride. Rather, it was a sheerly warrior's reaction, an instinct to fight back when attacked.

So, for a space, we stood there, locked in psychic combat.

And then—by Zair!—and then the horrifying numbness began to eat at my brain and the anteroom spun dizzily about me and I staggered, brought low as a tree is brought low when floods eat away its roots.

Chapter Four

Rovard the Murvish, Sorcerer of Murcroinim

The stink of smoke clinging in the anteroom mingled with the stench from Rovard. My head felt unscrewed, ready to lift off as a voller lifts off, and spin away and up into the vasty reaches beyond the stars. I had traveled between the stars, carried along by the Star Lords, and the queasy sensation in my guts acted as an unpleasant tonic to afford me an antidote to that drifting, rising, floating sensation of helplessness.

If the Star Lords who held such potent sway over my affairs on Kregen had given me protection, if Zena Iztar to whom I looked for help had spun a dazzling net of defense for me, I needed that help now.

One of the troubles with me, I often feel, is that I am not flesh, fowl or good red herring. I hover and drift between roles and if, as friends have assured me, that is a part of strength, it's a peculiar form of strength when compared with the single-mindedness of those who know exactly what they want and go hell for leather for it and devil take anyone who gets in their way.

Probably that feeling, dredged from the hidden themes fundamental to my nature, is why I take such joy in adopting disguises and assuming different names. My story so far will make much clear; I do know that when Rovard sought to dominate me and thrust his will power down over mine as a man cloaks a beast before he slits its throat, he aroused such a storm of rejection that I have the nasty feeling that even if the Star Lords and Zena Iztar had not pressed the sign of their protection upon me I might have resisted him.

And—I had sworn to myself not to lose my temper.

I staggered and almost fell. The waves of psychic power

beat upon me as the Tides of Kregen beat upon the rocks of the sea shores. I staggered; but I did not fall.

I glared back. My hand did not grope toward the rapier hilt. I made no physical move save to plant my feet firmly on the rugs. I battled. I used that same will power I had sought to use against the Star Lords and so prevent them from hurling me back to Earth. I struggled. It was done.

Do not ask me how it was done.

I was standing up, tall, wide-shouldered, and Rovard was vomiting all over the rugs, a vile stream as he retched and choked.

Norgoth let out a howl of pure frustration.

And Ralton laughed.

The woman screamed.

The Rapa touched a secret latch and the steel hoop sprang open and then, poor fool, he stood gaping witlessly as nothing sprang foaming and clawed in death toward my throat.

Norgoth glared around, his eyes rolling up as his sorcerer vomited and vomited upon the rugs.

"There is a greater sorcery here," he said. He looked wild, frightened and yet still bolstered by remnants of his own imagined strength. "A Wizard of Loh. There is a Wizard of Loh near and he thwarts all."

I shook my head. I was amused.

"Not so."

As though he took my words as a signal, for they were true as far as I knew, Norgoth acted.

For all the magical powers I believed assisted me, I remained a mortal man still. Maybe there were no sorcerous powers. Maybe my dip in the Pool of Baptism was enough. Perhaps the Savanti nal Aphrasöe had exerted some influence. But, for all that, I was a mere mortal man and could be slain by steel.

On those spindly legs Norgoth leaped.

He did not lack courage. His hand closed on my rapier hilt and I realized with a shock that the sorcerer's attack had left me weak, weak and slow.

My own hand clamped on his before he could draw. He would have done better to have tried for the left-hand dagger. For a space we struggled. He struck me in the face with the brass-studded back of his glove, and I took the blow and felt the sticky wetness and so gave him back the buffet. He sprawled back. His gross body balanced wonderfully upon those thin and ludicrous legs and he did not fall. But he collided with the woman. She pushed him off with a curse and tried to stick her nails into my eyes. I swayed and tripped her and I did not hit her as she went down.

Ralton remained standing, steadfast, unmoving.

The sorcerer now held his guts under the stinking pelts and groaned and gagged and rolled his eyes, which had reappeared from wherever they had been during his demonstration of sorcerous powers. The Rapa kept fiddling with his steel chain and collar and made no move against me.

I hauled the woman up by the collar of her tunic and stood her on her feet and pushed her at Norgoth. The two clung. Well, they were fit partners, I judged.

Then, with a fine swing and panache, the guards threw open the door and the anteroom filled with twinkling steel.

"Hold!" I bellowed. "All is in order. See that the deputation from Layco Jhansi is assisted on its way back. They are returning—*now!*"

At this Ralton Dwa-Erentor took a step forward, his face strained, puzzled, and his right hand half extended.

I looked at him, a straight, level, demanding glare.

"My thanks, Ralton Dwa-Erentor. I recall your sleeth—Silverscale, I think—gave my zorca a fine run. But sleeths will never best zorcas. Go back to Jhansi and remember this."

He took my meaning.

"I will, majister."

So I stood aside as the guards, tough, no-nonsense Pachaks, saw the embassy out. The woman favored me with a long look of loathing. The Rapa held the steel collar open, and his vulturine face with the arrogant beak exhibited expected joy at once more beholding his pet, whatever ferocious beast it might be. The sorcerer, Rovard the Murvish, had to be assisted out. Green foam-flecked slime dribbled from his beard. And, I swear it, his eyes were crossed as he left.

The last to leave was Malervo Norgoth.

He said, "I shall carry your words to Kov Layco. But I do not think he will be discomfited by them."

"Words won't hurt you," I said, most cheerfully, "unless a Wizard utters them, and then only if you are credulous. Tell him there is a length of rope waiting for him, with a loop at the end. I fancy it will snug right tightly up under his ear when the time comes."

"When the time comes, Dray Prescot, the rope will be around your neck."

"Oh, I don't doubt I deserve it. But Jhansi will be there first to show me the way."

So they left and there was no Remberees between us, and I was told that they did not observe the fantamyrrh—except Ralton Dwa-Erentor.

Taking myself off to the Sapphire Reception room I reflected that there was little in this to please. The exhibition to which I had just been treated ruled out the possibility of thinking about the offer of alliance from Jhansi. But then, could the offer have been genuine? My reactions in more or less having the embassy slung out must have been right, instinctively right. And I had promised myself not to flare up into that old intemperate rage. Almost, I had broken that promise. I tried not to feel smug as I went back to the people waiting for the news.

"So, majister," said Nath, somewhat heavily. "Does this mean you ally us with the Racters now that Jhansi is once more foresworn?"

"I don't see why you had to let the kleeshes go!" burst out Barty. He was furious, and, in his eyes, rightly so. "They betrayed their embassy, all their talk of heraldic immunity was a mere base trick. String 'em all up, that's the way of it—or should be."

Delia regarded him, for she favored him as a son-in-law when our daughter Dayra returned to the fold. Barty spluttered and splashed and covered his face drinking a cup of good vydra tea. Oh, yes, a right hellion our Barty Vessler in matters of chivalry and honor.

My people knew our ways well enough by now to talk freely among themselves discussing the offer from the Racters. Also, they knew that while I would take cognizance of what they said, the final decision was down to me. That was what being an emperor was about. I felt inclined to hear what Delia had to say. She was an emperor's daughter. But in all this idle chatter about emperors, I never forgot what I had promised myself on Voxyri Drinnik. The ways of emperors were not for me.

The talk flowed. The tea was quaffed. The food was eaten. We all had busy lives to lead with much to do and the few murs we could spare for this kind of pleasant interlude had already been exceeded. By ones and twos the company began to leave and the clepsydra on the shelf would have collapsed if worried stares carried physical force.

Nath Nazabhan and Barty Vessler were talking to Delia and I crossed to them, having had a few words with Jago De-Ka, a Pachak Jiktar who had come in from Zamra with news. The island was almost clear of the reiving mercenaries and flutsmen, he reported, and the Pachaks who had made a part of the island their home were now more than ever wedded to their new way of life. I expressed myself as satisfied, keeping a grave mien, as was seemly in so important a matter to a Pachak. Pachaks are a race of diffs with whom I delight in doing business.

Barty was still rather high on indignation, and Nath was as grimly ferocious as ever when I joined them.

Archolax the Bones, the deep lines in his face more pronounced than ever, walked across to us with a most determined air about him. I sighed. I could guess.

". . . until they dangled for two sennights!" quoth Barty.

"But you have friends up there, do you not?" inquired Delia with that devastating simplicity that snicks in like a rapier between the ribs.

"Friends? Oh, aye, friends. But if they wear the white and black these days, how can they be friends?"

Old Archolax sneezed. With great ceremony he withdrew an enormous square of yellow silk and blew. While the stentorian bellow was still echoing through the room he spoke up, swirling the yellow silk about grandly.

"Majister! The treasury is scraped to the bottom so hard I swear you would not get a single stiver out of the dust in the vaults. The Racters are all the grievous things we know them to be. But, majister! They have money. They are rich. Their estates up there are fabulously wealthy. An alliance there would fill our coffers. We could hire mercenaries and throw the damned mercenaries from Hamal out of Vallia."

He did not finish with: "I have spoken." Had he done so it would have fitted perfectly.

Delia's face bore that knowing, half-mocking, teasing smile.

The way these old buffers use their sneezing and their kerchiefs always amuses me—and causes me some facetious admiration, too, seeing that they thereby cloak their own highly individual designs. Old Evold Scavander, the wisest of the wise men of Valka, could always get that haughty and promising Wizard of Loh, Khe-Hi-Bjanching, going by a few splutters and sneezes and a whisk of bright cloth.

"I hear your words, Pallan Archolax, and they are indeed worthy of note. The embassy from Jhansi revealed their true purpose, and have left, with a zorca hoof up their rump." One of the Kregish ways of saying with a flea in their ear, that charming expression, and the others smiled. "But that does not tilt the balance down in favor of the Racters."

"Their gold tilts the balances."

About to give what I considered a stiff reply, Barty saved me the trouble, saying what was in my mind.

"But honor will tilt the balance back!"

So we wrangled for a space, and I think they could all see already the way my mind tended. Finally, I said, "We have the resources if we plan carefully. Gold to buy mercenaries will not set Vallia free. Our country must be set free by her own efforts. This is a cardinal principle."

Archolax opened his mouth ready to sneeze, saw me watching him, and merely swiped the yellow silk over his nose.

"Your commands, majister," he said. And then he added: "My fingers itch to feel Racter gold. But my heart would not be in it."

"Of course," put in Nath Nazabhan. "We could take the Racter gold, anyway."

"What, Nath!" exclaimed Barty. "Double deal 'em?" He screwed up that incredibly naive face, and one could almost see the wheels whizzing around in his head as he once more confronted the thrill of skullduggery in action.

The idea was intriguing; but it would not do, and we all saw that. Nath's flyer remained unsaddled.

Pallan Myer walked over from the door, and coughed, and stood waiting. He was youngish, stooped over from long hours of reading, with always a book or a scroll tucked under his arm or, to be honest, more often opened as he walked along reading, a constant terror to anyone else who did not look where they were going. I had put him in charge of education, the Pallan of Learning, and I was due to go with him to see about a group of new school buildings being fashioned quickly from materials left over from a slave bagnio, after it had burned, and many of the poor devils inside it, too.

Acknowledging Pallan Myer, I said: "Educating the children of Vallia is more important than wrangling. Nath. Do you go and see Strom Luthien and give him our word. And, Nath. Try to be gentle with the rast."

"Aye, majister. I will try."

Barty chuckled. "That'll be a pleasant surprise for him."

Myer started in eagerly talking away about the plan to give each child in the new building his or her very own desk. That way, he said, they'd do a lot more work without the jostling and larking you always found when the children sat on long benches, all scrunched up. I nodded, agreeing, and figuring out where we could find the artisans and the wood. Barty fell in with us as we went. Delia called across, saying she had work to do, and I smiled at her as we went out.

His face shining like one of those fabulous polished apples of Delphond, Barty Vessler strode along with us out into the suns shine. I saw Delia looking after him as I turned to give her a parting smile. Barty was deeply in love with Dayra and she was off somewhere adventuring on her own account and had been numbered in the ranks of those who opposed us. She had been or was still, for I did not know, a boon companion to Zankov and that crowd of cutthroats. Now that the Hawkwa country had declared for Jak the Drang and I was emperor in Vondium, now that Phu-Si-Yantong had withdrawn from this area, what in a Herrelldrin Hell Zankov was about posed a prickly problem.

Zankov had slain the old emperor. That emperor was Dayra's grandfather. I wondered if she knew that her comrade Zankov had murdered her grandfather.

Attitudes are easy to strike and damned difficult to unstrike.

Barty burbled on about the coming campaign as we mounted our zorcas to ride out to the new schools. We had already traveled a fair bit of the road in freeing all Vallia and we looked forward to riding side by side to finish the task. Every day Barty grew in stature, in wisdom and cunning. Of courage there had never been any doubt. You will perceive, I think, that I was looking with increasing favor on Barty Vessler, the Strom of Calimbrev. I knew practically nothing of my daughter Dayra. Yet the hope, barely formed and certainly not articulated, was that Barty would match up to Dayra, who was also Ros the Claw.

Ros the Claw. The suns slanted their radiance down about us and the day smiled with promise, and I thought of that wicked steel taloned glove she wore on her left hand. Those cruel curved claws could have your eyes out in a twinkling. A real right tiger-girl, Ros the Claw, a she-leem, clad in her black leathers hugging her skin tight, all grace and lithe lissomeness and striking feline beauty. And Barty had no idea that Dayra was Ros the Claw.

My own feelings muddled my thinking. I had not been on Kregen when Dayra and her twin brother, Jaidur, had been born, and Delia had shouldered a heavy burden—two heavy burdens. And there were the other children, also. The Everoinye had banished me, then, and I had now firmly made up my mind not to cross them again in any open way. The feelings about Dayra made me itchy, fretful, tearing open tender wounds I had thought long since scabbed over.

No matter where Dayra might be in Vallia, no matter what she was up to, it seemed to me right that I should talk to her in friendship and love. She hated me. I had had proof of that. And, also, I thought I had proof that she did not hate me, for she had drawn back and had not struck me from the instant she understood that I had at last recognized Ros the Claw as my daughter Dayra.

That gave me hope.

Emotions and feelings run all tangled, like disturbed water in a stream choked with fallen rock. We must have reliable news of Dayra soon. We must.

So I rode in the suns shine to see about facilities for educating the young, and I realized with a sober chill that I had few and contemptible qualifications for the task.

Chapter Five

Justice

Plots and counter-plots. Masks and disguises. The shadow in the night and the swift glitter of a blade. Well, they are all a part of Kregen, just as much as the pomp and grandeur, the armies, the brilliance of nobility and the shining of courage.

There was the matter of Renko the Murais.

Where I rode I noticed that the members of my choice band, those fighting men who were veterans now although so short a time ago being simple tradesmen or farmers, had strengthened their number by mustering more of the old comrades. They formed a powerful little mounted squadron riding at my back. And, with them, rode a formed and formidable body of upwards of fifty Pachaks. While welcoming this, I was puzzled. I mentioned the matter to Nath as we rode forward along the gutted Avenue of Hope and out into the virtually untouched Kyro of Taniths. This kyro was a particular pride of Vondium, being graceful in architecture, bright with color, a perfect place to take one's ease after the strife and turmoil of the day. The luxurious and headily perfumed trees and bushes growing in a profusion of beauty like a woman's hair and trailing splendor along the tessellated walks and cool colonnades always offered a welcome and a surcease. A man could expand his lungs here, and yet relax, safe and with the feeling he had come home. I smiled at Nath as I asked him, and he merely answered with a casual comment that, by Vox, a man needed friends at his back.

With this sentiment I agreed.

I did not press the matter. In truth, the thought that ferocious and loyal fighting men rode with me, keeping a weather eye open against assassins, stikitches dropping on us from any direction, was mightily comforting.

Each man of this impromptu bodyguard wore a tiny tuft of yellow and red feathers in his helmet, a brave show of color, highly evocative.

The business with the schools happily concluded and an old friend, Anko the Chisel, proving only too happy to place the entire resources of what was left of his workshops at our disposal, the matter of the desks was attended to. With them, also, grave details of ink and pens, of paper and tablets, and the correct clothes the youngsters should wear had all to be attended to with the same strict punctilio I might give to the decisions over the number of shafts an archer should carry in his quiver when we marched out, and how many with the regimental wagons, or the best method of ensuring next season's crop, or of how I might receive a deputation from a province seeking alliance. The work of empire is made up of details, great and small, and who is to mediate between them?

So, with the schools, and a faulty aqueduct to be seen to, and repairs to the walls where battering engines had breached them, and a swift and summary decision between a man and his brother over the rightful possession of a shop their father kept, he now being dead and nothing decided, I at last turned my zorca's head in the direction of the palace and a meal and the inquisition into Renko the Murais.

Well, the meal was a splendid affair, and I shall not spend time on such gourmet delights. Enevon Ob-Eye, Nath, Barty, the responsible officials and whoever else thought they had a hand in the affair all assembled in a relatively undamaged chamber where once music had flowed to delight lazy afternoons. The charred triangles of harps still stood in the corners, and the twisted remnants of many of the exotic musical instruments of Kregen had been hastily swept away into an alcove under the windows. I sat at a long table, with the dignitaries flanking me, and the condemned men were led in under guard.

I knew Renko the Murais. It was the same Renko who had fought with us as a Freedom Fighter in Valka.

I treated him as I treated the other miserable wights, showing no special favor.

"Have the charges and the findings read out."

This was done with due solemnity.

The contrast between the genuine solemnity of these proceedings despite the deliberate air of informality I had introduced, and the fascial solemnity of the twin embassies from our foes amused and depressed me. Nath had seen Strom Luthien off, treating him, as he reported hard-faced to me, with all due civility. The Racters, too, had been seen off with a zorca hoof up the rump.

The charges having been read out—a dismal catalogue of rapine and plunder and murder—the findings were studied. Here I welcomed the presence of Nath Nazabhan. His meticulous eye, his keen nose, his habitual and natural aptitude for turning over stones to discover the truth, were wonderfully displayed. The judges had judged fairly, we decided, in all but three cases of the thirteen. And all three had been dealt with in the court of Tyr Jando ti Faleravensmot.

I frowned.

"Is Tyr Jando here?" I spoke very mildly.

Enevon Ob-Eye shook his head. "He has been called away to his estates in Faleravensmot, majister. Some business of a cracked cistern and ruined flour."

"Important enough to warrant his absence, then, in a time of shortage." I pondered. Two of the wights standing in their gray breechclouts, chained, hang-dog before us, had been accused of raping two little Fristle fifis, and their story was that they had been over on the Walls of Opaz the Deliverer, hoisting stones, for they were powerful, hairy apims, with faces that would normally have been frank and open, and were now shattered and frightened and destroyed.

"Majister," said one, Tom the Stones. "False witness was borne against us by Tabshur the Talens—"

Nath, Barty and I listened and weighed the stories. A matter of a debt to this Tabshur the Talens, an inheritance, a squabble between siblings, and a charge of rape to remove Tom the Stones. The inheritance would then by default fall to Tabshur through the sibling. Tabhsur the Talens was a moneylender. Well, men must live in the world however they can shift. The unfortunate comrade of Tom the Stones, Nath the Ears—they were, indeed, remarkable—had been caught up in the plot because he was a comrade and could have borne counter-witness. Now we heard it all out and sent a guard of Pachaks to find this Tabshur the Talens and the sibling and hear their stories.

"Stand aside, Tom the Stones and Nath the Ears. Rest easy that justice will be done." How easy to say that! And how damned hard, by Vox, to make sure!

Then it was the turn of Renko the Murais.

He had been so dragged down by his ordeal that he kept his face lowered and his gaze on the floor, and so had not looked up once, being prodded into position by the guards. He wore a gray breechclout and was chained, and although the laws had seen to it that he was clean and deloused, he looked defeated and tattered.

Because he was an old blade comrade I must allow no favor to overbear my judgment.

The Relt stylor Renko had been found guilty of murdering had been discovered in the cellar of a ruined pothouse down on the Canal of the Cockroaches. The Relts with their birdlike faces are the more gentle cousins of the warlike Rapas, and are very often employed as clerks and accountants. This particular Relt appeared to be a stranger in Vondium. His satchel was missing and the leather straps had been slashed through. He had been searched, for his tunic had been ripped to shreds exposing the linings and the hems.

"Was the satchel discovered in the possession of Renko?"

Nath's words were pleasantly mild.

Enevon Ob-Eye said, "The records state the satchel was not recovered."

"And no one thought to search, or inquire?"

"The records state that Renko the Murais was discovered crouching over the body, as you have heard. There was a knife in his hand, and there was blood on the blade. The Relt had been stabbed six times in the small of the back. It does seem the proof was plain."

"Plain enough for me, by Opaz," declared Barty.

I said, "Was there blood on the cut straps?"

Renko the Murais jumped.

His shaggy head lifted with a snap. He looked up. He looked at me. An expression—a sunrise, dawn, the flowering of a bloom—shocked across his face. His eyes widened. His mouth abruptly trembled—trembled and then firmed.

"Strom Drak!"

"Aye, Renko, Strom Drak. And a pretty pickle you have got yourself into."

"I did not slay the Relt, strom! I swear it by Opaz the All-Glorious! I found the body and was set on, and so fought for my life, and was knocked on the head and left for dead. And when I woke—"

"You were taken up." I looked at Nath and then at Barty and the others at the table. "The law of Vallia—the new laws of Vallia that the new emperor will see maintained—demand absolute proof of guilt. No one saw this man slay the Relt. You must prove beyond all doubt he did the deed before you pronounce him guilty."

"But he was standing over the body with a bloody knife in his hand!" Barty spluttered, his face perplexed and yet clearly showing the way he struggled with preconceived notions.

"The chavnik knocks over the bowl of cream and the slave girl comes in to set it right and the mistress sees her and has her whipped for stealing and spilling the cream."

"Yes, majister, but—"

"Enevon. Read out the description of the wounds."

Enevon rustled his papers and then read: "Six stab wounds in the small of the back, close together, deep."

I looked at Renko. "You were an axeman, as I recall."

"That I was, strom." Renko, still disoriented, took a grip on remembered pride.

I nodded. "Are the clothes of the dead Relt available?"

They were not. They had been burned.

"Tell me of the men who attacked you."

Renko screwed his leathery face up. He wanted to rub his nose, I could see; but the chains stopped that.

"I saw three of them, strom. But there must have been another one at my back who hit me after I stuck the bastard in front. By Vox, but the whiptail was quick, and I'd have had him, too, but for that crack on my noodle."

I said, sharply: "A Kataki?"

"That's what I said, strom."

He'd said whiptail; but that was the slang term for a Kataki, a nasty member of a nasty race of diffs, slavers, with fierce brow-beating faces, and intemperate dispositions and with long sinuous tails to which they strapped six inches of bladed steel. There were Katakis on Kregen who had no other aim in life but to degut me. The ambition was reciprocated.

"Anything else? Clothes, faces, weapons—?"

"Rapiers, strom, but they kept them scabbarded. They hit me with what felt like the Lenk of Vox. The whiptail had a favor of black and green feathers clipped by a golden grascent—I think, strom, for I was taken by surprise."

For a space a silence fell. Then, to give Barty the due he deserved, he was the one to burst out: "By Vox! Under the

Gate of Voxyri—when I came running up—this Renko the Murais speaks the truth. I'll swear it!"

"Aye," said Nath. "The devil's work spreads itself."

After that we prosecuted further inquiries and a garbled story came out that made me itch with worry and with frustration. It seemed clear that the Relt stylor was bringing in a message and had been waylaid and slain and the message stolen. But from whom had the message been sent? The minions of Phu-Si-Yantong had heard of it, and we had not, and they had struck. There was no question now in anyone's mind that Renko the Murais was not guilty. His chains were ordered struck off at once. He expanded after that, and a cup of wine further restored him. But he could add nothing further to the story, being engaged in eking out a living scrounging scraps from the ruins, as so many were. Now there was a happy outcome to the adventure, we could feel thankful he had stumbled on the corpse of the stylor. Although, frustratingly, we knew no more than that there had been a message from someone.

"Anyway, majister—what made you—?" asked Barty.

"The blood. There was no blood on the cut straps. Had Renko stabbed him in the back, that would have been the beginning of the murder—or the end of the Relt—and then he'd have cut the satchel free. No blood meant a clean knife had been used." I smiled—I, Dray Prescot, smiled—across at Barty. "Anyway, Renko is an axeman. He wouldn't have stabbed with such a heavy knife. He'd have sliced the Relt's throat out."

"Yes," said Barty.

"And where stands Jando ti Faleravensmot in this?" demanded Nath.

"His judgments have always been impeccable," offered Enevon, shuffling his papers together. I rather think, as my chief stylor, he had been put out at the murder of a brother in his craft, and was pleased that at least some truth had been revealed.

A stir at the back of the chamber announced the arrival of Tabshur the Talens and the sibling who had won the inheritance, a lean fellow in an apron called Naghan the Tallow. They both looked as guilty as hell. But that must not be allowed to weigh against them. Somehow—and in this I do not boast but rather feel a sense of deflation and defeat—the news that the Emperor of Vallia himself had sent for them and was to look again at their stories, had unnerved them. And, in the case of Tabshur, at least, he was a hard-case, cunning and vicious in his extortions. Naghan the Tallow had been a mere tool in his hands, credulous and willing to be led into infamy.

They broke down and confessed. I think the jingle of chains as the Pachak guard waited added to their misery.

And then Tabshur said: "I paid Tyr Jando twenty golden talens for his judgment. The Fristle fifis was the case he chose. You cannot trust anyone these evil days."

In that he was right—or almost right. There are people I trust on Kregen. Not many; but they do exist.

As you will hear, there were some I should not have trusted, for betrayal touches high and low alike, friend and foe, and is indeed a foul stink over life.

I said: "Nath. Do you dispatch a guard to request Tyr Jando ti Faleravensmot to return to Vondium. There are questions to which he must give the answers. Oh—and tell the guard commander to make sure the cistern does not spoil any more flour."

"Quidang, majister!" barked Nath, and turned to one of the Pachak Jiktars.

There was no particular cleverness in the investigations we had made leading to the establishment of Renko's innocence. Had the questions been asked at the trial the outcome would surely have been different from what it had been. And people had made certain that Renko had been found guilty. He told us that he had been given no opportunity to speak then.

Another important detail had to be settled.

"Make further investigations into the Fristle fifis. The villain or villains must be brought to justice. Setting the innocent free is a half of the matter."

"Quidang, majister!"

Justice of a sort had been done here. That was cause for partial satisfaction. Jando ti Faleravensmot would have to answer for his conduct. Tabshur the Talens had paid Tyr Jando twenty gold pieces.

I wondered how much the minions of Phu-Si-Yantong had paid him.

Chapter Six

Yellow Sun, Silver Moon

When you live on a world as wild and ferocious as Kregen, for all its beauty and splendor, missions of mercy such as rescuing girls in distress or marching to the relief of a besieged city are a natural order of life, given the way of the world. Although I would not go so far as to claim they are of the same order as worrying about the overdraft, or the state of the automobile, or the parlous conditions of employment or where the next meal is coming from on this Earth, the parallels are clear and ominous.

One has to do what one can against the strokes of Fate and, really, that is all there is to it.

We all worked in those days as our plans matured. The crumbling walls of the city occasioned a great deal of worry, and much effort was expended in rebuilding the fortifications. Over the sennights what began as rumors hardened into facts. Unpalatable facts. Spies and scouts brought in sure word that a host marched on Vondium from the southwest.

All that wedge of Vallia remained locked in mystery since the victories there of the minions of Phu-Si-Yantong. His insane ambition to rule all Paz had received a set-back in the island, and he was set, with or without the help of the Empress of Hamal, on imposing his will on us all.

So we labored and set our house in order and sharpened our weapons.

With the new threat from the southwest there could be no thoughts of our marching north. The Racters and Layco Jhansi would still fight each other, no doubt, and the reverberations of that conflict would be felt in Inch's Black Mountains and in Delia's Blue Mountains. East of them across the Great River we held the land. There was, again, no thought of a westerly expansion for the time being.

A Life for Kregen

The imperial provinces around Vondium were now almost wholly in our hands, pockets and enclaves still being held by insurgents and reiving bands of aragorn, slavers. There remained also a number of roving gangs of flutsmen, mercenaries of the skies, who flew their great winged saddle animals in raiding descents wherever they sensed the pickings were easy. Strong detachments of the army had to be posted not only on the borders of the imperial provinces, but in strategic loci from whence they could march out forthwith against the threat wherever it might be found.

The whole island presented a patchwork of warring factions. How we were to bring peace to the whole land exercised our minds wonderfully.

And if you comment that the peace we brought merely represented the rule of me, Dray Prescot, well, then—yes, I suppose you are right. But I had fought that battle with myself and now my course having been set by the acclamation of the people, I could not in honor draw back. And I still devoutly believed that, blood or no blood, Vallia would prosper far more sweetly with my people to handle affairs than under the iron heel of Yantong or ripped apart by bandits and mercenaries and flutsmen who simply reived for their own benefit and no others.

As for Hamal—the Empress Thyllis would have to withdraw her iron legions, and see to her own internal problems. One day, and the quicker the sooner, by Zair, we would shake hands with the Hamalese in friendship. Until that time they were our bitter foes.

And Pandahem—well, the various countries of that island would have to serve as a friendly bridge to Hamal.

After Hamal the rest of the massive southern continent of Havilfar would ally together against our common enemies.

And there was Segesthes, and Turismond, and Loh. . . .

All Paz must stand shoulder to shoulder against the Shanks who raided and destroyed, sailing up over the curve of the world.

By Opaz! It was a task to daunt the stoutest heart. With all this mighty clangor of distant ambitions reverberating in our minds we were forced to deal with the here and now, the relatively minuscule problems of an army marching against our city.

As the reports came in we understood that the problem

was by no means minuscule. Given our resources, the odds against us were gigantic.

Mind you, the Star Lords might suddenly decide they had a sticky problem somewhere on Kregen they wished sorted out for them. Then I would find myself hoisted up out of Vondium whirled by the gigantic blue semblance of a Scorpion, thrust down all naked to get on with the job. So, as was my custom, as I planned and directed I molded men and women to handle the tasks that must be undertaken should I not be there, And, as always, they could not understand.

Only Delia grasped what I was doing, and sorrowed for it.

To the end of leaving everything in as apple pie an order as might be contrived should I be suddenly whisked away I looked carefully at the commanders available to us.

Nath—whose name of Nazabhan came as a courtesy from his father, who was a Nazab, an imperial appointment as governor of a province and equivalent to a kov—resolutely insisted that he wished to continue in command of the Phalanx. He put great store by that cutting instrument of war. I tried to make him see reason on both counts. But he would not leave the Phalanx command, and he would not allow that the Phalanx could be bested by infantry—as for cavalry, they were just a laugh.

Against aerial attack strong forces of archers were incorporated, and the artillery park was built up.

All Vondium and the imperial provinces surrounding the capital city resembled a gigantic beehive, humming with activity. What cheered me most was the demeanor of the people. Almost without exception they were cheerful, sprightly, utterly confident in themselves, their new army and their emperor. Feeling like a cheat and a fraud, and with profound doubts about the new army, but with pleased awareness of the new spirit of the citizens, I sorted out the folk to take over should the necessity arise. This is mere common-sense insurance when your name is Dray Prescot and you are Emperor of Vallia, and the Star Lords remain unsatisfied.

Messages carried swiftly by one of the few fast airboats we possessed assured me that the Lord Farris, the Kov of Vomansoir, prospered in his newly-restored kovnate. His people accepted him back with a warm welcome because he had been associated with Jak the Drang and was remembered and well-liked as a fair, just and generous man.

The airboat which brought him flying swiftly into Vondium bore the gray and yellow of Vomansoir. Alert, active, bronzed, he jumped down and saluted Delia and me as we waited to greet him.

"Lahal and Lahal," he called, smiling, brisk and yet with that sureness of purpose about him that marked him as a man who knew what was what and got on with it. "Majister—it is good to see you again. Majestrix, my eternal loyalty."

I wasted no time but spelled it out, right there and then, as we walked into the shambles of the palace to find refreshment.

"But, majister! Why should you go away again? Now all Vallia awaits your victorious arms."

"You will have Nath to handle the Phalanx—and if we persevere with him I think he will take on a larger command of the army. Barty Vessler will be of help—he is a fine if headstrong aide-de-camp—more than that, really—and there is Enevon to handle all the finicky details of daily administration."

"But—"

"There are pallans appointed to all the departments of government and they can function autonomously with only an occasional eye." We told him of the sad business of Tyr Jando ti Faleravensmot, and of how he had hanged himself rather than return to Vondium. That meant another possible lead to the Wizard of Loh who sought to destroy us had been lost.

"But—"

"You will have Laka Pa-Re to run the mercenaries for you. He is a fine example of the best of the Pachaks. He remained after the nikobi was discharged and I have promoted him Chuktar. You may repose complete confidence in him. And there is Naghan Strandar, and Larghos the Left-Handed, and there are all those ruffianly companions of the choice band. Only if I am called away, Lord Farris, will your services be needed in this. I ask it as a favor."

"But, majister—your sons. Prince Drak, Prince Jaidur—"

He knew that Zeg was away somewhere and had heard us refer to him as the King of Zandikar.

"Drak is off in Faol looking for Kardo and Melow, and Jaidur—well—" I cocked an eye at Delia and she smiled, both radiantly and ruefully.

"The last I heard of that rapscallion son of ours he was seeking the whereabouts of his sister."

My ears pricked up at this. These women and their infernal secret societies are one thing; but now they had inveigled a brash fighting man in the person of Jaidur into their schemes. I saw that, and quickly enough, if you please.

At last I overbore Farris by saying around a goblet of the best Gremivoh, the wine favored by the Vallian Air Service, in a voice I made as neutral as possible: "Anyway, I need you here to keep an eye on things and on the Empress Delia, also." Farris was a man whose life had been dedicated to the emperor and whose fanatical loyalty to Delia was a part of his makeup. "An army marches against us from the southwest and I've a mind to go out there and spy them out. Perhaps—"

"Aye, Dray Prescot," quoth Delia, sharply. "Aye! And you've a mind to crack a few of their villainous skulls, too, while you're at it. I know."

"Mayhap, my love," I said, unrepentantly. "Mayhap."

So, the matter being settled, we passed onto a more detailed assessment of the situation, which was pretty fraught, as I have explained.

Reports from our scouts indicated that the army had landed in Vallia on the coast of Kaldi to the west of the Island of Wenhartdrin. This gave the invading host a long distance to march, for they might have landed much nearer the capital, and I surmised that they hoped to pick up recruits as they advanced. Just how the honest burghers and farmers of Vallia would react to this hope remained to be seen. Certainly, the southwest had not, to my knowledge, shared the ambitions toward self-determination of the northeast.

In a direct line—as the fluttrell flies as they say in Havilfar—the invaders had six hundred and fifty miles to cover to Vondium. It seemed clear they would not march a direct line. At an average speed of ten miles a day—more or less—at which a spry army can march with its baggage and artillery and followers and all the rest of the baffling impedimenta that so slow up armies on the march, they would take better than seventy or eighty days. The latest reports gave their position as being at the border between Ovvend and Thadelm. They had come, therefore, roughly halfway.

Estimates of their numbers varied enormously. This was partly due to the inexperience of some of our volunteer scouts and partly to the complexity of an army on the march, where thousands of followers confuse the eye. A sagacious Khibil, a paktun with many battle scars, had told me that he estimated the core of the army—the formed ranks of fighting men and the wings of cavalry—at fifty thousand. This was an army, therefore, of indeterminate strength, not so small as to be contemptible, and not so large as to be truly overpowering.

My reaction to that information had been to cast the net of scouts wider, suspecting another army marching parallel to the first. So far no confirming reports had reached me.

Nath was white with fury at my decision not to take a single brumbyte from the Phalanx. And, because I would not take any pikemen from the files, the Hakkodin, who flanked them, would not be touched, either.

"But majister! We *are* the army—the heart and sinew and core. If we march out, now, in all our strength, we can crush them—"

"Utterly?"

"By Vox! Yes!"

"I think not."

"But they are just an army—cavalry with zorcas and these white-coated hersanys, and infantry with nothing untoward in the way of weapons or formations. Fifty thousand! We will go through them as a cleaver goes through beef!"

"And you're like to strike a bone, in the middle, Kyr Nath."

The invading army flew no colors that had been reported to me. The hersanys present, those shaggy, six-legged, chalky-white riding animals, indicated there were contingents from Pandahem. And Phu-Si-Yantong had set his ferocious seal on the whole island of Pandahem, subjugating all its kings and rulers to his despotic sway. I wished him joy of it. He must be mad, for that seemed to me the only way to explain the ambitions he cherished. As for the good in him, that must lie so deep that Cottmer's Caverns brushed the heavens.

"Well," said Nath, breathing deeply and the whiteness denting the corners of his nostrils. "If I may not march my Phalanx, then, at the least, majister, let me come with you."

With a sorrow tinged with affectionate amusement, I said: "And leave the Phalanx without the leader? Come now, Nath, surely you see I cannot do that?"

He was in a cleft stick and he knew it, and the knowledge

made him barge off with a parting remberee and I did not doubt that his Relianchuns would skip and dance to his tunes and give their brumbytes in the ranks a little stick, also. Well, that is the way of it. He kept his men in fighting trim and I was unsure if I really did want him to hand over control of the Phalanx to somebody else. There were plenty of superb fighting men who could handle that immense and crushingly destructive mass of men with their pikes and shields and deadly onrushing force, naturally; but the sight of Nath commanding had power to instill perfect confidence.

The business of the day being settled for the time being, for alarums and excursions cropped up at any hour, I was free to give thought to what Delia had said about Jaidur. The notion in my mind that there must be more than one army advancing on Vondium had, for the moment, to be pushed aside. I left it with the thought that the mercenaries and the detachments from Hamal who had taken over the southwest had not obstructed the landing of the new army from Pandahem, and this argued they were in league and mutually assisting each other.

But, Jaidur. . . .

As we sat to a private meal in what would be called our withdrawing room, with Delia superb in a long sheer laypom-colored gown, and I lounging in a white wrap, the whole small room limned with gold from the samphron-oil lamps, I found her as reticent on this as I had on other occasions touching the Sisters of the Rose. That secret society of women demanded much of their members, and had a hand in a great deal of what went on in Vallia.

"You know I am under vows, my heart."

"I know. At least reassure me that Jaidur is—well—" I gestured helplessly. "That he is not likely to be chopped and eaten at any moment."

Delia laughed. The line of her throat caught at mine.

"No, no, you hairy old graint. You worry too much over the children, and yet—"

"And yet they have been woefully neglected by me, I know. Some people, looking at our family, might well say they have turned out a thoroughly bad lot. Well, not Drak. I except him, of course, and, I suppose, Zeg, seeing he is fully occupied in the Eye of the World being the king of Zandikar."

"A bad lot? We-ell . . . Lela bides her manners and is so mewed up with the SoR she hasn't been home for—"

"I haven't seen her since I got back—" I choked on my words, and seized up a crystal glass of best Jholaix—for we had unearthed a cellarfull of the superb wine in a ruined wing of the palace—and drank it off, scarlet-faced, I have no doubt.

Gravely, Delia regarded me. Her gown slipped demurely from one rounded shoulder. The lamps caught flecks of gold in her brown hair. She looked gorgeous.

"From where, my heart?"

I swallowed down. Sudden, it was, sudden and quick and fierce, like a first love.

"From that world I told you of. That world with only one sun, and only one moon, and only apims."

She caught her breath, and was still. And that was her only reaction.

Then: "You have spoken to me of this strange world which boasts but one small yellow sun, and one small silver moon, and lacks any kind of humans save apims, without a single diff to make life interesting. And is it real? And is it—?"

"It is real. It is called Earth. And it is where I was born." I reached over the table and took her fingers. They were warm, alive, trembling only a little. "And, my heart, it is many and many a dwabur away from Kregen, lost among the stars of the heavens."

"Your home—is among the stars. . . ."

"No, Delia, no. My home is here, on Kregen. With you."

Her smile transformed her face, making what was beauty into a radiance so all-encompassing the loveliness dizzied me. I closed my eyes, and opened them, and Delia still smiled on me.

"And this weird crippled world is where you go when you leave me?"

"I am sent there. Against my will. Because I defy those who wield the power. I shall not defy them so stupidly again." We talked then, quick questions and answers, and I told her much. She was fascinated by the idea of Earth, and quite beyond any childish feelings of guilt that the pure religions of Opaz would frown on her or condemn her conduct.

We talked through many burs of the night.

And, when at last we slept, we still had not talked enough to satisfy her curiosity or relieve my mind of those years of guilty secrecy. But, when all was said and done, what difference would this make in our relationship? We were a twinned whole, a twosome that transcended one-ness. She had always been aware that I left her from time to time, without explanation, and always returned. She always waited. No moist-mouthed seducer from Quergey the Murgey could sway her love away from me, as he had so often done with lesser women from their husbands. We remained still Dray and Delia. We were. But I felt a deal easier in my mind now that Delia knew. And, when she did know, I saw all my previous fears as the childish phantasms they were. To be brutally honest, the truth had come out and the whole episode smacked of anti-climax.

And, to be equally truthful, that was exactly how it should be.

The next day I mounted up and rode out at the head of my little band, aiming to get on with the hard business of rebuilding an empire, not for the glory of empire but because it was a task that had been set to my hand by the people of Vallia.

Chapter Seven

Jilian

Barty reined up and swung his zorca about to fall in with me.

"They're three ulms away, off beyond that ridge of trees."

He pointed ahead. The trees lined the horizon, barring off forward vision. The clouded sky towered above and, I fancied, when the wind dropped there would be rain. The turf compacted firmly beneath hooves of the zorcas and nikvoves, the breeze rustled bushes and small trees among the grassland, and we were approaching Dogansmot, which is a lively enough little town in the vadvarate of Thadelm in the southwest of Vallia.

I said to Volodu the Lungs: "Do not lift your trumpet, Volodu. Word of mouth, and quietly. Dismount."

Approaching us walked three zorcas, one of whom had a broken horn, carrying two dead men and two wounded. I looked at them and felt the anger, and repressed it.

"Close, Barty. You did well."

He nodded and was enough of a veteran now to say, merely: "Our patrol was ambushed. They left two dead men, three zorcas. The Pandaheem know we are about."

"Surely." At our backs the long columns were dismounting. "Get the men away into what cover they can find. Spread out. Strict silence." I swung to Targon the Tapster and Naghan ti Lodkwara who rode with Korero the Shield. "Come, and quietly as you value your hides."

The four of us cantered out across the turf, making very little sound. The zorca hooves beat softly. And I would have no truck with junk like jingling accoutrements and flying tassels and nonsense of that sort. Our harness and gear made no sound as we cantered out to scout the enemy.

"Gallop," I said, in a harsh penetrating sort of way, and

with a swift look back, which assured me that the troops were finding cover and making themselves and their mounts invisible, clapped in my heels and took off. The others followed.

We reached the line of trees without strain.

The situation was as I had expected.

The enemy general had sent forward a patrol to the line of trees and their distance beyond gave us time to reach the trees first. But only just.

We saw the green and blue uniforms, the brilliance of bronze and silver, as the zorcas broke up the ridge from the far side. There were ten of them, riding hard, and their plumes nodded very bravely.

"Let them get in among the trees," I said, most mildly. "Ten. Well, whoever gets himself a third man will be right merry and quick." From which, you will perceive, I was in a grim humor that needed a little skull-bashing to relieve the tensions. Vondium had burned and Vallia had been ripped into shreds. Somehow we had to start rebuilding, and here and now was a tiny fracas along the way....

The trees rose tall and heavily foliaged, their roots no doubt drinking deeply of a subterranean stream. The shadows fell bafflingly, and we waited in silence, completely confident.

The ten cavalrymen spread out a trifle as they reached the crest of the ridge and plunged boldly in among the trees, and this made me think they had once been good soldiers but were now by reason of easy marching and the absence of fighting grown somewhat careless. That carelessness cost them their lives.

After the first surprise and sudden onset they fought well. But four of them were down on the instant before they had drawn, and the next four, wheeling their mounts and setting up an outcry, barely had time to clear scabbard. The remaining two, those on the wings, fought their zorcas under control and attempted flight.

I reined in. The brand smoked red in my fist. Targon, Naghan and Korero whooped up their mounts and went flying in and out among the trees, like bats. They caught the last two Pandaheem before they quitted the tree-lined crest, and I did not wish to see who claimed three.

My desperadoes trotted back, looking mightily pleased with themselves. I was already dismounted, the reins slung over a handy branch, examing the dead men and their equipment.

Their zorcas stood by the corpses, which made me think we dealt here with an army of professionals, or hardened mercenary veterans. By this I mean men accustomed to working with zorcas for most of their lives, and not levies scraped up for a quick and cheaply promised conquest. Their carelessness had been a self-confident carelessness, when all was said and done.

"Summon up Karidge's regiment," I told my men, without looking up. One of them would ride with my orders. "Silently. The rest to move up in order to the ridge."

Rising, with what I wanted to know already tucked away, I walked to the far edge of the ridge. Fallen leaves kicked underfoot. The shadows dropped down, and then a chink in the overspreading leaves rained a colorfall of ruby and emerald. The army advancing down there were still two ulms away, that is to say around three thousand yards, and I could make out with the aid of my Kregen spyglass the way they came on.

Well. An army is an army. And there are all kinds, and, as I must have remarked, they are all the same and all different.

This ridge with its awkward traverse would make them trend away, following the easier ride to the north, and already the outriders were swinging. As my scouts had reported, there were no banners displayed. The cavalry screened the infantry. The artillery was mostly small wheeled varters, drawn by hirvels and quoffas, with just the two big catapults. These were drawn by teams of twenty four krahniks apiece.

The infantry were predominantly sword and shield men. This made a frown of black fury and exasperation cross my face, whereat Targon said: "Have you the gut ache, then, majister?"

"Sword and shield men," I said, grinding the words out. "From Pandahem."

"They learn," said Korero in his aloof way. A Kildoi, a man of that race of diffs from far Balintol that are little known beside so many other of the brilliant diffs of Kregen, Korero the Shield moved always at my back. His lithe limber physique was that of the master in martial arts of all kinds, with a command of the Disciplines. He had four arms and a tail equipped with a hand, and his handsome face with its golden beard overtopped me by four clear inches. Withdrawn, Korero, yet ready with a quip that would dart to the heart of the situation. Now, with a nod of his head, he finished: "There will be Hamalese drill instructors with that little lot. And a rascally gang of masichieri, too, if I am not mistaken."

"I do not think, Korero the Shield, you are mistaken."

Odd, when you thought about it, how in a world where men swore all the time by gods and spirits and phantom beings dredged from their various racial pools of unconsciousness, Korero hardly ever let fall a good round oath. That, I surmised, was a part of that aloofness bred in him in Balintol.

And when I say he was an adept of the Disciplines, I did not at that time know which particular set had trained and molded him. They were not those of my old comrade—never a blade comrade, of course—Turko the Shield, who was a Khamorro. Nor were they of the Kem-Brysuang of the land of Jeveroinen. We had a fellow from Jeveroinen in the ranks who was an adept of the fifth degree of Kem-Brysuang, and he was a most peculiar fellow indeed. His name was Bengi-Trenoimian and he had been bested in two falls out of three by Korero who had, by mutual arrangement, not employed his tail hand in the bouts.

Now I stared with concern at that army trending away to the north to pass the tree-crowned ridge. Shields were not a common article found in the armories of Pandahem or Vallia and we still had a deal of trouble to persuade men who regarded a shield as a coward's article of equipment to use them. One of the earliest regiments formed in Vondium after we re-captured the capital and filled with eager young volunteers had proved that point. Rank after rank, they had thrown down the shields we had just issued. The shields lay on the grass of the drinnik like pathetic flower-heads slashed down wantonly. Well, as you may imagine, there was a hell of a fuss, and a great hullabaloo and in the end we reached a compromise.

That was one of the many times I regretted the enforced absence through sorcery of Balass the Hawk, for that kyrkaidur could demonstrate sword and shield work to perfection.

It seemed that the fighting men of Pandahem had heeded the lessons brought to their discomfiture by the iron legions of Hamal. The sword and shield men—we generally called them churgur infantry—marching down there looked as though they were not yet completely sure of their weapons. You can usually tell.

The blocks of color moving all together represented massed regiments, five hundred or so men apiece, swinging along in column. We spied on them from the ridge of trees and marked their progress and the little breeze flicked and flecked the leaves about us and the slanting rays of the suns flickered opaz light upon the world. Kregen—ah, me, Kregen. . . .

"Nearer sixty than fifty," said Korero.

I nodded.

"And a good quarter cavalry."

As though the name cavalry conjured him from the ground Karidge moved up at my side. He breathed only a little more heavily than usual, being a sprightly fellow with a tufty beard that bristled even when he sang. A consummate artist with a zorca, he was turning into a good cavalry commander. His regiment was always impeccable and meticulously turned out. They wore the red and yellow, for they were an imperial regiment, all three hundred and sixty of the jutmen, organized into six squadrons plus ancillaries. Karidge employed a long curved sword, and his dolman and pelisse were marvels of gold and silver lace and embroidery.

"A damned great gang of them, majister, by the Spurs of Lasal the Vakka."

"Aye, Jiktar Karidge."

"We could knock a few feathers out of their tail."

"Aye. We could."

Targon the Tapster grunted. "Then let us mount up and ride."

"Tsleetha-tsleethi," I said. "Let us watch them for a space."

The obvious plan was so obvious my men grumbled and fidgeted as we waited in the shade of the trees and watched the army march past below the ridge.

Easy enough to knock a few feathers out of the tail, to ride down whooping and cut up the long straggling baggage lines and provender wagons. That was the way of the raiding cavalry. But I hungered for more. I hungered for the complete destruction of this damned army that had invaded our country.

And that must wait until they were within easier striking distance and we could bring greater power down on them. I mentioned this to Karidge and to Jiktar Nalgre Randur, the numim commander of the nikvove regiment. They thought about the situation, and then Randur stroked his ferocious lion-man's whiskers and gave his opinion that, as usual, the emperor was right; but that it was hard on a man to show him a mangy gaggle of foemen and then forbid him to unsheath his sword.

Jiktar Wando Varon ti GrollenDen, commanding the second zorca regiment, left his command strung out to guard our rear and walked through to join us. He wanted to know why we were not mounting up and riding down and, as he put it, letting some good Vallian air into those Opaz-forsaken Pandaheem down there.

Another fiery-tempered, audacious, sword-swinging cavalryman was Wando Varon, who maintained his regiment smartly enough but harped all the time on spear work from the saddle.

Holding these men in check now that they had set eyes on their enemy was like trying to hold an armful of kittens. I sighed.

"Very well. But toward dusk, when the chances favor a swift and determined attack. And, for the sweet sake of Opaz, do not get entangled. Quickly in, quickly out, and avoid taking plunder." I meant what I said. "They have regiments of zorcas down there. We will have to move like the Flame Winds of Father Tolki when you have had your fun."

Following my words there was a quantity of pelisse-swinging and feather ruffling and sword slapping, together with a deal of boot banging and moustache stroking. The cavalrymen swelled their chests. Their faces appeared to fill out, grow larger and firmer, and the brightness of their eyes matched the brilliance of their appearance. Yes, your dyed-in-the-wool jutman, your cavalryman who gallops in with a skirl and a whoop, knows how to ruffle it.

The two regiments of zorcas and the single regiment of nikvoves totaled around a thousand riders. There were fifty or so of my choice band with me, together with the Pachaks. These last two sets of ruffians, and I joke most feebly there, I cautioned off to another duty.

So, and for our mounts in a literal sense champing at the bit, we waited out the long descent of the suns.

Dorgo the Clis, his scar giving him the look of a desperado who would as lief slit your throat as doff his hat, was sent off to Dogansmot with a few riders to find out what the invading army's mischief had been there. This would be the first place they had bivouacked in that we had found and I felt the heaviness of heart that the usual rapine and plunder would have taken place. Dorgo rode circumspectly around toward the south before cutting west. The breeze at last died away and the rain gentled down, lustring all the greenery with a veil of silver.

Dogansmot lies not too far from the eastern border of Thadelm where that vadvarate marches with the imperial province of vond. Vond was solidly with the new emperor in Vondium, and we had ridden through from town to town and village to village in a kind of triumphal procession. We had left in our wake a determined intention of resistance to the invaders. A good blow here by this small cavalry force, the success of my own plan for the night, and then we could return and set our own army in motion.

And, all the time I schemed, that irritating little itch persisted. There had to be another plot by our foemen afoot. This army below us was in one sense derisory for the sack of a great capital city. There just had to be other forces in the field.

The army was from Pandahem, that seemed clear and would explain the absence of saddle flyers and vollers. We had seen not a single aerial force, and our own couple of airboats were at a discreet distance, waiting the signal. There was something afoot, something nasty and something that boded ill for Vondium.

When I told Barty that he might ride with the three regiments in command he said in his eager way: "That is very fine of you, Dray. But I'd rather ride with you. I know you're up to some kind of deviltry and that sounds much more interesting than beating up a baggage train and firing tents."

I regarded him stonily. A stout-hearted young man, the Strom of Calimbrev, if a little hasty and not over-inclined to think of consequences. But I could not find it in me to deny his request to join in my little spot of mayhem.

So Jiktar Nath Karidge, as the senior regimental commander, would conduct the cavalry. I gave him strict instructions and we checked sand-glasses, and then I led out my choice band and the Pachaks. The suns were drifting down behind banks of vermilion and emerald clouds, and the rain sifted in as though shaken from a trag's pelt. We rode silently. Ahead of us lay an army preparing to bed down for the night.

"They're pretty free and easy with their lights," observed Barty as we jogged down.

Indeed, there was plenty of light from lanterns and torches, whereat I frowned. What I purposed needed the shrouding cloak of Notor Zan.

"They act," said Targon with all the wisdom of his newly won state as a veteran warrior, "as though they're a friendly host. They didn't even investigate the disappearance of their patrol."

"Whatever the explanation," I said, "it must wait for now. Shastum!" Which is to say, "Silence!"

The sand trickled away and by the last of the light we saw the final grains tumble through. In the growing shadows flames licked up from the baggage lines and tents began to burn.

No need for further orders. Everyone knew what had to be done and their part in the operation. The expertise we had laboriously acquired during those hectic and wearing times clearing out the Radvakkas and the Hamalese and their mercenaries was once again put to the test. Barty and the others led off, their mounts going quietly through the night, only an occasional stray chink of reflected light striking up from steel or armor.

The sky faded in a dying riot of color. A few stars began to prick out. The tents burned splendidly and already an uproar was beginning that would cloak our designs. Straight for the sumptuous marquee we rode, with its pennons of colors that held no heraldic significance, its pearl lights shining through the cloth, its armed guards, its total air of munificence. This, we were confident, was the marquee of the army commander.

Guards rose to challenge us, cloak-flaring shadows in the night. We rode through or over them and the alarm was up. But we went galloping on, striking down opposition, intent on our target and our tasks.

The thumping onrush of the zorcas, the sound of steel on iron, the shrieks of men, the bluster of wind and the frantic flicker of flames out of the corner of the eye melded to make a bedlam—a familiar bedlam that released inner compulsions together with the blood that coursed around the body, freely, stimulating us all to greater exertions.

A Life for Kregen

Two Chuliks disputed the cloth-of-gold entrance to the marquee. Their comrades were down. Targon and Naghan struck horizontally, lethal sweeping blows. The Chuliks tumbled away; but one was only half-dead, and his flung spear took Naghan in the shoulder. He yelped, more in surprise than pain. That would bite him later.

"Take Naghan," I yelled at Targon. "You too, Korero. Ride on."

In the bedlam about us as men struggled and died they obeyed instantly. I leaped off the zorca and tumbled pell-mell into the cloth-of-gold opening. Lamps burned in mellow blazes and I could see only a Rapa at the far end of the tunnel-like entrance about to loose a shaft. The bow snapped and the arrow sped. My rapier shisked up and the shaft caromed away, to slice through that precious cloth-of-gold. I was up and past the Rapa before he could draw, and left him coughing on the carpets. The inner cloths flung back. I strode through.

This was a tented antechamber. Stout wooden posts had been driven into the ground and beautiful slave girls, practically naked, were chained by their necks to the posts. There were eleven posts and ten girls, and the odd post's iron chain lay like a serpent upon the ground. I walked on past with a stony face and two more Rapas fell away, screeching.

The girls were all screaming and caterwauling away, and I hoped I might release them if I returned this way. But ahead another tented chamber within the marquee revealed other men, sumptuously uniformed, relaxing with chased goblets of wine, and the girl who danced for them. She danced unwillingly, and a greasy slave-master snapped a whip at her buttocks, from time to time, to remind her of her duties.

The men were slow to react to my presence.

They displayed the same casual carelessness we had observed in the cavalry patrol and the general attitude of this army.

Firmly convinced that the solution to the mystery must lie with the commander, I moved on. They saw the rapier in my fist, they saw the slender blade and the crimson stains, and they started to lumber to their feet. Their reactions began with surprise, went through startlement, anger, furious rage—and then went on to dismay and fear and a babbling rush to get away, anywhere away. Those who could escaped. Those who could not, including the slave-master with his whip, remained stretched out in the tented enclosure. I did not think many would sup wine and watch a girl being whipped into dancing for their pleasure again.

"Hai, Jikai," said the girl, very calmly. Her body was lithe and lissome, remarkable, firm and curved, and she swayed with natural grace as she picked up a discarded cloth to cover her nakedness.

I gestured the rapier.

"The commander?"

"Oh, Lango is in there with his painted boys. You will have no trouble with him. Your men will destroy this army with ease."

"Mayhap," I said. I went across to the inner opening which was fastened with more cloth-of-gold. The girl picked up a rapier and by the way she handled the blade it was clear she had used weapons before. She smiled at me.

"But, I think, jikai, you will let me deal with him."

"He is of concern to me only as an enemy of Vallia."

"So ho! A patriot. I had thought all patriots long since fled. Your name, jikai?"

"As to that, I have been called Jak the Drang. And you?"

"Lahal, Jak the Drang. You may call me Jilian."

"Lahal, Jilian. Now, for the sweet sake of Opaz, let us get on and do this Lango's business for him."

The close atmosphere with the lamps shining evenly, the long lines of drapes against the tent walls, the gold and silver goblets spilled across the rugs and the wine soaking into the priceless fabrics, the stink of blood, the sprawled bodies of the men, clung about us. Her coolness both amazed and amused me—the amusement a genuine feeling, the amazement stupid in a world where I had already encountered Jikai Vuvushis—Battle Maidens.

I noticed without comment that Jilian selected from among the pile of tumbled clothes a red length of cloth to wrap around herself, ignoring the lustrous golds and silvers, the greens and blues.

She called me jikai, which in the connotation she used meant great warrior, and understood that I commanded men. She would get a shock, I thought, when she discovered I had merely three cavalry regiments with me. But all that must wait. We moved together toward the inner opening.

Her face was pale. I thought that to be a natural part of her beauty and not brought on by the circumstances. There was color there, a palest tinge of rose along the cheekbones. Her face was artfully formed, low-browed, wide, with deep eyes that appeared in the lamps' glow to burn with the desire to exact revenge. Well, there were red and angry weal marks on her buttocks and thighs, and I did not doubt she felt she had good cause to give back what had been taken out on her body.

Her dark hair reached low over that broad white forehead, adding a luster to the eyes, giving an air of intenseness to her whole face, the features clear and pleasing, the mouth warm and red and mobile. She moved with grace. We stood together by the entrance and from beyond the muffling drapes of cloth-of-gold the sound of light laughter reached us.

Jilian's rapier flickered like the tail of a leem.

"They laugh, those rasts. But now we will smoke them out."

"We must hurry. There is a whole army encamped about us and there will be many guards."

Her dark eyes flayed into me, and I could feel the pressure of her thoughts.

"And do you, Jak the Drang, jikai, fear an army?"

"Assuredly so—when I have other irons in the fire."

She reached out and ripped away the cloth-of-gold.

"Then let us heat this iron, together, and soon!"

Chapter Eight

Kov Colun Mogper of Mursham

Wherever Jilian had sprung from, the people there had taught her swordplay. Also, and this I found highly intriguing, she stopped to pick up the thick black whip the slave-master had wielded. When we burst through into the inner tented enclosure of the army commander, Fat Lango, it was the whip which, cracking out like a striking risslaca tongue, barbed, lashed him into painful movement. He shrieked. The lash coiled and lifted and struck, and again Fat Lango shrieked.

Jilian laughed.

Her teeth were very white and even.

The guards here were apim, slothful, over-dressed and arrogant to the point of stupidity. They did not interfere as Jilian lashed Lango.

And, still, I carried the Krozair longsword scabbarded over my back.

The painted and perfumed boys fled screaming from the wide pillow-strewn bed. Lango was bleeding. He tried to scramble away on all fours, like a dog, and the whip belted chunks of skin from his rump. Again Jilian laughed, drawing her arm up so that her whole body tensed, cracking the whip forward in a long raking slash that sliced all across Lango and made him shriek in agony.

He fell face down, and now the whip rose and fell, rose and fell, and I saw the last of the guards run. I turned back.

"Time to go, Jilian."

"I," she said, panting only a little, magnificent in her barbarism, "have not yet finished."

"Then, lady, I must leave without you."

She looked up, and the whip trailed.

"You would?"

"Believe it."

"I do, jikai, I do. And, I am ready." With this she struck not, as she had done, in the pain-ways of the whip, but in the death-ways. I have described this vile kind of Kregen whip before, like a Russian knout or a sjambok. A thick, tapering instrument of agony and death. Fat Lango jerked, abruptly, rearing up like a praying mantis; then he slumped and he was dead.

"Now," said Jilian, and she coiled that thick rope of vileness along her white arm. "Now, jikai, I am ready."

She moved like a stalking chavonth toward the cloth-of-gold entrance. I went the other way, toward the rear, where blue and green striped cottons covered the thicker material of the marquee. She stared after me.

"I go this way."

The bloody rapier licked out and stripped away the cloth, ripped in a lunge and a twisting tear down, and then across and down again. An opening gaped onto the starshot night.

"I," said Jilian, with some amused acerbity, "will go with you, Jak the Drang, jikai."

"You may call me Jak, Jilian. And I welcome you. You are, I think, a mistress of the Jikai Vuvushis."

"Yes."

Together, shoulder to shoulder, we stepped out. Guy ropes angled, glimmering whitely, to catch unwary feet. The commotion boomed away and the flames were still shooting up, orange and lurid, blurring the luminous stars. I headed directly away from the sumptuous marquee of the commander, the late and unlamented Fat Lango, and I kept my eyes peeled for sight of my men. The uproar was prodigious, and once away from the marquee and only four dead men to betray that anyone had passed, we were able to slow down. But there was no sign of my men.

"Where, Jak, is your army?"

We stood by a line of picketed hersanys, their white coats ghostly in that eerie light. Jilian looked completely composed, the red cloth wrapped about her waist, the rapier in her left hand held negligently, the whip coiled up along the right arm, ready to be shaken down in an instant.

"Why do you think I have an army?"

She smiled. "Men like you always command armies."

"That may be. But my army is not here. We must find mounts and ride."

She threw her head back and laughed. Then, abruptly, her head came forward and her face lowered on me, intense, demanding, challenging. "Yes, Jak. Yes. I think—I think I would ride with you."

I was turning away, ready to free the nearest couple of hersanys, and cursing one that tried to take a bite out of my arm. The six-legged beasts are as intractable as any of the trix family of saddle animals, but thicker in the body and, certainly according to my lion-man comrade, Rees, thicker in the skull. I gave the hersany a pat along the neck, soothing him, and swiftly freed the tether. I handed the rope to Jilian, not doubting that she could ride bareback.

A Fristle guard came running up, yelling, his whiskery cat-face outraged. Jilian felled him with a single slicing blow from her whip. It had sprung from her arm and struck as though impelled by an inner life of its own.

The Fristle fell against my hersany. I took the opportunity to wipe my rapier clean on the fellow's tunic, before I thrust the blade away in its scabbard. And Jilian laughed.

As we mounted up I reflected on her intense and brooding face, almost fierce—not quite fierce, I remark, but intent and concentrated—and compared that with the wild passion of her laughter. This was a girl whose inner spirit held much within her opaque depths. Maybe no man had plumbed her fully yet. Well, that was no job for me. I had not envisaged rescuing a girl, anyway, in this night's work. And that, of course, brought to mind the other girls chained to their posts, terrified and shrieking in their nakedness.

I turned the hersany's head back.

Jilian said: "You may be a jikai, Jak; but your bump of direction is sadly misplaced."

"Your friends," I said, most mildly. "I think I should see if their chains may be removed."

She stared at me, and, I think for the first time, saw me as other than a hulking warrior.

Silently, she turned her hersany, too, and together we trotted back to the marquee.

Many a time I have ridden quietly through a shrieking bedlam, an uproarious furor, and marveled at the maniacal things poor crazed wights will do in times of stress. We saw sights that would have amazed your solid stay-at-home citizen; men yelling and crying, women rushing about with streaming hair oblivious to anything, anything at all, so that they ran all a-crying into blazing tents, animals driven mad with fear and trampling down men too crazed to step out of their way. Other things there were too that it would be kinder not to talk about. Through it all Jilian rode with that intense, lowering look on her face that was not a frown, not quite. We reached the marquee and saw how the guards were.

A windrow lay in blood. Others were reeling and staggering, desolated by wounds. The shambles showed a fight had raged here that must have been terrible in its ferocity. Among the corpses I saw a twisted figure, wearing the brave old red and yellow, and I dismounted and turned him over gently. It was Yallan the Iron-throated, a good comrade, who had ridden with us since the Battle of Sabbator. A spear had penetrated between the hooped plates of his kax tralkish and done for him.

Jilian dismounted and walked across to stand at my side.

"One of your men?"

"Aye. Just the one. The wounded would have been carried off. That is the way my men are."

She said, "There are many dead here. Yet you mourn just the one?"

The flash of feeling I experienced shook me. We had just met and I had thought—and now, how little she knew of me! I knew nothing of her, save that she had courage, and a beauty to set a man's pulses thumping, and a cool appraisal of life that, I suspected, had brought her through many a dangerous turn.

So, just as gently, I said, "I mourn for all men slain in battle or dead in bed. Yet some must, I think in nature, mean more than others. Is that so strange?"

"No. But they look so—so pathetic. Like the offal a butcher throws to the dogs."

I marked her words.

She was right. And, by saying that, she revealed more of herself.

Inside the marquee we found more dead guards, blegs and numims and Fristles, and all the slave girls had gone. The chains had been parted by savage blows, the cut edges of the links bright and glittering. So I knew Barty and the others, looking for me, had taken the time.

"We must leave. My men have saved your friends."

As we mounted up—and the whip chopped two Rapas who would have taken our mounts, as the rapier snicked the life from a third—she said, "I pray you, Jak. Do not call them my friends. They were poor little shishis, slave-girls by nature. I am not as they are."

I restrained my anger.

"No one is a slave by nature unless they are told this. A baby is born and must learn—"

"Slaves are born slaves."

"On this, Jilian, you and I must have words later."

"With you, jikai, mayhap words will not be enough."

The tip of the rapier snicked up the warrior-cloak from a body, and a flick sent it sailing like a zizil of The Stratemsk toward Jilian, who caught it deftly and wrapped its blue and green check folds about herself. Another blue and green check enfolded my red and yellow. We turned the hersany's heads away from the marquee and the windrows of dead as soldiers with torches ran across from the bivouac lines, shouting.

Into the shadows we rode, but gently, gently, restraining the impulses of our mounts to gallop in frenzy from the bedlam.

The noise of genuine combat floated up in a clangor of iron from the east and that, therefore, was the way my men had gone and the way I must go, too. I glanced at the girl.

Erect, she sat her steed, bareback, grasping the coarse rope with a slender hand that, I could guess, would have a grip of steel. She looked across at me and the redness of her mouth, purple plum in that light, curved into a smile. And then her eyes widened and she stared across my shoulder.

I switched around on the beast's back and saw riding among torches carried by a body of zorcamen a man in armor who glittered like a golden idol, resplendent, radiant, his sword lifted high as he bellowed orders. The zorcamen surrounding him looked more competent than any of the soldiers I had yet encountered in this army. They rode hard and they trampled down anyone and anything that chanced to get in their way.

It seemed prudent for us to sidle into the shadows of an undamaged tent until this formed body of hardened veterans passed.

Jilian's face screwed up into a fist. The whip snapped free. Her naked heels lifted out. I reached out and grabbed for the rope and her heels kicked in and the hersany leaped.

My clutching fingers missed the rope. The animal bounded

away. Jilian made straight for that body of zorcamen and straight for that shining golden figure. The fury in her face was colder than the Ice Floes of Sicce.

"By the disgusting diseased liver and lights of Makki Grodno!" I yelled, clapping in my heels. "Can't you control your temper, girl!"

With Julian in the lead we hurtled toward the zorcamen. If the Fates, who play with us poor mortals as children play with insects, inspecting a wing here and a leg there, had a hand in it I do not know. But Jilian's hersany caught a hoof in a guy rope and staggered sideways, twisting, hurling her from his back. The beast went down thrashing and I had time only to haul my own away. I checked him with a vicious tug on the rope and swung down. Jillian lay winded, glaring up with such a look of vindictive hatred as would make a man's innards turn to treacle.

"Kov Colun," she said. She spoke in a whisper. "I have sworn to have his manhood and have it I will—I will make him into a nithing, a mewling spineless ninny, and then perhaps, if it pleases me, will I kill him."

The zorcamen rode on, not seeing us in the shadows, our falling commotion merely a part of the greater confusion.

Jilian stood up with my hand under her armpit. She breathed deeply, magnificently. "The bastard came from that marquee, the unburned one with the golden flags. He has something of mine I would have back."

With that, without a look at me or another word, she started for the marquee. The cloth-of-gold was not as lavish as that festooning the marquee of Fat Lango; but everything spoke of wealth and refinement and a lavish expenditure of money and the labor of slaves. Jillian's whip lashed the life from two Rhaclaw guards, their heads shining, domed and as wide as their shoulders, bursting under the impetuous ferocity of the lash. Jilian ran on past them and entered the marquee, the whip black and cutting striking before her.

Whatever was so important as to warrant this risk was no doubt somewhere in there, if she said so. This Kov Colun had looked a different prospect from the others of this army and I deemed it expedient to stand on guard by the marquee entrance. Jilian would find what she wanted, so I contented myself by a harshly shouted: "Hurry, girl!"

She re-appeared and color stained her cheeks like flame.

"By the Rod of Halron and the Mount of Mampe!" She

spoke in a breathy whisper, as though drunk, and yet she moved with a sureness that told me she was vibrantly alive with her own personal triumph. Under her arm she carried a silver-mounted balass box, about eighteen inches long. The rapier in her left hand snouted parallel to the ground and even with the box under her arm I fancied she could give an account of herself. The whip was recoiled up her arm, and her white skin was blotched and stained with blood.

I said: "You are quite ready?"

"More ready than those cramphs within."

"No doubt," I said, handing her across a couple of corpses and a pool of spilled blood. "They are also without."

She laughed.

"Aye! Without much."

The blue and green checks swathing us would serve for a space yet. But the sounds of distant strife wavered on the night air, faded and were gone. A silver trumpet note sounded, tiny and far, signaling the "Recall" and the "Reform." The way the notes trilled told me that was not Volodu the Lungs but one of the trumpeters of Karidge's Regiment. They had done well, for the army encampment was in a leem's mess; but we were left here, alone, and must make shift to get out of this ourselves. In thus pulling his men out, Nath Karidge was strictly obeying my orders. I took Jilian's arm again and we moved silently into the shadows between the tent lines.

"Zorcas, I think," I said.

"With a saddle this time, Jak."

"Aye."

With a bitterness she made no effort to supress, she said, "You marked that tapo in the golden armor?"

"You called him Kov Colun."

"Yes. A piece of dirt that walks about on two legs. Colun Mogper, Kov of Mursham. Never turn your back on him, never trust him. If you can, try to stamp his face flat in the mud—after I have done with him."

"Mursham," I said. "In Menaham. That explains the difference, for if he is one of the Bloody Menahem then he would be affronted by the sloth of this army."

Her bitter anger had been partly mollified by her success in recovering her property, and my words finally brought her thoughts back into some kind of coherence. "You know Menaham?"

"I have fought the Bloody Menahem before. They are one people of Pandahem we will have trouble with in the future—"

"One! All of the rasts in that Opaz-forsaken island."

"I do not think so."

"You think because this army is a farce they are all like this?"

We passed beyond a smoke pall from burning forage and the Maiden with the Many Smiles shone out, plunging between cloud wrack, the moon shedding down her fuzzy pink light upon scenes of desolation and death. We saw zorcas moving and headed that way, ready.

"No. There is something almighty strange about this little lot—"

"Of course. They are the dregs of the gutters and the wharves, dressed up as soldiers. The Chulik paktuns they have engaged as drill instructors left en masse, disgusted. There are no Pachaks and a few Khibils in this sorry army. Pandahem breathed easier when these cramphs were shipped out."

These words gave me serious concern—more than concern, an all panic stations alarm. I saw it—not all of it, but a deal of it and the core of it. The plan against Vallia. . . . This army was the decoy, a rabble dressed up in fine fancy uniforms and taught to march together and then let loose into Vallia. They were expendable. They had been provided with a cavalry screen composed of men who had once been soldiers and who had been told off for this duty probably for dire misdeeds, or indiscipline or some fault. There are always these men who take the letter of Vikatu the Dodger and fail to see the spirit of that archetypal old sweat of the armies of mythology. That explained the conduct of the patrol we had ambushed. It explained why the army was as it was. But it did not do one very vital and overmasteringly fearful thing.

This knowledge newly given into my hands did not tell me where the real armies were, where the blow aimed to destroy us all would be struck at Vallia.

Chapter Nine

The Whip and the Claw

Jilian kept singing snatches of a silly little song as we jogged along in the suns shine the next day. We had all the world to ourselves, it seemed. The sky stretched emptily and the unending grassland was studded only with small trees and bushes, a wide heath that was, in truth, deceptive, for it extended merely between towns here in eastern Thadelm. The song concerned the comical efforts of a little Och maiden and a strapping young Tlochu youth to sort out the twelve limbs they possessed between them. I found Jilian's song silly but enchanting. It is called *The Conundrum of the Hyrshiv*. The eventual solution the Och girl and the Tlochu boy worked out for themselves is ironical and funny; it is touching and true, though, for it illustrates that despite difficulties love, what is sometimes ludicrously called "True Love," will find a way around problems of this physical kind.

She broke off singing and with that graceful turn of her head looked across at me and said, "You could, at least, Jak the Drang, jikai, have found us zorcas."

Her use of jikai here was entirely sarcastic.

We rode hirvels. Now the hirvel is a perfectly good saddle animal. He is a stubby, four-legged beast looking not unlike a nightmare version of a llama with his tall round neck, cup-shaped ears and shaggy body and twitching snout. But he will carry you along if not as fleetly as a zorca or as powerfully as a nikvove in some comfort and despatch.

I said, "There had been enough killing for one night."

"Deaths don't frighten me."

"I saw that. Can you tell me where you were trained?"

By my phraseology she understood that I was circumspect about the sororities. She laughed.

"There is no secret about *where,* Jak. That was at Lancival. Oh, a wonderful place, all red roofs and ivied walls and the gentle cooing of doves and the sliding gleam from the water well, that is a long time ago now." She sighed and her laughter died. I judged that to a man with a thousand years of life, as I had awaiting me, her memory of a long time ago might seem as yesterday. Or not, given the terrors and the pains of the intervening period. She flashed her eyes at me. "But as to *how,* that you may ask and never get an answer."

"I do not think I would choose to ask."

"And you?"

"Here and there about the world—"

"Oh, really, Jak! If we are to be friends, as I sincerely hope, you must do better than that."

"You would wish to be friends with me?"

Her regard on me wavered and she looked away. She shivered. "Better a friend than an enemy."

"Well," I said, trying not to be offended. "And I think if we are to be friends you must do better than that."

"Mayhap I do not wish to be—friends."

"As to that, we must let Opaz guide us."

"Yes."

"So how was it you were slave with the Pandaheem?"

Her face flushed up again in remembered terror and anguish, and, too, recollected anger.

"I served the Sisters well. At least, I think I did. I have some skill. But when the Troubles fell on Vallia, flutsmen came and I was taken. They dropped from the air like stones. We fought but were overborne. They are not—not nice, flutsmen."

"Most, not all," I agreed, equably. "And this Kov Colun?"

"I will say nothing of him save that I shall sink my talons into him, and rip him, and may then, if it pleases me, kill him."

I nodded and the conversation died for a space.

After a time as we rode along and the motion of the hirvels jolted our livers we regained a more pleasant atmosphere and she told me she was one of six children born to a shop keeper in Frelensmot. He had been a happy, jolly man, and just rich enough to buy three slaves for the shop, which was, she said with a funny little toss of the head, a Banje store, a place where you could buy candy and sweets and toffee-apples and miscils and all manner of toothsome, mouthwatering trifles. But the shop fell on evil days and her father spilled a vat of boiling treacle on his foot and it never healed and that broke him. She herself was sent at first to the Little Sisters of Opaz, where she learned a great deal of how to be demure and polite and sew a fine stitch. Later she went—and here she hauled herself up in her tale, and regarded me with those eyes of hers slanting on me with the telltale surprise for herself that she had said so much.

"When I went to Lancival I learned what to do with a length of steel somewhat longer than a sewing needle."

She laughed. "And I learned other things, also, and one day Kov Colun will find out how I can rip him up in a twinkling."

Her hand reached back and stroked down the polished balass of the box. A sensuousness in the gesture reminded me of the way a great cat will turn her head and rub a paw down past her ear. Then Jilian laughed again, her head thrown back and the long line of her throat bared and free to the breeze.

"And you are just Jilian?"

"For you, Jak, just Jilian."

"I see." Well, it was no business of mine. Although she wouldn't understand, I did not think we would go up the hill to fetch a pail of water together.

We would have to avoid habitations until we reached Vond and any other riders we encountered would without doubt be hostile. The rendezvous with Barty and the others lay some way ahead and although I was in a fever of impatience to reach Vondium and attempt to discover where the main threat to the city would come, I had to tread cautiously. So we covered the dwaburs, talking and laughing, and keeping our weapons loose in their scabbards.

A scatter of black-winged warvols rose ahead of us. The scavenging birds would rip a body up, dead or half-dead; but they were a part of nature fulfilling a function and so must be treated on their own merits. We rode up to the mess hunkered by a grassy hillock.

The three zorcas were almost stripped down to the bone. The three jutmen because of their armor were not in so detailed a state of dissolution, although their faces were gone, and only three yellow skulls jutted above the corselet rims. Their weapons were gone, and although two of the arrows had been withdrawn, the third, broken in half, still shafted from the gaping eyesocket of a skull. One always, in these circumstances, inspects the fletchings.

There was no sense in grieving over the three zorcamen. By their uniforms and insignia they were of the Second, Jiktar Wando Varon's regiment. Stragglers, they must have been attempting to catch up with the main body, as we were, heading for the rendezvous.

The arrows were fletched with natural gray and brown feathers, and were of the length to be shot from a standard compound bow. "Hamalese?" said Jilian.

"Very likely, or their mercenary allies. We have a ways to go before we reach Vond. The river will set a barrier of some sort between us. Keep your eyes skinned."

And that was an unnecessary injunction, to be sure.

The mercenaries turned out to be masichieri, very cheap and nasty examples of men earning a living hiring out as killers and pretending to be soldiers, and they found us as the twin suns were sinking into banks of bruised clouds and streaming a choked, opaline, smoky light over the grass.

"I make ten of them, Jak."

"Yes."

"Will that be five each, d'you think?"

They were infantry, armored in an assortment of harnesses, bearing a variety of weapons, and their bristly ferocious faces exhibited their joy at thus finding two lonely strangers at this time of the evening. They rose from the bushes and four of them bent bows upon us. They were joking among themselves.

"Best step down nice and easy, horter and hortera," one shouted, very jocose, calling us gentleman and lady.

"Had I a bow—" began Jilian.

I said: "Put your head down, girl!"

I clapped in my heels, the Krozair longsword flamed a single brand of livid light against the sky and I leaped forward.

Three of the arrows were caught and deflected as the masichieri, startled, loosed. The third whistled past out of reach to my rear. Then I was in among them. The Krozair longsword—well, that brand of destruction is indeed a marvel, and this was a true Krozairbrand, brought from Valka, the blade and hilt so cunningly wrought that the steel sings of itself as it thrusts and cuts. Four, five and then six were down before they even had time to consider what manner of retribution they had brought on themselves. I kneed the hirvel to the side and the Krozair blade hissed. Back the other way and a thraxter that came down at me abruptly checked, snapped across, and its owner went smashing backwards without a face.

The remaining two were to my rear and I hauled the hirvel up squealing on his haunches and swung him about. His hooves clawed at the sunset. We were down and I was belting back, and saw a sight, by Krun!

One of the masichieri staggered away his hands to his face and between his clenching fingers spurted a crimson flood.

The other screamed as the whip coiled around his neck. He was dragged bodily up to Jilian's hirvel. I saw her face. It was drawn and intent. I saw her left hand.

She did not wield a rapier.

As the shrieking wight was dragged in, struggling futilely against the coils of the lash, a steel taloned left hand raked out, glinting in the dying light, slashed all down his face. That cruel, steel curved claw ripped his face off as a mummer takes off a mask. Blood spouted. Jilian reined back and flicked her whip and allowed the body to drop.

She laughed.

Her left hand, gloved with taloned steel, a razor claw of destruction, glimmered darkly as she lifted it to me in triumph.

Chapter Ten

What Difference Does an Emperor Make?

"By Vox! I do not know. I've no idea at all."

"Us and Sogandar the Upright," said Nath at Barty's wail of despair.

We stood in that book-lined room glaring in baffled fury at the map of Vallia. The colors mocked us. No scouts reported an invading army, we had had not a whisper from our spies in the occupied territories. We knew nothing. And yet, I was convinced, there had to be the real invasion force from which that ludicrous gaggle of men masquerading as an army under command of Fat Lango had been intended to decoy us away.

"Where among all the Ice Floes are they?" said Barty.

He stood with his hands on his hips and his head thrown back and he looked as though he'd just tried to eat a five-fathom eel lengthways.

"There's only one way to find out." Nath slapped his rapier up and down in the scabbard, fretfully. "And we're doing that right now. Scouts, spies, aerial observation. What else can we do?"

"Wait," I said.

"Aye, majister. Wait. And the men grow lean and hungry although we fill their bellies six times a day."

"The fight will come. We must ensure we fight it where we choose."

Most of my joy at rejoining the force and then of marching back to Vondium had evaporated when I discovered that Delia had taken herself off again about important and secret business of the Sisters of the Rose. Always I felt irritable and half-lost when she was away. This is natural, if foolish, behavior and I do not choose either to defend or curse at it. It just is.

The arrow that had winged past me in that short sharp

fight had sliced a chunk out from under Jilian's breast and I'd had a fair old game with her at the end, just before we joined up with the rest of the retreating force. She'd fought her two masichieri well. But she'd become a little delirious and I'd had to strap her down to the hirvel. It was a most undignified young lady who was decanted in Vondium and hustled off by the ladies to their own wing where the doctors could attend more effectively than I had done. Had Seg's wife Thelda been here the to-do would have been much greater, of course.

The trouble was—this meant I could not question Jilian about her steel claw which was a twin to that worn by Dayra.

Jilian had kept the clawed glove strapped to her hand and wrist after the fight. That had caused some of the bother, for she'd taken it into her head to slash at anyone who came near. Well, that was all over and she was safely asleep festooned with acupuncture needles. When she awoke, poulticed, bandaged, dosed and medicated, she'd be herself again.

So we pondered the dark designs of those who sought to topple Vallia, and, besides wondering where they would strike, wondered who in a Herrelldrin Hell they were.

One thing I could do, and that was make sure the army was up to scratch. We were forming regiments at a fair pace, of course; but it takes time to turn a man into a soldier. I offer no excuses for this conduct in a land where always before in living memory gold had been used instead of warriors. Now we must free ourselves by our own efforts. The response of the Vallians was immediate and generous and we had no difficulty in filling the muster lists of any regiment on the day they were opened. Cavalry, infantry, artillery, we formed fresh bodies and trained them. For air—well, I had found myself one of the wise men of Vallia, who are not to be confused with sorcerers although often termed wizards, and he was busily producing the substances necessary to fill the silver vaol-paol boxes that lift and power fliers. We would build ourselves a fleet of sailing fliers, able to lift into the air but dependent on the breeze for sailing. At the least, they would give us some support, and at the best would help us rout the enemy.

In the great waters of Kregen there are perhaps only the devil Shanks from over the curve of the world who can teach Vallians much about sailing ships. From the fleets of great Vallian galleons would come eager volunteers to sail the ships of the sky.

The map of Vallia as well as remaining blank as to the intentions of our foes showed not a single mention of any place called Lancival. I had not commented to Jilian that I did not know it. And she, the minx, had known all along that I could not. No smot, den or village, no province or estate that I could find was called Lancival, and none of the men I questioned had heard of the place, no, by Vox, never!

The Lady Winfree, a charming girl and married to a Chuktar newly appointed to command a brigade, looked right through me when I mentioned the name to her. She excused herself rapidly and made off, her skirts swaying, her head high. So that was that. Lancival was another of these damned secrets the women held so close to them. Well, they were entitled to secrets, of course, that went without a say-so. And, equally of course, there are secrets wives hold that they are not entitled to, just as their husbands hold remembered guilt. I felt the thankfulness in me I had told Delia of Earth, that weird little planet with one tiny yellow sun, one small silver moon and not a diff in sight.

I went to see Jilian in her yellow-sheeted bed with the flowers banked around the suns-filled room. She lay white and lovely and completely unconscious of anyone or anything save what paraded before her in dreams. I sighed.

The doctor said: "Give her another two days, majister."

Long before I left the ladies' quarters, which had been among the first of the palace ruins to be rebuilt, Barty met me bubbling with an enthusiasm and a joyful eagerness I found despite my mood to be wonderfully infectious.

The first thought was that one of the invading armies had been discovered.

But Barty called out: "Dayra!" He waved his arms, his face almost bursting, and fell in beside me to trot along babbling out the news. "She has been seen. It must be her, definitely—the spy was well paid. She rode into Werven with a rascally gang buying supplies. I am sure, Dray, there can be no doubt."

"Werven. That is in Falinur, Seg's kovnate."

"Wherever it is, Dray—I must be off. This is the chance we have been waiting for."

He was right. And the devils of temptation leered and beckoned to me. My daughter, my elfin wayward daughter who wore a steel-taloned claw and slashed men to pieces, Ros the Claw—how could I not rush instantly to find her and how could I not stay in Vondium in her time of trial? What to do?

Barty must have sensed that indecision in me, for he was becoming more and more attuned to the delicacies of personal relationships these days. He cocked an eye at me, and stopped speaking, and for a dozen strides we marched side by side out of the women's quarters. In silence we continued through the Mother of Pearl Court, under the colonnades where purple-flowered ibithses glowed against the limewash, and so over tessellated paving into the cool blue shade of the Goldfish Court where the tanks rippled ghostly flickers of orange-gold like sparks against the milky silver.

"You must go, Barty." I spoke heavily. "And my heart goes with you. But for me, I must stay here."

He understood.

There was no way of telling if he was pleased or sorry I would not be with him, for we had gone through a few hairy moments together, and to do him credit he expressed immediate understanding and determination to talk to Dayra. He was aware of problems. He did not know Dayra was Ros the Claw. I felt it right that he should know before he went, and found little sense in my withholding the information previously.

"By Vox!" he said. "You mean—like that ghastly steel claw your friend Jilian was wearing?"

I nodded.

He shook his head. "What a girl. I've romped with her when we were very young—before I knew you, Dray. I think she must be very—grown up—now."

"Yes." I spoke dryly, and my throat choked up. "Very."

Barty had owned a number of airboats and all the survivors of the troubles had been placed at the disposal of the Vondium Defense Forces, as was proper. The Lord Farris was reluctant to release a single unit from the small forces we had; but he understood from what I did not say and from my demeanor that the need was pressing. Barty was fully supplied with all that a man needs to survive on Kregen and with a party of his own men was sent off in fine style. He called down the remberees, which were answered with bellows of well wishes, and the flier fleeted up and away into the radiance of the Suns of Scorpio. A fine, headstrong, courageous young man, Barty Vessler, the Strom of Calimbrev.

But, all the same, the thought occurred to me and I could

not halt it, that it ought to be me who flew off with such high hopes. And, come to think of it, where the hell was Delia?

The next few days passed most miserably.

There were, at the least, no more ghostly visitations from that infernal Wizard of Loh, spying on us in lupu; but even that would have been a welcome interruption. As it was, and despite the people around me who worked hard and with a will, I felt alone, isolated, cut off from all the things that seemed of worth. So when Nath, who as the commander of the Phalanx was now called a Kapt, a general, wanted me to inspect the new bodies he had formed, I was glad to go.

Now, as you know, a Phalanx consists of two Kerchuris, the two wings, each of five thousand one hundred eighty-four pikemen, the brumbytes. Flanking them are the Hakkodin, the axemen and halberdiers, eight hundred sixty-four strong. Because we now had access to adequate supplies of iron, and Vondium's forges produced first quality carbon-steel, we had incorporated bodies of men equipped with the big two-handed sword. With these fearful weapons they could knock a jutman from his saddle with a single blow, if they did not slice him in half.

In addition, and because of the promised threat from the air, the Phalanx had attached strong forces of archers. These were not, alas, the famed and feared Bowmen of Loh armed with the superb Lohvian longbow. They used the compound reflex bow, powerful, accurate, flat in the loose, and they had been drilled and trained until shooting oozed from their ears. They had been given particular attention. The Vallians were now aware of the danger from the skies.

As for artillery, wheeled varters, the Kregan ballistae, were manufactured and artillerymen drilled and practiced with a keen desire to make their battery the best in the army. The superior Vallian gros-varters, too, were produced. There just was not time to have the wise men go into the problems of design and manufacture of the repeating-varters I had set my heart on. They would have to come later—if Vallia survived.

The two Kerchurivaxes came up to report, massive and brilliant in armor and a profusion of ornamentation. I never stinted on the amount of decoration a fightingman cared to wear, provided always that nothing was allowed to interfere with his efficiency. The long period of waiting was trying, but as the two Kerchuri commanders saluted and I looked beyond them, with a welcoming word, to the massed blocks of the Phalanx, I saw with a lift of elation that the men showed not a sign of boredom or slothfulness. Of course, Nath kept them up to the mark. But, all the same, idleness breeds slackness. We would have to take a little stroll in the suns shine of Antares and give the brumbytes and the Hakkodin a modicum of exercise.

Each Kerchuri contains six Jodhris, and the twelve Jodhrivaxes were wheeled up smartly to me to be received with a Vallian handshake after the formal salute. They were all tough-looking men, sweating a little in their armor; but big, bold, bulky, fit men to stand in rank and file and handle the long deadly pike. Pikemen need bulk as well as muscle. The Hakkodin, as I received their commanders, were lither; but still big men, still men who could swing a halberd and take the legs from under a charging totrix or benhoff.

The archer force attached to this Phalanx was under the command of Log Logashtorio. He was a Bowman of Loh, from Erthyrdrin, Seg's homeland, and he did not know whether to laugh at the antics of his men with the smaller bow or to be proud of their achievements. He was an old professional, a man I had known for some time and who had remained loyal throughout the Time of the Troubles. I had promoted him to the command with the rank of Chodkuvax. A few words quickly revealed his delight in his command and the work involved and his whole-hearted support of his bowmen, despite that they were not Bowmen of Loh and did not pull the fabled Lohvian longbow. I shook hands and said, "Now if Seg Segutorio were here, Chodkuvax Logashtorio . . ."

And his seamed face split into a massive smile and he beamed and said: "By the Veiled Froyvil, majister! Seg would say never a word of praise; but he would see, he would see!"

And, as you will readily perceive, Log Logashtorio was anxious that Seg should know of his good fortune in gaining a command himself. So with the shouted words of command and the long blam-blam-berram rataplan of the massed drums, the Third Phalanx marched past. Everywhere I went where men spoke to me the "majister's" flew thicker than swallows in spring. I had grown partly used to it, as the Prince Majister; but now, every now and then, I'd be pulled up sharply as I was addressed as emperor. That was a job I'd not sought, and meant to do and have done with, and shuffle it off onto my splendid son Drak.

This Third Phalanx presented a fine stirring sight. But, as Nath said: "They have not been blooded yet, majister."

"Come the day, Nath, and they'll do as well as we did with the old Phalanx of Therminsax."

"They will, by a Brumbyte's Elbow! They will!"

The next day it was the turn of the churgur infantry, long flexible lines of sword and shield men, splendid in their crimson and yellow. By example and exhortation we were gradually dinning into their heads that shields were not cowards' weapons, and the success of the Phalanx at the Battle of Voxyri had done much to impress all. These men were organized into regiments under a Jiktar, four hundred eighty strong, although some were still short while others contained as many as six hundred in their ranks. This situation I tolerated; time would straighten all that out. And every minute of every live-long day was spent in training these men and drilling them and turning highly individual citizenry who were habituated to working together when profits were involved into that fierce, demoniac, cutting machine of an army that would be vital to our survival.

Also, at this time, members of the Order of Kroveres of Iztar began to trickle in from wild adventurings around the country. I welcomed them with the utmost warmth, for these were the men with whom I sought to change the ways of a world. I shall have much more to say of the KRVI later; but suffice it for now to say that they formed a powerful if small band of devoted comrades, beautifully complementing that choice band who had followed me in the Times of Troubles. And, from time to time, when a man proved himself, fresh candidates were taken in and, slowly, the strength of the KRVI grew.

The Grand Archbold of the Kroveres of Iztar did not put in an appearance in Vondium which saddened me mightily.

So, events were happening thick and fast every day; but the events I hungered for did not happen. Delia did not return. Dayra and Barty did not return. The damned ghost invasion remained invisible. And my friends did not show their faces in Vondium, as I would have wished. As for the rest of my family—enough for them that I wished them well and, indeed, messages had been sent to Zeg, the King of Zandikar.

Jaidur, of course, was prancing around running errands for the women.

The sailing fliers were built with the utmost urgency and the yards turned them out by the handful. Mere clumsy wooden boxes, they seemed, square-ended, blunt, and yet purposeful, designed to do a job and adequate for the demands that would be placed upon them. The silver boxes were readied and installed. The masts were raised and all the complicated rigging of the sealanes was dispensed with; we rigged them with foremast, main and mizzen, courses, topsails and royals only with spinnaker and jib. I had decided it was scarcely worth the complications to rig masts extending from the sides at right angles, as we had done in the past. With these sailing boxes stuffed with varters and catapults and gros-varters, aswarm with aerial sailors and fighting men, I fancied we would give another nasty shock to the invading armies, as we had trounced the army of Hamal at the Battle of Jholaix.

The silver boxes lifted the skyships only. The lines of force—ethero-magnetic force, old San Evold sometimes called them—which crisscrossed the world, were gripped onto and held by the power of the silver boxes, as though a keel was extended. By this means the skyships could tack against the wind, unlike free-flight balloons which are helpless in a breeze.

I went to see Jilian on the day of the departure of part of the army in a fleet of skyships. It was an evolution only, to see how quickly we could transport and disembark a Phalanx into battle. The ships were not all the same, naturally; being the work of individuals; but they were of a size. There were the smaller vessels, sloops of the sky, and the mediumsized, frigates of the air. And there were the mammoths. These were four and five decks high, with towering superstructures studded with varter ports. Flung together, they were crossbeamed and buttressed, their knees sturdy, their scarphs rudimentary and reinforced with bronze, their planking coarse and heavy. Without the need to combat the hogging and sagging motion to which a ship is subjected in the sea, without the need for fine lines, they could be built cheaply and efficiently as hulking great boxes stuffed with fighting potential.

Each of the larger ships could carry a Jodhri from the Phalanx or two regiments of churgur infantry or a regiment of cavalry. I needed to know how swiftly the whole force could be brought into a concentration, landing and disembarking and the troops forming. This kind of exercise was vital to our planning. We took that Third Phalanx that had looked so fine on parade, two brigades of churgurs, and four regiments of cavalry, two of zorcas, and one each of totrixes and nikvoves.

At the last minute, by design to test the men, I added the Fourth and Sixth Regiments of Totrixes. That, at the least, gave a more equable balance as between infantry and cavalry. With the bedlam going on as the two regiments frantically loaded themselves into their ships, I went to see Jilian.

She looked up from the yellow pillows and she did not smile.

"So, Jak the Drang, jikai—you are the Emperor of Vallia."

"You are feeling better? The wound has healed?"

Her claw was removed; but the end of the balass box stuck out from under the bed. The scent of roses overpowered in the room. The quietness fell soothingly after the uproar outside.

"Yes. You bound up my wound—and the doctor says you sucked out the poison."

"Yes."

Her hand moved under the yellow sheet, across her breast, and was still. Still she did not smile.

"And—the emperor?"

"What difference does that make?"

"To you—or to me?"

"To either of us."

"Nothing." And then she smiled. "No difference at all."

"When you are fully recovered I want to talk to you about Lancival, and other things." I licked my lips. "About a girl called Ros the Claw—"

She half sat up. Her dark hair shimmered in the light.

"Ros? How do you know her?"

I felt the leap in me. I kept my face composed. "I have met her."

"Well, steer clear of her. She has a leem temper." Jilian lay back, and I could see she was still very weak. "It is something to do with her father. A right cramph, by her account. But she is good with the—" Here Jilian halted herself again, and then said, "With her claw." And so I knew she had nearly told me the secret name these women called that vicious weapon.

"The people here will look after you well. Get strong again. The poison weakened you—"

She saw the way I was clad, the harness, the colors, the weaponry. "You march out to war?"

"No. An exercise only."

She laughed. It was a small, pale laugh; but it reminded me of the way she threw her head back and laughed, fine and full and free, as we rode across the grasslands.

"You look as grim as though you ride out to confront the legions of Hodan-Set."

Chapter Eleven

Of Lahals After Battle

Fifty immense sailing skyships lifted out of Vondium and spread their wings and with a good breeze set course southeast. I had a mind to find out what was going on in that corner of Vallia.

Crossing Hyrvond, the imperial province which extends a finger to the south alongside the Great River, we were over friendly territory and the people, looking up in wonder and seeing our flags, waved in greeting. Next came Valhotra, of which Genal Arclay was Vad. Continuing on with the breeze backing a trifle and making us slant our yards to catch the best of it, we crossed the Vadvarate of Procul. Procul, and the Vadvarate of Gremivoh to the southwest of it, lies at the heart of superb wine country. But our thoughts were not on fine wines as we neared the border with Mai Yenizar. This kovnate, which was then fairly large, extending from a wide loop of the Great River southwards to the coast, was firmly in enemy hands.

That enemy, we had reliable reports, consisted of a multiplicity of fortresses set up by the aragorn, lordly slave masters terrorizing the districts under their heels. They descended on weak and undefended places and set up their centers and decimated the countryside. The border had been patrolled by us and defended as best we could with the forces at our disposal, as I have related. I fancied we might drop down on an aragorn fortress or two, near at hand, and give the men a taste of real action. At the least, that operation would relieve some of the pressure.

North of that wide-ranging loop of She of the Fecundity, Vallia's chiefest river, lay the imperial province of Bryvondrin. Over the River again and north and eastward lay lands held by our foes that interposed a buffer between us in the provinces around Vondium and our allies in the northeast. A goodly stroke might be brought about here if we did not become entangled. Always, the fear that mighty hosts converged on us had to be lived with, making my days, at the least, dark with the forebodings of coming diaster.

We in Vondium were like blindfolded men who are attacked from out of the darkness and do not know in which direction to strike, for fear that a blow one way will expose the back to the deadly stab from another.

I had told Jilian this was a mere exercise, and the men believed that, and here was I already planning a miniature campaign in which real blows would be struck and real blood shed. From such shoddy stuff are emperors made.

Nath, who as the Kapt of the Phalanx, had insisted on his right to fly with us, said to me: "We fly well to the east, majister. Aragorn down there."

"Aye, Nath. A visit from us might tone up their muscles."

"Amen to that. But, I would suggest, before the suns set."

"Assuredly. Have the captain signal preparation for descent." I pointed over the rail. "There is a wide swathe of land all set out for us. And the trees are far enough away. There is not a sign of a habitation anywhere." I looked at Nath as I spoke, and he braced up, knowing I summed him up.

"With respect, majister. I would prefer to land nearer the target."

"When you see a damned aragorn fortress, Nath, you may descend. Be prepared to have your men disembark smartly. I am going below. Call me the instant anything happens."

"Quidang, majister!"

As I went down the companionway I reflected that the exercise would reveal faults in the most glaring way. We proposed a disembarkation in sight of the enemy. Interesting. Most.

The deep end is very often a capital way of learning to swim. Not always, though, and so as was to be expected I merely fretted and fumed in the stateroom, and could get scant comfort from a pot of superb Kregen tea.

The hails, floating in with a joyous raucousness, came as a blessed relief. But I waited before going on deck for Nath's report.

When I stepped onto the quarterdeck with the wind blustering the canvas and the busy activity of bringing the ship in to land, I was struck by the similarities and the differences in this sailing ship of the air and all those other ships I have sailed on the seas of two worlds.

"Not so much a fortress, emperor!" sang out Nath, mightily pleased at his discovery. "More a whole stinking town of 'em!"

And, indeed, as I looked over the rail there was a town spread out below, slate-roofed, granite-walled, huddled behind battlements. Smoke rose from the evening meal cooking fires. A bell sounded, faintly, borne away by the wind. We could see flocks of cattle being driven along white roads toward the gates. The smells rose up, some appetizing, some bringing a gushing memory of slaughterhouses. I frowned.

We had determined to drill the men in the evolution of disembarking as speedily as might be contrived. Then I had thought it would be salutary to teach the aragorn the lesson that Vondium still survived. And now Nath was bringing us down onto a town, where a full-scale battle could be expected, and where his beloved Phalanx would be of little use.

I expressed these thoughts to him.

He smiled triumphantly, and pointed past the long gray walls of the town below.

Men rode toward the town. They were aragorn, haughty in their armor, proud with weaponry, and there were many of them. But the miserable crowds of slaves who lurched and staggered on numbered many many more, and we watched the end result of a slave drive here, a successful slave roundup that brought in the miserable wights from a very large area. I nodded, convinced.

"Churgur infantry to the town with a regiment of zorcas," I said. "The Phalanx and the rest of the cavalry to form ready to stop those cramphs down there. *Move!*"

The signals hoisted away from the yardarms, scraps of colored bunting in true-blue navy style. I had taught my own aerial sailors much. Signaling, even then, was smart and accurate.

The sword and shield infantry ships wheeled away, their canvas swinging free as they slipped sheets, heading down to the gray confusion of the town. The Phalanx ships dropped ponderously to a long sloping meadow. I watched the aragorn.

Their confusion must be expected to be immense. But in a very short space of time they had shaken out into line, formed, their spears all slanting, and their helmets catching the light of the suns. Whoever ran this town was a man who knew what he wanted and made damned sure he got it.

The ships were touching down, massive argosies landing as light as thistledown. The men leaped out, running to form their files on their faxuls, their file leaders, each file of twelve men forming in twelve ranks to give the one hundred forty four brumbytes of the Relianch. The Relianchun stood at the head of the right hand file. As the Relianches formed they joined with others, so that six Relianches formed the Jodhri. Flanking them the Hakkodin fell in, and the archers took up their places in the intervals.

It was all done with a smartness, a panache, a cracking sense of style and occasion. These men had never been in action before—only a few in positions of command—and so that had to be taken into consideration. All the same, they handled themselves well, and the solid bulk of the two Kerchuris was wonderfully reassuring.

I had the oddest feeling that I would have liked Delia to see the Phalanx in operation. Not fighting, but in maneuver.

"Send a totrix regiment back up to the town," I yelled. "Volodu—signal Jiktar Karidge to keep his men back." For that intemperate commander was edging forward and forward, ready to get a good smack at the aragorn before anyone else could get in. Volodu put his silver trumpet to his lips and blew Karidge's Regiment and Hold Fast, and I saw the distant figure astride the zorca, all a glitter of gold and crimson, turn indignantly in the saddle and glare back. And I smiled.

It was quite clear that the aragorn, who are always completely assured of themselves, arrogant past arrogance, did not quite know what to make of this sudden descent from the sky. They were abruptly confronted by a thick body of men forming up into solid masses, and carrying damned great long spears. They were, by Krun, highly perplexed. They could understand the wings of cavalry, and being sensible fighting men would give great care and caution to the movements of our nikvove regiment. But, as for the stolid brumbytes, no. No, they didn't know what to make of them.

One thing the aragorn did understand. If they attacked they won. Or, to be more accurate, those aragorn who had not so far lost had won. I fancied it was the turn of this little lot to experience defeat.

A Life for Kregen

The notion seemed pleasing to me to see what our new archers might do.

Volodu blew Archers Forward and Log Logashtorio led his men out. The new Chodkuvax rode a zorca and gave signals with his very own Lohvian longbow. The bowmen spread out and, at the signal, drew and loosed, sweetly, as they had been taught.

The shafts glinted against the sky like shoals of barracuda. Up and over and down, they plunged, volley following volley. Chodkuvax Logashtorio's Third Phalanx Archers shot five smashing volleys, and then they were running back, haring between the intervals of the Phalanx, pelting out to their new positions on the flanks. As a sheer demonstration, of textbook drill and controlled shooting, it was masterful.

But it did not stop the aragorn.

As that avalanche of cavalry smoked down the hill toward the Phalanx it was the turn of the brumbytes. The aragorn rode the usual mix of saddle animals, but they modified speeds and kept together, rank on rank, so I judged they had been fighting drilled troops at some time recently. That was not altogether a marked trait among the aragorn. They liked to raid and slave and pen their captives in barracoons. If they met drilled and disciplined opposition they would decamp and set up shop elsewhere.

I sweated, suddenly.

Had I made a ghastly mistake? The onrushing host of aragorn were almost on the Phalanx now. The Phalanx was composed of green troops. Were these aragorn different from the usual? Were they about to topple my massed brumbytes into bloody ruin? I sat my zorca and I trembled. Pride, pride, what a stupid thing to do—and I had done it, I, Dray Prescot called Jak the Drang, Emperor of Vallia—Emperor of Nothing!

But how splendid the Phalanx looked. . . .

With fierce down-bent heads, their helmets all in line, plumes nodding, the pikes thrust forward into a glittering hedge of steel—yes, yes, the old words, the old words. But, by Zair! How they stood, clamped to the earth, like a primeval cliff face, adamant against the sea. A song rose from their packed ranks, a paean, a soaring battle hymn. The words were the old words, and they set the blood to pulsing. With the front rank pikes firmly bedded in the earth, the next thrust over the first, and the next in two-handed grips, shoulder high, twelve men deep, the Third Vallian Phalanx took the shock. As the rolling thunders of the ocean break in spume and fury against those weathered cliff faces, so the aragorn foamed against the pikes. A welter of uprearing steel, of screaming animals, of blood, of noise and bedlam and then of a receding wash of sound, as the recoiling waves break and flow and surge away, rippling, spreading, so those Opaz-forsaken aragorn, damned slavers to a man, broke and fled.

The trumpets rang out, crashing notes of silver urgency.

The Phalanx formed, became a cohesive whole, surged upright, moved, advanced—charged!

And on the flanks the Hakkodin hacked and slashed and carved a path through the fleeing cavalry.

"Time for our cavalry, Volodu," I said.

Volodu the Lungs blew Cavalry, General Chase.

The Vallian zorcas, totrixes and nikvoves leaped forward.

Spuming down in their turn like the returning tide, they roared on after the fleeing aragorn.

Everything now could be left to Nath. And here came a zorcaman, red-faced, exhilarated, racing down from the town, roaring out that the place was in our hands. I acknowledged him, shouted, "Well done!" and turned my zorca toward the mob of chained slaves crouched in long rows of misery.

As I trotted carefully across I reflected that the aragorn had not known how heavily, man for man, we outnumbered them. The close-packed blocks of the Phalanx tended to conceal the numbers. But, for all that disparity, there had been a sizable crowd of slavers, and their captives stretched in row after row, chained, naked, hairy and filthy, crooning those soul-songs of misery and inwardness that pass beyond mere despair.

The naked bodies sprawled on the dirt in postures of abandonment. Calloused elbows and knees, sores, scars, the brutal signatures of whips, the matted forests of hair in which lice roamed, miniature denizens of miniature jungles, yes, the trademark of the slaver is far-removed from the fictions written and believed by the wilfully blinkered. Looking at those bare, bruised and begrimed bodies, exposed in nakedness, I was reminded of Jilian's comments outside the marquee of Fat Lango. And, also, of nakedness I recalled what a dowager, quivering in repulsion and outraged moral rectitude had said, speaking with that plummy voice of conscious refinement. "Going naked," she had said, "is disgusting. Why, if God had intended us to go naked we would have been born like it."

The contrast between these bundles of half-starved naked wretches in their filth and degradation, and the well-fed, smart and sumptuously-clothed men who had rescued them could not have been more marked. Everywhere the movement of crimson and yellow as the troops busied themselves about humanitarian tasks seemed—at least to me—to bring a glow of glory to the field. And my views on glory are well known and hardly repeatable in mixed company. Crimson is the imperial color. The cavalry attired in scarlet and yellow formed a kind of personal body—not a bodyguard—and the brave old scarlet struck a distinctive spark as Targon took the choice band trotting out.

Karidge's Regiment streamed past heading up to the town to make sure of the place. We knew it from our maps as Yervismot, and I was damned sure Nath knew what he was doing when he'd brought the aerial squadron here.

The totrix regiments and the nikvoves were distant figures under the slanting rays of the suns, dispersing the last of the aragorn. Their uniform colors varied, for according to long tradition the cavalry wore regimental colors distinct from those of the infantry. This practice had been allowed to continue. In the glittering group of riders surrounding me were representatives from all the regiments to act as messengers, in addition to my own aides de camp. So as I rode toward the slaves, where a fresh hullabaloo started up with a deal of chain swinging, I moved in the midst of a tapestry of color in which the scarlet and yellow predominated.

A group of Gons who habitually shave their heads to leave bare and shining skulls were frantically digging out handfuls of mud and plastering it into that bone-white hair of which they are so ashamed. A person's beliefs are a private affair, and who would deride a man for removing his hat when he enters a church, or keeping his hat firmly on his head and removing his shoes?

There were so many slaves chained in their long rows that it seemed to me natural to guide my zorca toward the scene of the commotion. Here a fleeing posse of aragorn had tripped across outstretched chains. Steel against bare hands—well, there were dead bodies here, naked and bleeding; but, also, there were riderless animals and aragorn on the ground being beaten to death. The anger of slaves moves like a choked watercourse, a blocked drain, and when the obstructing filth is removed, the outburst smashes forth, unchecked.

Grimed naked bodies slashed iron chains. Heads burst and limbs broke and ribs caved in. But swords bit deeply in return and I urged my zorca on more smartly. To lose one slave after we had liberated them seemed to me to be offensive to the order of life.

The sword I drew was a Valkan-built weapon, brought by Delia from our arsenal in the stromnate. With master-smiths, and notably Naghan the Gnat, we had designed and built the brand. Owing much to the Havilfarese thraxter and to the Vallian clanxer, it also shared as much as I could contrive of the master-weapon, the Savanti Sword. Men called this new sword the drexer. I swung it forward as I rode, deeming it suitable for employment here, and jumped off the zorca to get in among a clumped group of aragorn who speared and slashed away at slaves who screeched and fell, bloodied and stumped, and could not break through to the slavers.

The men at my back broke out in yells of concern.

"Majister! Hold back. Wait for us." And: "Emperor! You endanger your life."

The last of the light flared deceptively as the twin suns speared their emerald and ruby fires erratically through tortured cloud castles. The aragorn were confident against the naked slaves and were busying themselves in collecting riderless animals. Those who caught a steed mounted up and galloped off, although slaves hung onto them and lapped them in chains, and brought some down. It was all a shadowy, bloody, confusing fracas, the kind of nonsense in which a fellow can get knocked on the head and never know he was dead.

Not all the slavers were apim, and I crossed swords with a Rapa, who went down as I jumped past. A bleg beyond him staggered back on his four legs, and a chain tripped him and another slashed his guts out, and I helped knock him down—for their four legs make blegs mightily resistant—and jumped on past to get at an aragorn who lifted a sword against two women, naked, screaming, hugging each other in a last paroxysm of terror.

The aragorn turned to meet me. All about us men and women shrilled in horror, and chains clashed and the spears drove in. My men were still racketing away and coming on, for my last savage lunge astride the zorca had distanced them. The aragorn fancied himself as a swordsman; but I chopped him without finesse and saw another from the corner of my eye, and ducked, and swirled back. A naked figure, with a mass of dark hair and a superb body, leaped on the slaver and hauled a chain around his neck. Entangled like a wild beast trapped in iron nets, the slaver choked back.

He went down and two more came at us, desperate now, determined to break past and get at the totrixes who stood, shivering in terror at the blood and noise. Together, the naked man and I met them. The drexer drank the life from one and the chains crushed the life from the other.

"Majister! Emperor!" The yells lifted and the men of my retinue were there, slashing aside a last frantic attempt by the aragorn. The light shifted, dying in an opaz haze. The dirt ran with blood. Naked flesh stained crimson. The slave with the dark hair and the body of a fighting man slumped, and he collapsed to his knees and I saw he was wounded, a jagged rent across his back.

Half-kneeling, he looked up.

The brilliantly attired soldiers of the new Vallia crowded about me. They were profuse in their expressions of concern. "Majisters" and "emperors" filled the evening air. And I looked at the slave, collapsed there in his blood and filth still gripping the harsh iron chains.

"Majister—the risks you take. . . . Emperor, we are here to protect you. . . ." Oh, yes, majister this and majister that, emperor and emperor. . . .

The slave looked up and spoke.

"Lahal, my old dom," he said. "I might have known you'd get here—given time."

He coughed, then, and a spittle of blood trickled down his chin.

It was extraordinarily difficult for me to speak.

The babble of voices at my back, with their continual interlarded majisters and emperors. . . . I straightened my shoulders. I found my voice.

"Lahal, Seg," I said.

Chapter Twelve

Jikaida over Vallia

We flew back to Vondium. The odd little thought occurred to me that had I known it was Seg Segutorio struggling all naked with his chains, I would have unlimbered the Krozair longsword and gone in raging like a maniac.

And that was a demeaning thought, to be sure; but it adequately expresses my own confessed confusion in personal relationships.

"By the Veiled Froyvil, my old dom, but that is good," said Seg as he took the goblet from his lips. His mouth shone with fine Gremivoh, and I instantly refilled the goblet for him. We sat in my study, with the books and the maps, and Seg looked more like my old friend than a sodden wrung-out chained-up slave.

The doctors had seen to him and patched him up, declaring he needed rest. His first words after that typical greeting had been: "And Thelda?" Whereat I had shaken my head. "There has been no news of her, none at all."

"I went up to Evir," said Seg, now, as we brought each other up to date with our doings since we had parted on the way to the Sacred Pool of Baptism in Aphrasöe. "I went into that damned pool with Delia and the emperor and the others, and then I was back home in Erthyrdrin." He drank again, and shook his head. "Mightily discomposing, I can tell you."

"I know."

He looked up. "Well, you would, wouldn't you?"

"So you made your way back to Vallia and went to Evir?"

"Yes. If I'd been sorcerously transported home, then Thelda would, too—or so I thought."

"You were right." I told him a little of the power of Vanti, the Guardian of the Pool, enough to allow him to understand that we had been caught up in a wizardly manifestation. He seemed satisfied with my explanation. "She'd been there. They told me. An uncouth bunch, all right, those Evirese."

"And?"

He moved his left hand emptily.

"I went to Falinur, then. After all, I am supposed to be their damned kov. But, for me, they can keep their kovnate and their mangy ways. I was taken up by flutsmen, and escaped, and then, being a trifle down, was easy prey for the aragorn. We'd been marching for days on end. I think—I'm not sure—I escaped a couple of times. But the lot I was with when you came up were the last."

"You are home now, Seg."

He gripped that empty hand into a fist. A Bowman of Loh, Seg Segutorio, for my money the best bowman on Kregen, and a kov, the Kov of Falinur. Yet he was the truest friend a man can have, and be thankful to all the Gods of Kregen he may call a friend. Now he looked down, shrunken, fearful of the terrors the future must bring.

"Home—yes, Dray, I made Vallia my home. And, now— my wife, my children, where are they?"

"You have returned. They will, too."

"I believe that. I have to believe that. But the whole business has been a nightmare."

He had heard the news, how the emperor's life had been saved by his immersion in the Sacred Pool, of how all those who had taken him there had been sorcerously dispatched to their homes, of how the emperor had at last been slain in the final moments of the Fall of Vondium. He had listened stony-faced as the story of Kov Layco Jhansi's treachery was told, and of how Zankov, the mysterious agitator, had killed the emperor. He heard about Queen Lushfymi of Lome, and expressed no great desire to meet her, despite that she worked hard and devotedly for Vallia. I knew that Seg loved his Thelda very deeply. For all her faults she was a good comrade and I often castigated myself for my treatment of her, for the supposedly funny remarks I made about her. She tried desperately hard to be a good friend to Delia, and Delia loved her, too, in her own way.

And now she was missing and might be anywhere, not only in Vallia, either. Anywhere at all on Kregen. . . .

Seg fetched up a sigh. "Well, Thelda always means well,"

he said, at which I shot him a hard look. "I just pray Erthyr the Bow has her in his keeping."

"Amen to that, Seg, and Opaz and Zair, too."

The doctors having told me that the Kov of Falinur needed a proper convalescence, which was not at all surprising, I made Seg see sense. In addition to seeking Thelda he wanted to know what had happened to his children, Dray and the twins. From my own bitter experiences of the past, and more recently in attempting to trace Dayra, I knew the wait might well be a long and agonizing one before any news was received. And, all this time, the work of preparing Vondium and the provinces loyal to us to resist the coming attack had to go on.

I said to Seg: "I am particularly pleased that the Grand Archbold of the Kroveres of Iztar is now with us."

Seg showed a flicker of interest.

"The Order has admitted a number of new brothers lately. The work goes on. It seems to me, as a mere member, seemly for the Grand Archbold to welcome the new brothers."

"Yes, my old dom," said Seg, but he spoke heavily. "You are right. I value your words in this. You made me the Grand Archbold—for my sins, I suspect, as you so often say. But I will perform my duty." He brightened. "Anyway, it seems to me a perfectly proper function of the KRVI to search out and rescue ladies in distress."

"Ah!" I said.

If I thought then that this work with the KRVI might help Seg, I feel the thought to be just and proper. If, as I suspect may have been the case, I also thought it would get him out of my hair, the thought was not only unjust and improper—it was despicable. Still, as they say, only Zair knows the cleanliness of a human heart.

Seg did say, with a flash of his old spirit, that, as for the new army, they were a fine, frilled, lavendered bunch of popinjays with their laces and decorations and brilliance of ornamentation. "I mind the days when you and I, Dray, marched out with a couple of rags to clothe us. Provided our weapons were fit for inspection by Erthanfydd the Meticulous, we didn't care what we looked like."

"Ah, but, my old dom," I said, somewhat wickedly, to be sure: "That was before you met Thelda."

Which was, to my damnation, a confounded stupid thing to say.

Seg took himself off to meet the brothers of the Order and discuss plans and, no doubt, take a stoup or two, and I went back to the paperwork. Blue was a color not in favor in Vallia save in the northeast, where it had been adopted in provincial badges and insignia as a kind of silent insult to the south, and in certain seacoast provinces where the ocean gave ample reason for its inclusion. These color-coded badges and banded sleeves and insignia of Vallia can be lumped together under the general name of schturvals, and by the schturval a man wore you could tell his allegiances. Nath Orcantor, known as Nath the Frolus, came to see me, highly indignant, determined that the fine spanking regiment of totrixmen he was raising should wear blue tunics over their armor, and red breeches.

Enevon Ob-Eye and Nath were in the room with me at the time, going over sumptuary lists, and they looked on, more than a little astonished.

"Blue?" said Nath. "In the Vallian Army?"

"And why not, Kapt Nath?" said Nath Orcantor the Frolus. "I am from Ovvend, as you very well know, and our colors were granted in the long ago by the emperor then."

"Oh," said Enevon, and he smiled. "You mean sky-blue."

"Done, Jiktar Orcantor," I said. "Your totrixmen may wear sky-blue tunics and red breeches—but let the red be more a madder, or a maroon, rather than a crimson."

Nath Orcantor the Frolus nodded, well pleased. He was not a whit put out that his regiment could not wear the imperial crimson, for that was an understood part of the hoary traditions of Vallia. The emperor said what was what, and crimson was the imperial color, and Nath the Frolus was raising a private regiment—for which, I add with great emphasis, I was most glad. We needed every man with us in this fight.

And there, in this piddling little frivolous-seeming incident, was another example of the way the imperium was eating away at my brain.

Nath Perrin the Oivon was raising a regiment of light-armed infantry who would act as skirmishers before the main line. When Jiktar Perrin wanted to clothe his regiment in green no one could see any objection. So, neither could I. After all, as I have reiterated, green is a fine color—for some people and in some areas. So Jiktar Nath the Oivon's five hundred drilled in a leaf-green tunic, with minimun armor and armed with stuxes, spear and swords only. They did not carry shields and, for a space, I was willing to allow that.

The army grew.

A regulation had to be promulgated setting the largest size of epaulettes it was permissible to wear. The normal male Vallian's outfit in civilian life is the wide-shouldered buff tunic, with breeches and tall black boots. The size of these wings gives a fine dramatic effect. But now, with the blaze of uniforms to play with, and bronze or steel wings to clamp over the shoulders, the Vallians seemed to have gone mad. I saw a Hikdar with silver epaulettes stretching out a full hand's length beyond his shoulder. A sensible size had to be established, for these enormous shoulder-boards with their fantastic decorations could seriously impede the sword arm, or the spear-wielding sweep, if unchecked. Truth to tell, the wide metallic wings of the soldiers became a kind of trademark of the Vallian army. No one wanted to be without bronze, iron or steel epaulettes, and their use was demonstrated in battle where they saved many a slashing blow from taking off an arm. They complemented the leather, bronze-studded jerkins admirably.

When the fellows of my choice band ceremoniously presented me with a golden pair, I caved in, and wore them when in a certain uniform which they suited. But how I thought of the days when, clad only in the old scarlet breechclout, I went swinging off to the fight!

The food situation had now eased enormously. This was due in no small measure to the wise precautions we had taken to return agriculture and husbandry to their usual high state of efficiency. The pallans, that is ministers or secretaries, appointed to the various posts of government, functioned well. I had told them what was needed and they had done their best to do the job. In truth, Vallia, or that part of it still owing allegiance to Vondium, had been ruled by decree. Now, in conversations with the Lord Farris and the other pallans and responsible officials, I announced that the Presidio would be reformed.

Farris was delighted.

"That takes a load off my shoulders!"

"Mayhap, Farris. But you are still the imperial crebent-justicar—when I am away, the responsibility is yours."

"Do you anticipate—?"

Farris could not be told of my real fears. I said, "I am

fretful. Everything runs here in Vondium. We remain in the dark. Perhaps I will tour around the frontiers." And, at that, we all felt the pain. Those frontiers were tightly drawn around us now, well inside what had once been a united country. And, again, I could not tell him that some itch in me, an ache in my bones, told me that I would soon have news from Barty.

Two fresh regiments of archers had been formed and their Jiktars besought me to present the standards and to inspect their men. Sitting at my desk—that infernal desk with its never-ending avalanche of papers—I looked up most pleased when Seg came in, smiling.

"You look—look better, Seg."

"Aye. I have been working. I know Thelda will be found."

"Good." I nodded vigorously. "These bowmen this morning, Seg. I have to inspect them. Will you. . . ?"

"Delighted. I shall, of course, say nothing."

"You may say nothing to them or their Jiktars. But to me, you will speak and I shall take heed of your words."

"Well, then, let me go to Loh and recruit Bowmen of Loh."

"No!"

He was surprised at my tone.

"But, Dray—why not? Always Vallia has paid gold for mercenaries. And the Bowmen of Loh are the best archers in the world. Why not?"

"Vallia must free herself by her own efforts."

"If there is not gold enough in the treasury, why—"

"Aye!" I said, and my bitterness shocked Seg. "Aye! If the mercenaries cannot be paid honestly, they may take their pay in loot."

"From your enemies. That has always been the way of it."

"You saw the Phalanx when we met again? Each brumbyte, each Hakkodin, is a free man of Vallia. They take their silver stivers in pay, and they know if they loot Vallian property they will dance on air for it."

He shook his head. "But it is enemy—"

"Look, Seg. All Vallia is like a gigantic Jikaida board. The drins are set out, the squares colored, the men in action. We fight and struggle for possession of drins and advantageous positions. Men die in the real world, instead of being swept up and replaced in the Jikaida box. This is not a game. And, remember, this enormous Jikaida board is Vallia, all of it, all

Vallian. When you destroy a town full of foemen you destroy a Vallian town."

We had played Jikaida the evening before and Seg had lost disastrously. This game which is just about the most popular board game among most Kregens can become a disease, taking up all a fellow's time and thoughts, move and counter-move obsessing his every waking moment. It is, in most people's estimation, far superior to Jikalla. And the image it brought to mind, of men marching and counter-marching from square to square, of the player concentrating on every move and trying to outguess his opponent, was an image of our present position in Vallia. We played a real life flesh and blood Jikaida on the giant board of Vallia, and our opponents would have no mercy if we played a false move. And, as you shall hear, I was to play another and altogether more personal game of flesh and blood Jikaida. But, then, that lay in my troubled future.

Seg started to say in his forthright way, "Well, all right, my old dom, I can see that plain enough—" when the door burst open and Jilian ran in, laughing, excited, her pale face flushed with happiness.

"Jak, Jak—the Lady Franci's rark has had puppies and here is—oh!"

She saw Seg, big, handsome, yelling at me, worked up at my stupidity in not hiring a strong force of the finest bowmen in the world, and Jilian halted and the rark puppy wriggled and squirmed against her breast.

Very mildly, I said: "Jilian, you should meet Seg Segutorio, the Kov of Falinur, who is a blade comrade and the truest of friends. Seg, this is Jilian, who is just Jilian and who I am sure would love to shoot a round with you."

Seg stared at her. "A bowgirl?"

"Among other accomplishments."

I had not told Seg about Ros the Claw. His daughter Silda had been mixed up with the wild gang with whom Dayra ran, and I was not sure quite what his reactions would be. He had hauled his daughter out of it; I had not.

They made pappattu and exchanged Llahals and then Lahals.

Seg eyed me.

"So, and pardon me, Jilian, for finishing this subject, you will not, Dray, hire Bowmen of Loh?"

"No."

"And if they are brought against us by our enemies?"
"Then the Archers of Vallia must outshoot them."
"Impossible."
"I know. But it will be done."

Jilian watched us, stroking the puppy. She wore a laypom-colored tunic with silver edging, one of Delia's, and the four pin holes made a square punctuation, empty of the brooches usually pinned there.

The moment was broken as the puppy at last broke free and, a lightning-fast ball of ginger fur, led us a dance around the room before we caught him. Jilian gathered him up, crooning to him, stroking his fur. I smiled.

Seg saw the smile.

"These two regiments of these marvelous archers of yours?"

I glanced at the clepsydra.

"Yes. Time to go. You will excuse us, Jilian?"

She put her head on one side, her hair dark and low over that broad white forehead, and all her intent look returned.

"I think, Jak, that I shall raise a regiment of Jikai Vuvushis. We can fight for Vallia."

Seg looked at her, and then at me, and I said: "That would be interesting, anyway. They have Battle Maidens up in the northeast who have declared for our foemen. It would be—both amusing and horrible—to see Jikai Vuvushis in line against one another."

Jilian tossed her head. She laughed. "That will be no new thing."

"Kregen," I said, but to myself. "Kregen...."

As we went out I noticed Jilian's sandals. Light and airy, they were thonged with golden straps to the knee. Those sandals were never Delia's.

Jiktars Stormwill and Brentarch met us on the parade ground and the inspection went off faultlessly. Everyone knew the Kov of Falinur was a Bowman of Loh, and the ranks stiffened up wonderfully. Their shooting was good. It was not excellent; just good, and I knew Seg would be highly dissatisfied. But these were green regiments, and must learn. Their Jiktars would keep them at training, making sure the Hikdars ran their pastangs firmly and fairly, and the Deldars would run along the ranks bellowing and shouting as all Deldars bellow and shout.

The standards were presented, the trumpets blew, and a

band from the Second Archers, a seasoned outfit, played stirring marches. By my express wish they played "The Bowmen of Loh." Seg looked at me. Then he looked away. Well, in this life we all have to learn, and it is always the hard way, and painful.

The parade marched off to the strains of "Old Drak Himself," which was by way of being a growing habit, and would soon be a tradition, when a flier circled across the rooftops, obviously searching. Seg had been given a Lohvian longbow by Log and his other comrades, for he felt naked without, and the great bow was out of its scabbard, strung, and an arrow nocked at a speed which would have dizzied the green archers marching off the parade ground.

I saw the schturval painted up on the side of the flier. Gray, red and green, with a black bar.

"Lower your bow, Seg. Those are the colors of Calimbrev. The flier is from Barty Vessler."

Seg lowered the bow; but he only half unbent it and he kept the shaft ready in that casual, superbly competent way of a true Bowman of Loh, the master archers of Kregen.

The men in the voller spotted us. What with Cleitar holding my own flag aloft, and with Ortyg the Tresh lifting the new flag of Vallia, and the blaze of scarlet and gold about, it was pretty clear where stood the Emperor of Vallia.

Targon the Tapster and Naghan ti Lodkwara, who had rejoined after his wound had half-healed, exchanged remarks. The others of my choice band, also, expressed opinions. I sat, looking forward and up, stony-faced. These staunch companions of the choice band and Seg had lived and worked with me in different times, and, it seemed, times centuries apart. Seg was not himself. If anyone questioned me, and no one did, I was prepared to be reasonable on the point. But Seg Segutorio meant a great deal, a very great deal, as you will know. As, to be sure, did every single one of the choice band.

The flier landed and Hikdar Douron jumped down and ran across, saluting as he hauled up before me.

"Majister!"

"Spit it out, Hikdar Douron."

"The strom begs to report," he started off. I killed my smile. That, for a certainty, was not the way Barty had given his message.

"Yes?"

"The—person—he sought has left certain signs so that the

strom is confident he knows where she is. But the strom has been wounded and is mewed up in the fortress of the Stony Korf. He cannot leave our wounded."

I said: "Why did you not all leave in the flier?"

"We have been joined by freedom fighters—we could not bring them all and the strom would not abandon them. Honor—"

Barty's honor! Well, the lad was in the right of it.

I turned to speak and Seg said: "Stony Korf! I know that devil's eyrie. It is in Falinur, that is supposed to be my kovnate, may it rot in the Ice Floes of Sicce."

The decision was made without thinking about it.

Farris was told he was to take over. No attack was imminent, everyone was sure. I would take a pruned down group of the most ferocious desperadoes of my band. Seg would come. We were at last going to find my daughter Dayra. We were going to talk to Ros the Claw.

And about time, too.

Chapter Thirteen

A Bowman Topples a Blazing Brand

To be free of the cares of empire! Once more to ride the winds and with a cutthroat band of loyal companions to hurtle across the face of Kregen, speeding beneath the Moons, and sword in hand once more to plunge into headlong adventure. Ah! This was the old Dray Prescot, a fellow with whom I had barely been on nodding acquaintance lately.

We had packed Barty's flier with men and supplies and, Hikdar Douron having assured us we were adequate for the job ahead, I had not pressed Farris to release any more vollers from his small and hard-pressed fleet. Our sailing skyships would be, by days, too slow.

Now in fading light, Douron pointed ahead, where a jagged line of peaks rose against the star-glitter. This was an uncomfortable little corner of Seg's kovnate, a sour, dull place inhabited by sour, dull people. They insisted on keeping slaves and all Seg's attempts had failed to convince them otherwise. I knew that toward the end, before the Time of Troubles, he had been at his wits' end, unwilling to use the force at his disposal against the people of his new kovnate, and yet, sharing my views, desperate to end the blasphemy against human nature that slavery was, in very truth, in our eyes.

"I remember this fortress," said Seg. He wiped his lips and peered ahead. "When I asked its chief, a bent-nosed rascal called Andir the Ornc, to manumit his slaves, he threw my messenger out, a fine young fellow, Naghan Larjester, and sent him back to me with a nose as bent as his own. It was a jest. I was screwing up my mind to march on him with my people and make an example of him, when the emperor was poisoned."

"I think, Seg," I said with some gravity as we flew down—"I really do think you are well out of Falinur. It is a kovnate of which much may be made. But slavery has to be ended. And there has been far too much water under the bridge."

"If you mean, Dray," said the Kov of Falinur, "that you wish to strip my kovnate from me, why, then, I will be the first to throw my hat in the air."

"I will do what you wish. You are still a kov, that is something useful to be, in this world, as you know. And a kov must have estates. There is a province ready for you, once—"

"Aye," he said, his wild blue eyes bright in that mingled light. "Aye, dom! I know! Once we have cleared out whatever bunch of rasts is sucking it dry now."

"Aye. And there will be a lot of that, by Krun."

He did not ask where away this new kovnate of his might be and, truth to tell, I was in nowise sure myself. But, I was firmly convinced, unalterably convinced; Seg Segutorio was a kov and would have a kovnate.

He told me something of conditions he had found north of the Mountains of the North when he had gone seeking Thelda in Evir, the northernmost province. A fellow had taken over up there and was calling himself the King of Urn Vallia. He controlled Durheim and Huvadu although running into some trouble from the High Kov of Erstveheim. Venga, of which the hapless Ashti Melekhi had been the vadnicha, had been invaded and her twin brother, the vad, was on the run. It was all a mess up there, and, that was true of the southwest and the southeast and the mountains, also. There was no profit in worrying over those broader problems now when the stone fortress below rushed up toward us as the flier dropped, and we saw the men waving below, waiting for us.

We were in enemy territory here. That was a foul note, to be sure. Enemy territory, in Falinur, one of the heartlands of Vallia!

Almost, we got through unobserved. Almost....

As we skimmed for the stone ramparts a volley of arrows whisked up toward us. Campfires burned in a circle about the fortress of the Stony Korf. A few shafts punched into the flier; but no one was hit. Varter bolts lanced the dusky air. We even saw two catapult stones come arching up, like balls tossed high in sport, and curve over and so fall away. But the arrows persisted. Seg perked up, taking a professional interest.

"Undurkers," said Seg. The fascinating information in his

comment was the comparative lack of contempt. I wondered what scrapes he'd pulled out of since we'd parted that might have given him this new outlook. Certainly, he was scathing enough about the short bow, as was I. "Undurkers. Well, my old dom, we've seen them off before."

"And will again, despite that we have no Bowmen of Loh with us, save yourself."

He did not laugh. The voller whooshed air over the crumbled stone battlements and circled once, losing speed, before dropping to a mossy patch of stone at the center of the tower. That was just about all this place was, a tower. Seg said, quietly, as the besieged folk came up: "You may not be a Bowman of Loh; but you'd give most of them a run for their money."

Well, of course, from Seg Segutorio, that was high praise.

Then we were exchanging Lahals and jumping from the flier and I was being led off to where Barty sat under a canvas awning, looking most disgruntled, with an arrow-wound in his shoulder.

The people clustered around, their bearded grimy faces reflecting villainously in the torchlights. They were smiling a little, now, thinking rescue had reached them. The scene was like a witch's coven. Barty waved a hand.

"The emperor and I would speak in private." He had not risen to greet me—and the reason for that was plain enough. His people backed off. My own desperadoes were busily engaged in estimating the defenses and getting an idea of the enemy out there in the darkness that shut down with the last of the suns. It was not a night of Notor Zan; but for a space the star glitter and two of Kregen's smaller moons gave the impression of a night darker than it really was. Seg stood at my shoulder. Barty looked up. His face looked odd; his usual high color had fled; but his pallor was made more leaden by the red stains under the skin, high on each cheekbone. He looked at Seg.

"I said the emperor and I would be alone."

Seg did not move.

I said, "Seg, this handsome young man who has fallen so low is Barty Vessler, the Strom of Calimbrev. And, Barty, you have the honor and pleasure of meeting Seg Segutorio, the Kov of Falinur."

Barty opened his mouth; shut his mouth, extended his hand as the pappattu was made. My new friends had said harsh words about Falinur and its kov. But, as always, I could not be harsh on Barty. So I added, casually, "Seg is with us in this." Here I had to trip daintily around certain subjects. "He is aware of the problem and—"

"Oh, them," said Seg. "My girl Silda wanted to go off and be some kind of Jikai Vuvushi. But Thelda didn't like the idea and I had to bring Silda home." He glanced at me, and, amazingly, laughed. "She is not at all pleased that Drak has gone off adventuring in Faol."

So ho, I said to myself, so the weathervane spins that way, does it. . . ?

Barty's news was both stimulating and depressing. Dayra had most certainly been seen and then the local gang of mercenaries who held the district for Layco Jhansi had mewed him and his men up here, together with the local Freedom Fighters. And, one of these, the guerilla chief, was in a right state over his wife. I said: "Dayra first. Then the others, all of them, as many as we can contrive."

"I agree. But Dayra isn't with this bunch of cramphs trying to burn us out." His words were not idle. Every now and then a varter bolt tied with burning flax would arch up and over and fall into the tower. Sand was flung in strewed winnowed falls to quench the flames. "Well, young Barty! Where the hell is she, then?" At this he spread his hands helplessly, and winced, and looked more gray and drawn than I liked. "My spies got wind of what she came for. That kleesh Zankov has been thoroughly rejected by the Northeast Parties, and so he is seeking an alliance with Jhansi."

Seg ran a hand along his longbow. "It will be interesting to meet this Zankov."

"But now," I said. "Right now!"

"Majister," said Barty, and his voice shook. "I do not know."

"These cramphs are getting troublesome," said Seg, brushing sparks away as a blazing bolt hit and bounced near us.

"Where was she last seen, Barty?"

"Trakon's Pillars. Jhansi was supposed to be meeting her at a summer villa the old kov had there."

"Him," said Seg, and sniffed. "I'd as lief Naghan Furtway had his Opaz-forsaken kovnate back again."

"You know the place, Seg?"

"Yes. Damned degenerate pest hole. Furtway was a great Jikaida player—you know that, Dray—and the whole place was built like a Jikaida board. Most odd. And devilish, too. I can take you there. But our friends outside grow impatient."

A few words soon showed that the mercenaries outside the tower had been reinforced after Hikdar Douron had left for Vondium. We had brought men, yes; but had we brought enough to break through the ring? Barty was all for getting up and bashing on. There were saddle animals stabled in the lower floors. But the Jiktar who ran his guards, a man who could have sat for a portrait to represent the professional, life-time fighting man, shook his head.

"In my view we are still too few," said Jiktar Noronfer.

"Um," said Seg.

"We must break out!"

Barty sank back on the blankets. He looked in bad case.

Then Jiktar Noronfer, with the infuriating ability of the professional to state a situation as though it was not a matter of life and death affecting him no less than anyone else, said: "They will break in before the flier can return to Vondium for help."

Another iron-headed bolt arched over the ancient stone battlements and hit, bouncing. The flames from the tar and bitumen-soaked flax blazed up. The brand skated across the stones straight for us like a comet on a collision course.

Barty let out a feeble yell. Jiktar Noronfer dived out of the way. The caroming bolt leaped, like a fractious zorca, spat sparks, sizzling with a noise like a cage full of serpents. It roared directly at us.

I leaped for Barty. Seg—the infernal idiot!—seized up Noronfer's dropped spear and swung toward the blazing brand. Even as I got Barty up and scrambled him out of the way so Seg with a beautifully lithe skip and jump got the spear point under the iron head of the bolt and heaved. Then he, too, jumped for safety. His cloak was alight. He landed and rolled and I put Barty down as gently as I could contrive and as the flaming bolt reared up and spilled over the stones at our back I leaped on Seg. With my bare hands I batted at the flames and got his cloak ripped off and tossed aside. I was not burned, thank Zair—well, not much, not enough to notice.

Seg sat up.

"Thanks, my old dom. We've enough light as it is without using me as a living torch."

"You maniacal Erthyr nitwit! Why didn't you jump out of the way?"

"Never thought you'd get the youngster out of it in time. You were damned quick."

"Not as quick as you, you—"

Seg's face drew in with pain. His eyes misted. Torchlight hung shadows along his jaw and his cheeks hollowed.

"Get that tunic off! And the kax! Your wound, when you were slave—"

"Aye, Dray, aye. It's plaguing me, devil take it."

Seg's wound had opened and the bloody mess made me go cold. Barty's needleman was summoned and we kept everyone else away and I made up my mind.

I made up my mind not as the Emperor of Vallia, not as Dayra's father, not as a friend to young Barty. I made up my mind because Seg needed immediate and expert attention which the needleman here was not equipped to give. He could insert his acupuncture needles and dull Seg's pain. But that was not enough. This was just another obstacle and, like all obstacles, must be evaluated and the best course chosen.

Seg protested vehemently. But I would not be swayed.

"And Jiktar Noronfer," I said with emphasis, my face I am sure as hard and merciless as it had ever been. "I see you are a shebov-Jiktar. If you wish to gain the remaining three steps in the Jiktar grade to make zan-Jiktar and, if you are lucky and live, ob-Chuktar, you had best pick up the spear you dropped and fight with us."

"I will fight, majister. I do not seek to excuse my conduct."

"Make it so."

I thought he would come through and fight well, better than well, after the spectacle he had made. But I would keep my eye on him.

Barty and Seg, of course, both of them, kicked up a frightful indignant racket. But I was prepared in this to be highhanded, very high-handed, even going to the ridiculous length of reminding them that I was, for Vox's sake, the Emperor of Vallia. Thankfully, it did not come to that sorry pass and they agreed. I turned on Jiktar Nonfer.

"Wheel me up the leader of the local Freedom Fighters, Jiktar. He ought to know his way around."

"Quidang, majister!" barked Noronfer, very businesslike, and clattered off down the stairs to the lower stories.

Seg looked mighty sullen. Because he, like me, had dipped

in the Sacred Pool of Baptism he would live a thousand years and his wounds would heal swiftly and cleanly, leaving no scars. But nature will not always be baulked and his wound had been far more serious than I evidently had realized. He would heal. But that last foolhardy, heroic act had burst the fragile adhesions of the wound's surfaces. He needed proper rest and attention and that, by Krun, was that. As Kregens say, the situation was Queyd-arn-tung! No more need be said on the subject.

Barty, too, as I say, had to have his lines read to him. The two wounded men lay side by side, Seg on his side, and glowered at me. At last Seg said, "That flint-fodder outside. You have a good longbow? Mine—"

"Rest easy and stop chaffering like a loloo over chicks!"

"Thelda—"

"I know. In this short time we've been away there could be news in Vondium. The whole world can change in an instant." By Zair! But wasn't that right! I knew, perhaps none better, how in a twinkling life can make a one-hundred-eighty-degree turn, and stand you on your head, gasping, with nothing ever the same again. "And you can go see if Delia is back, too."

"I will. And getting out of here?"

"The plan calls for us to rush 'em and knife through. It will knock over a dermiflon." Which is a cast-iron guarantee of success. "Now shut your great fanged wine-spout and let yourself be loaded aboard the voller. And, Seg—"

"Yes, my old dom?"

"Take care of yourself. You hear?"

His smile might be a wan ghost of his old reckless fey laugh; but he mustered up a smile for me. "I hear." And then, being Seg Segutorio and the best comrade a man could have on two worlds, he barbed in a cutting: "Majister!"

I winced, and then they came and took Seg and Barty and the other wounded and loaded them into the voller.

As the flier rose into the air I saw a dark hunched shape lift in an embrasure and the thin pencil mark of a great Lohvian longbow being fully drawn. That was Seg Segutorio, for you. Despite his lacerated and bleeding back he was up there and ready to cast down a few deadly shafts to help us. The cramphs out there were flint-fodder, no doubt of it, and I crossed to the battlements and looked down. Three dark figures spun away, arms wide, screeching soundlessly as She of the Veils rose through wreathing mists and shed her fuzzy pink and golden light. Now we would have light enough to see by, light enough to kill by—if we were unlucky or unskilled, light enough to die by.

The voller vanished into the night and another besieger toppled with a long Lohvian arrow through him. Four times, Seg had shot. I do not think there was another archer in the whole world who could have loosed three—and hit with every shot.

Losing Seg like this naturally made me think of Inch and Turko and Balass and Oby and the rest. By Krun! Devil take these troubles consuming Vallia. I ought to be out scouring Kregen for my friends.

Going down to the lower stories I found them choked with saddle animals and calsanys. Jiktar Noronfer was just about to climb back up. He looked annoyed.

"Beg to report, majister! The local chief—Lol Polisto ti Sygurd—has just got back." He paused, waiting. I did not amuse him by bursting out with a hot-headed: "Back from where, by Vox!" I looked at him. Noronfer wet his lips, suddenly, and finished in a rush: "His wife has been taken by these rasts and they sent a message. He tried to fight through; but was beaten back."

I said: "Was he wounded?"

"No, majister."

I looked again at Noronfer, and, again, he wet his lips.

I wondered what Barty was coming to. Noronfer was a mercenary, although not yet a paktun despite his rank of Jiktar, and he must have seen the way we were ceasing to employ mercenaries in Vallia. Yes, more than an eye would have to be kept on this one. . . .

Lol Polisto ti Sygurd lay exhausted on a straw pallet, smothered in blood, not his own, and looked savage and wan and distraught and, also, a useful-appearing fighting man. As the leader of the local resistance fighters warring in guerilla fashion against the minions of Layco Jhansi he must have a fair amount of the yrium, the power to move men to actions of which they deem themselves incapable. I did not smile; but I bent down to shake hands, saying: "Lahal, Tyr Lol Polisto. Tell me; their numbers, their strengths—their weaknesses?"

"Cramphs, the lot of them!" He struggled to stand up; but I pushed him down, gently. He whooped in a breath. He was a fit, limber man, with dark hair and he reminded me, with

Seg in my mind, very much of that master bowman. Now he got out: "At least two hundred of them, swordsmen and Undurkers. Layco Jhansi is determined to have my head and uses the Lady Thelda as bait. By Opaz the Deliverer! I pray she is still safe, she and the child they took with them, the Opaz-forsaken kleeshes."

My response was instant, particularly as thinking of Seg's Thelda brought the plight of this man more sharply into focus. He was clearly suffering anguish. If Jhansi had taken Lol Polisto's wife Thelda as a hostage, I, for one, had no sanguine hopes for her survival, hers or the child's.

I told Lol Polisto the plan and he expressed the opinion that as a plan it would sieve greens very well, which warmed me to him; but that if we swung our swords right merrily enough we should break through with the warriors I had brought. We had, as yet, no wounded to worry our heads over. The saddle animals were made ready, a mixed bunch, and I was found a zorca who, although his single spiral horn was broken, appeared a spirited-enough beast and anxious to get out of the dark and fetid hole in which he found himself penned. We mounted up and the rest grasped the stirrup leathers. Talk about the 92nd charging on the stirrups of the Scots Greys at Waterloo! The big lenken double doors were thrown open with a smash and golden moonlight splashed in. Then we were out, a dark mass of men and animals, roaring out and slap bang into the surprised mercenaries opposite us. It was all a sheerly onward-surging mass tumbling the foe left and right.

We racketed on, leaping shadows, swarming on, sweeping away in an instant a line of Undurkers who were thrown down and shattered, sent reeling, before they could pull string to chin. We hit the mercenaries and pulped them and then went on, striking fiercely left and right, leaving a trail of bloody corpses bleeding on the churned up dirt.

The drexer proved admirable for this foul work; and, to be sure, I did my share. But I kept both Lol Polisto and Jiktar Noronfer in my sights as we galloped fiercely on.

A quick bellow to Polisto directed him to lead on. I hauled my maddened beast up, his polished hooves striking the air, swung him about. The tail of our company pressed swiftly on and now the mercenary cavalry was reacting. Totrixmen appeared like lumbering phantasms from the golden-fretted shadows.

"Jhansi! Jhansi!" They screeched as they came on. The golden glitter of moonlight ran down their blades.

"You make a man twist to follow you!" exclaimed Korero, hauling his twin shields up. Only a few arrows sported down. Dorgo the Clis reined up beside me, and Naghan and Targon the other side. Others of the choice band clumped. We formed a small but very knobbly afterguard, a nut these cramphs of mercenary totrixmen would find extraordinarily hard to crack.

Dorgo had reported on the blasphemies he had witnessed in Dogansmot. These men we faced tonight were very different from that fatuous army of Fat Lango's, which had sat down and vegetated after the death of its leader; but they shared the same avariciousness for rapine and pillage. We were sharp set for them. On they came, heads bent, weapons glittering, and we faced them, and if I say we were the more vicious and savage and barbaric, well, I think that to be true if understandable, Zair forgive us.

The two lines clashed and there was a moment of tinkerwork before we belted them, belted them in true style, hip and thigh. The totrixmen turned and fled. Someone set up a cheer, but I bellowed out intemperately: "Stow your gab! There will be more of 'em. Now, ride. Ride!"

We swung our mounts' heads and gladly galloped off into the golden-tinged darkness.

Chapter Fourteen

Lol Polisto ti Sygurd

Having outdistanced the pursuit we eased our mounts. We intended to be long away from this neighborhood by dawn. We had suffered six casualties, and carried with us ten or so who bore wounds, light or serious. Not one, thank Zair, of my choice band had taken so much as a scratch. They were by way of becoming your well-accomplished band of desperadoes, to be sure.

Lol Polisto said with a matter-of-fact simplicity that carried more chill conviction than any amount of loud-mouthed bragging: "The cramphs have my wife Thelda and our child and I am going to get them out."

"Where?" I said to him, just as quietly.

"In a camp they've set up at Trakon's Pillars."

"Ah!"

"You know of the accursed place? Surrounded by bogs, deep and dark and treacherous. And decadent too, once you get there. They were proud and gleeful in their triumph." He held out a bracelet, a heavy silver thing engraved with strigicaws and graints. "This is a trinket I gave to Thelda, in remembrance of our adventures and our love. They flung it into the fortress of the Stony Korf, with a note tied to it. See." The note was obscene. It mentioned Trakon's Pillars. I understood the feelings torturing Lol Polisto.

"We will ride there, Lol. I think we can perhaps pay a call they do not expect."

"Majister!"

"Aye," I said. "Aye. Of all Vallia. A thing I do not easily forget."

We rode hard all the rest of that night and rested up a couple of burs before dawn. The wounded with a strong escort went off to one of the hide-outs the freedom fighters had set up. Among them was a lop-eared rascal with a lewd grin exposing snaggle-teeth, by name Inky the Chops, who, having been born hereabouts laid claim to a working knowledge of the treacherous pathways through the quagmire of Trakon's niksuth, the bog area surrounding Trakon's Pillars. There was no holding Lol, who appealed to me as a fighting man battling for his homeland and his people, and a family man tortured by fears for his wife and child. It was clear that he loved them both deeply, and, I could see, the love was returned. So, in daylight, we pressed on into the bog.

Mists wreathed the pewter-placid waters and green scum floated and laid carpets for our feet that would have pitched us into the stinking depths had we been foolish enough to trust them. Bladderworts burst, it seemed, just as we passed them, in succession like a royal salute on Earth, and the smells clashed and stank. We wrapped scarves around our noses and pressed on along the spongy ways, with lop-eared Inky the Chops loping ahead. He prodded with a long tufa-tree stick he had slashed off, and every now and again he stopped, and sniffed, and picked his nose, and heaved up a gob, and spat, and then started off along a fresh trail. I put my trust in Zair and followed on, letting the zorca sink his feet where he would, knowing he had sense enough in this.

Ashy-trees hovered over the ways, their spectral branches splotched, dripping with green and orange slime, like Spanish moss. Clumps of scraggy rusty-black birds rose, squawking in indignation at our trespass. These last I eyed with exasperation and concern. A watchful sentry could mark our progress by those betrayers. They were, in very truth, not unlike the magbirds of Magdag, inhabitants of the land of betrayal and treachery, as I considered them.

Presently Inky the Chops halted. The way, such as it was, stretched ahead between water-grasses and bulrushes and clumps of floating weeds. The stink offended man and beast alike. Mist wreathed and there was nothing silvery in that oily, greenish-black effluvium.

"Well, Inky?"

"It gets a bit tricky hereabouts," said Inky, flashing his snaggle teeth. "There's risslaca in some of these stretches of open water. Real nasty 'uns."

The risslacas come in a fantastic variety of sizes and shapes, and only some are akin to Earthly dinosaurs. I could see the wriggle of a leepitix as it chased a fish in a pool to our left. Oily mist swirled down on the other side, and a vast and creaking giant of an un-named tree hung over the squelchy trail. I cocked an eye at Inky.

"Do you wish me to lead?"

He had no time to answer before Korero—and Targon and Naghan and Dorgo and Magin—were up and pushing to get to the point position. I let the corner of my mouth twitch.

"Go on, Inky. You will have spears to protect you."

"Spears!" He spat—most accurately, overwhelming a dragonfly. "If'n you get a real big 'un—don't git in my way when I runs!"

"I won't," I promised him. An engaging rascal, Inky the Chops, in the style of Kregen rascals I have known.

We pushed on for a space in this fashion, my men taking it in turns for the dubious honor of leading out. I made good and sure I was up near the head of the column. The beasts did not like it at all, and were growing increasingly restive. What happened, when it did, at last, happen, reflected scant credit on any of us. The labyrinth of boggy pathways and precarious footholds along the compacted dirt gathered between tree roots mazed in its complexity. Inky seemed to know where he was going. We reached an open space that bore the marks of solid land. Trees bowered it in that green and orange dangling slime, and mist coiled, and no birds sang.

But the risslacas were waiting.

Equally at home on land or in water, they charged us with clawed and webbed feet expanded to give them perfect support on the treacherous boggy surface. Squamous hides gleamed in orange and green, camouflage colors, and bright and glittering eyes measured us for size. Talons raked. In an instant we were battling desperately with spear and sword against talon and fang.

The noise spurted. Ichor smoked as sword strokes opened up reptilian inwards. We were fortunate in only one thing; they had attacked head on instead of lying in wait.

With the drexer slicing away and the zorca a live coal between my knees I was forced to pirouette away, and felt the beast sliding dangerously, hock-deep, into slime. With a convulsive heave he was up and out of the muck. On a semblance of dry ground he gathered himself. Lol Polisto had stayed near me throughout this nightmare journey. His zorca collided with mine. Both animals squealed their fears.

As though impelled by the same evil spirit they took to their heels. Heads down, spiral horns thrusting, they bolted.

No effort of sawing on the reins would halt my zorca. He went baldheaded up the trail, brushing past Inky, and I got in a good thwack at a reptilian head, all scales and eyes and fangs, as we racketed past. Lol led. We were both carried on and away and into the shrouding mists and we left the sounds of that desperate combat far in our rear.

As I say, little credit to any of us—and least of all to me.

By the time we had the zorcas under control once more we were well and truly lost.

"Well," said Lol. "I am not giving up."

"Nor me. There is a—girl—who was at Trakon's Pillars. She may have left there by now; but I hope to find someone who saw her, who perhaps knows where she has gone."

"And I will fetch my Thelda and the child out of that filthy den."

"Then let us go forward. This lead looks promising."

We led our mounts for a space, quieting them down, and walked with careful feet along the shuddery trail between quagmires. We walked with naked steel in our fists, and, because I was now afoot, considered it more fitting to unlimber the Krozair longsword. Lol stared.

"I know I am in the best of company with Jak the Drang," he said. His own clanxer glimmered. "Men have heard of the deeds of Jak the Drang."

"And you?"

"I was tending my estate of Sygurd when the Troubles began. I had no truck with politics. But in evil times a man must turn his hand when he can. And then I was able to help my Thelda, and we married and we carried on the fight as guerillas. At times, I think, you could almost call us drikingers."

"I have used bandits, Lol. Properly motivated they are just people—it is those who seek only self-gratification who pose the problems."

"Aye. We have been fighting Layco Jhansi's men for a long time, now, and never seem to gain an advantage."

"And the Kov of Falinur? How stands your allegiance?"

"He is dead—" Lol started to say and then he swung about sharply and the clanxer flashed and a tendrillous mass of fleshy pseudopods writhed onto the trail. In the next instant we were fighting together, shoulder to shoulder, almost, to

"A mass of fleshy pseudopods writhed onto the trail."

clear the path as bulbous growths, half-flesh, half-plant, descended on us from the dank recesses of the overhanging trees. I say almost shoulder to shoulder. I like to stand with a free space so as to get a good swing with the longsword. So, together, as comrades in arms, we fought, and cleared a passage through for ourselves and our zorcas.

When at last we burst free Lol drew the back of his hand across his brow, and ichor dripped from the blade of the sword.

"That weapon, Jak the Drang, is incredible."

"It has been called an old bar of iron."

"Would we had a thousand such to face Jhansi and his lurfings."

"We shall deal with Jhansi, if the Racters have not done so first, in due time. What d'you know of this fellow Zankov?"

"Only that he is a devil. He seeks an alliance with Jhansi. There is some foeman they both fear—apart, that is, majister, from you."

"Aye, me. They mock me, I know." I told him about Yantong and his crazy schemes. "If Zankov has fallen out with his Hyr Notor, he is in parlous case and must seek fresh allies."

"They could form a powerful combine across the center of Vallia. If—"

"You said, Lol, you were not a political."

"I said, if you will pardon me, majister, that a man must turn his hand to the business of the moment in evil days."

"And so you did, Lol, so you did. And what is that, striking a hard corner through the mist?"

On the instant we halted and remained perfectly still and silent.

Strands of spiderweb drifted from tree to tree, intertwined bundles of gold-glinting threads like gilded thistledown floating on the breath of the breeze, and at the center of each small aerial maze the darkly red body of the spider, crouched and ready, feeling the currents of the air upon his senses and the trapped thrashings of insects on his hairs. Beyond the drifting spider-silk puffballs and the down-drooped trees, beyond the last curl of orange and green mist, the hard outline of a blockhouse thrust a manmade objection into the running deliquescence of the marsh.

"The first outpost," breathed Lol. I barely heard him. "Now may Opaz be praised."

"Amen to that. D'you know the best place to hit 'em?"

"No. But I guess we should circle around—"

"They'll be wary of that trick, I'd guess. Mantraps, stavrers, spikes. Let's just stroll up to the front door and knock. What say you, Lol?"

His features brightened and took on a fierce look of joy. He moved his sword, freely, liberated from worry over trivialities. "By Vox, majister! I am with you!"

So, as calm as you please, we strolled up to the front door of the blockhouse, leading our zorcas. Yes, we were an impudent pair, or a foolhardy pair; but we did it.

A Rapa stepped out, a dwa-Deldar, big and vulture-like in his leather and bronze harness. His sword pointed at us.

"Llanitch!" he shouted when we were within a dozen paces. "Llanitch!" Which is by way of being an intemperate order to halt.

We moved on a full four paces before we hauled up and I said: "Llahal, dom. This bog! It is enough to give the Reiver of Souls a touch of the black dog. Layco Jhansi is expecting us." Then, as though that little halt had fully obeyed his order and as though it was the most natural thing in the world, still speaking, I started to move on. "This bog—it tires the sword arm and that is the truth, by Krun!"

The Havilfarese oath must have gone a little way to reassure him, perhaps, even to soothe him, for he lowered his sword and half turned to call back into the blockhouse.

I sprang. I was on him like a leem. He went down, unconscious, gathered under the black cloak of Notor Zan, and Lol and I were into the ominously gaping doorway.

There were four others inside, lolling on bunks, and another two who contested fiercely over Jikalla. We dispatched them all after a short and not very bloody struggle. We did not slay them all. I was pleased at the way Lol worked. Short, efficient strokes, a minimum of fuss, and a neatness about his fighting told me he might have been a peaceful farmer before the Time of Troubles but, like so many Vallians, he had been forced to take up the sword instead of the ploughshare and found in the new occupation an aptitude that, while it must please him, left him also with that dark and hollow feeling of self-disgust and despair.

We surveyed the interior of the blockhouse, then Lol went out and dragged the Rapa in. The Rapa's big cruel beak of a nose was dented in where he had hit the dirt face-down. It had been his misfortune to find a solid chunk of earth instead of the ubiquitous mud.

"This one is half-conscious," I said, and hauled the fellow up. He was an apim, like us, and wore a fine fancy uniform of leather and bronze with a short and ridiculous cloak of ochre and umbre in checkerboard style.

"Wha—?" he said in immemorial stupid question.

"We did," I said, cheerfully.

"Uh?"

"I assume you were asking who or what hit you?"

It was a little too much for him. He decided to tell us what we wanted to know when Lol, very casually, asked which portion of his anatomy he fancied he could best do without.

The trail opened out past the blockhouse, becoming firmer and less treacherous and there were no more risslacas. That, at the least, was good news. The openness was something else again. We put him to sleep, gently, and bound and gagged all those still alive and, going out and bolting the door and wedging it with a half-rotten log covered with woodlice and limpet-like sucking slugs, we took ourselves and our zorcas off along the trail to Trakon's Pillars.

Presently Lol, who had been showing acute symptoms of earnest thought, said: "Why not take a couple of their uniforms? We could pass muster for guards, you and I."

"Aye, Lol. We could. I think you have been a farmer and a guerilla. Those guards back there—their uniforms. They are outpost men, exterior details. If Jhansi is still as slippery as I think, he will have arranged first-rate and differenly accoutred guards for inside."

"Oh," said Lol. Then, "I see."

"We'll try the same trick again, and this time say we have been passed on by the outpost guards. It should serve to bring us within range for handstrokes. I'm loath to shaft 'em without warning."

The wide-eyed and incredulous gape Lol favored me with indicated, truly enough, the flabbiness of this my later self and the unwelcome realization that I would have to stiffen up, brassud! in the near future.

To attempt some limping explanation of my words and thus reveal my hopeless confusion seemed to me an enormous task and one from which I shrank. I was saved further emotional turmoil of that nature by the simple-minded and cunning lie the guard we had questioned had told us, seeking in

"The beast bopped up out of the bog."

his professionally loyal way to encompass our downfall. He had said there were no more risslacas.

Quite evidently, the beastie which hopped up out of the bog, dripping slime and stinking like a Rapa barracks the night after, had not heard the guard. He opened his gapers and charged, hissing.

"My Vall!" shouted Lol. He let go of his zorca and swung his sword forward. I stepped up to his shoulder on the narrow trail and held the longsword, two-handed, pointed front and center. There was no room to dodge, no time to run and only a squidgy and slime-sucking death in the swamp on each side. So we had to face the monster.

His clawed and webbed feet slapped like suction pads against the ground. His hisses were boiler-punctures. His fetid breath hit us like a furnace blast from hell. His fangs glinted yellow and green, choked with bits of rotting flesh. Without a coherent thought I took a step forward and swung the Krozairbrand.

That magnificent steel bit. It chunked solidly alongside the risslaca's head and then I was knocked lengthwise. The mud sprayed. I near choked on the slime and was on my feet and hacking at the beast's underside. His back was armored with spines a foot long, draped with trailing weeds. Lol had struck and was down and stabbing away from underneath. Green ichor flowed, bubbling. Together we worked on the dinosaur, hacking and spearing, and avoiding the desperate tramplings and slashings of his feet. Luckily—and I mean that fervently—he was a four-footed fellow, and so we did not have that extra or those two extra pairs of death-dealing talons to worry about. He sagged to his chest, and we stood to either side, hacking away as though we chopped down trees in a primeval forest. Lol took a razor slash along his thigh, and cursed, and set to again with a will. We did not shout or rave; just got on with the disgusting job.

By the time the beast decided he had had enough and attempted to evade us, sliding like a parcel of rotten cabbages into the marsh, we, too, had had our fill.

Lol sagged back. His face showed a greenish pallor.

"By Vox! He nearly had us."

"And the zorcas have gone, Drig take it."

"Yes." And Lol Polisto laughed. "Now Thelda will have to walk out. She will not like that, if I know her."

"Well, let us go on. Now we look enough like half-crazed fugitives from the niksuth to make our story watertight."

"Which," observed Lol with another laugh, "is more than that sorry beastie is right now."

As I say, Lol Polisto was quite a character when he got a head of steam up.

We padded on soundlessly with ready weapons as the mist gyrated and swung oily green and orange streamers about us, mingling in confusing gossamers with the trailing slime from arching tree branches. We met no more risslacas. The trail gleamed like a cobbled street after rain. The smells lessened. The mist still clung, dank and miasmic; but the way opened ahead and the next guard was, most unfortunately, a bleg. He and his companions came trotting along in that weird jerky way of the four-legged blegs, and while they were no doubt anxious to traverse the trail through the bog and reach the outpost where they would relieve the guards on duty there, we were as anxious that they should not betray us. The unfortune circumstance lay in that they were blegs. With their Persian Leaf Bat faces and four legs like Chippendale chairs, they were clad in uniforms that, although we might make shift to don, would never serve to fool another guard. So we fought and passed on, and looked always ahead.

A parcel of slaves lurched lugubriously across a side trail. They were burdened with sacks and staggered as they struggled on under the whips and goads of Och guards. One tends to talk of slaves in this context in terms of parcels; no disrespect is meant by it. The Och guards were disposed of and the slaves, dully incurious, went on their lurching way. We walked on into the mist. A Fristle astride a totrix came lolloping along singing a song, his feet jutting out at arrogant angles. He went whiskers first into the quagmire. Lol stood back and put his hands on his hips.

"I," he said, "just do not believe this."

"You may ride, Lol," I told him. "We're bound to run across a couple of decent uniforms soon."

We found the uniforms stretched across the broad backs of three Chuliks. These diffs were a different proposition, and we had a nice little set to before we could claim their garments for ourselves.

"I see what you meant about the uniforms and gear," observed Lol as we dressed in the fancy ochre and umbre and buckled up the lesten-hide harness. The sleeves were ochr and white—the serving swod's approximation to Layco Jhansi's kovnate colors of ochre and silver—and the accoutrements of the men were of good quality. I nodded and stowed the longsword and longbow and quiver over my shoulder, draping a checkerboard cloak across them.

"We'll penetrate a good long way dressed like this. But do you keep your own sword, also."

"I understand."

When we reached the artificial lake surrounding Trakon's Pillars and surveyed the narrow wooden bridge that connected the pillared stronghold to the land—so-called—we realized what a foolhardy errand we were on. But there was nothing else for it now but to press on as cheerfully as might be. So, singing that silly little ditty about Forbenard and the Rokrel, we pushed on over the bridge. At the far side under the overhanging wooden gateway a Fristle guard awaited us.

"Six of 'em, majister," said Lol, leaning down from the saddle. "I'll rush 'em, and then—"

"Hold, Lol! You may rush 'em, with my blessing. But I shall feather three of them for you as you ride. And, once inside, make for the deepest darkest dirtiest shadow and await me. I shall not be long."

"Majister!" He looked stricken. "I did not mean—"

"I know what you mean, Lol Polisto, and I welcome your thought. Now, as you love Vallia, do as you are bid."

He grunted, and said, softly, "As I love my Thelda and my son." But he waited until I had unlimbered the bow. Then he clapped in his heels and was away and I hauled back the string and snapped three arrows across the gap, whistling past Lol's down-bent head. Three of the Fristles coughed bright blood and collapsed. Lol took two more and the last turned to run. Lol's totrix, tangling his stupid six-legs, stumbled the wrong way. The Fristle, screeching, his whiskers flaring, would escape and arouse the castle—all I could do was call on Seg's Supreme Being, Erthyr the Bow, and cast a last shaft.

It sped true.

Lol spurred on swiftly, as we had agreed, and I ran in after him, hurdling the fallen men, for the Fristles may have cat-faces, but they are men and can prove it. Inside the gateway the wooden walls stretched and ahead showed shadows under brickwork, arches and galleries. That looked promising and so I ran—fast, you may be sure—expecting an arrow to float silently down any mur and knock my brains out. I reached the brick, gray with age and round-edged, and ducked into the shadows. A totrix snuffled and Lol said, "All clear."

"Well done. Now let us get on."

From previous experience of the uniquely Kregen architecture of palace and castle I expected us to be able to move about with comparative freedom provided no alarm was raised. The alarm was going to be raised in no uncertain fashion the moment the first of the Fristle guards was discovered. So we must tailor our cloth to suit the narrowness of our movements.

This rat's warren of Trakon's Pillars turned out to be something of a surprise, in the end, for we ventured through courts of mouldering brick and past colonnades of gilded wood where every motif shrieked of one thing and one thing only.

Jikaida.

Our bedraggled appearance which had served to give us time to fell the Chuliks had vanished with the donning of their guard uniforms provided by Jhansi. We moved smartly, with that unmistakable swagger of the mercenary drawing swift, half-averted glances from serving wenches, free and slave alike. For a space we could proceed unmolested. The totrix was like to be a hindrance but we were loath to part with the steed against his immediate and urgent need in the near future. Past tumbled ruins, past brand-new buildings, freshly lime-washed, we went, seeking always to come to the center. There, we both felt, lay the answers to our dual questions.

We skirted several courts laid out as Jikaida boards of various sizes. Not one was in use this early in the morning. An ob-Deldar moved bulkily out of an arched doorway and bellowed at us, and we ignored him and marched on as though about the kov's business. Later on we were accosted again, this time by a thin-nosed and supercilious Hikdar. His misfortune was that he snapped at us in an alleyway between ochreberry bushes, and so had no protection from inquisitive eyes as we clapped him down in his cape and sat on him. He struggled like a landed fish.

"Dom," I said, very friendly. "Tell us where the captives are stowed away and you may live."

He started to bluster and then to yell as soon as Lol took

his clamping hand away. Lol tapped him alongside the skull, gently, put his fist back over the fellow's mouth, and, leaning down with a fierceness that perfectly complemented my apparent gentleness, said, "If you do not instantly tell us what we wish to know, and do so quietly, you will miss—" Well, what he would miss would make him miss a lot of life hereafter. The Hikdar was happy, most happy, to tell Lol what he wanted to know.

Leaving the Hikdar stuffed under the ochreberry bushes we led the totrix through ways advised us until we passed a neat little pavilion reflected in a goldfish pool. Past a tall yew hedge a gravel path led to a small wicket set in a creeper-bowered brick wall. Here the sentry eyed us as Lol, most officiously, said: "We have news for the kov, dom. You had best not keep him waiting."

The guard—one of that nameless band of heroes whose sole function, as I have pointed out before, seems to be to stand all puffed in gold and silver finery, with a spear, and to be knocked on the head—was inclined to argue. He was also incautious enough to open the wicket to make his point with great vehemence. Lol hit him, whereupon he ceased to be an obstacle and we were able to pass inside.

"Now where?"

"We must ask again, and keep asking, until we get the answer we seek."

"You have, majister, I think," said Lol. "Done this before."

"On and off," I said. "On and off."

But, the truth is, and will remain, that no two occasions are ever the same. And, every time, the old gut-tightening sensations afflict you and you have to keep a damned sharp lookout behind you. Damned sharp.

The bustle of the place was refreshing after the dolorous dragging down effect of the bogs. Slaves and servants and guards moved about and we were able to make our way forward. A swod with purple and green sleeves told us that, he thought, the prisoners were confined in dungeons where the rasts nested and the schrafters sharpened their teeth on the bones of corpses.

"The lady prisoner, cramph!"

The swod rolled his eyes down, trying to focus the dagger pressing into his throat. "In the Lattice House," he squeaked.

So we went to the Lattice House.

This turned out to be a brick-built structure whose bricks

were still sharp-cornered, and whose roof was tile rather than wood or thatch. We stopped by the corner of a gravel path, where brilliantly plumaged arboras strutted, and took in the prospects of breaking in. Lol was shaking.

"Easy, Lol. We are almost there."

"Aye. I haven't even thought of getting out."

"One thing at a time."

A dozen guards sweating with effort ran past, and their Deldar bellowed at them to spread out and search the Ladies Quarter. I frowned. "The hunt is up."

"Just let us break in. Then—"

We glared from the shadows of the foliage, and I saw that Lol's shaking had stopped. I rather fancied he would make a good companion, even a member of the KRVI, if we got out of this in one piece apiece, so to say. For the life of me I couldn't take it seriously, and this, I vaguely realized, was because Lol was the kind of fellow to make you do things you wouldn't dream of doing in more staid moments. He was a lot like Seg, and Inch, in that. . . .

"Bluff," I said. "It will work if you believe it will."

With that and giving Lol no time to argue I straightened up, gave the stolen uniform a flick, and marched very arrogantly toward the entrance door. This was of lenken wood with bronze bolt heads, and each side stood an apim swod, brilliant in the ochre and white livery of Layco Jhansi.

"Llahal, doms," I called out. "There are two madmen at large and the kov has sent us to protect the prisoners. Let us in and be quick about it."

The two rankers frowned at us, and their swords twitched up. You couldn't blame them. Now I have been accused, here and there, of saying that a certain man was a fool to draw a sword against me, and this has been alleged against me as proof positive of my overweening self-pride and pompousness. This is not so, as you who have heard my story will know. The truth is rather that I sorrow at his foolishness and take no pride from it whatsoever—how can one man take pride in the exposure of another? These two swods would have fallen into the category of fools, but that Lol stepped in first, feverish with frustrated impatience, and belted them, one, two, and knocked them flying.

"Very pretty," I said. "Now we must drag them in and find someone else to ask where away is your lady wife."

"We will," he growled. As we dragged the guards in

through the doorway I reflected that Lol was picking up my ways with a pleasing aptitude.

The lenken door closed with only the wheezingest of groans and as the wood latched shut a posse of Rapa guards ran past, swords and spears at the ready. I cursed them and turned to follow Lol into the interior of the Lattice House.

The place was lushly furnished, carpeted, lit by skylights well out of reach of even my Earthly muscles. We found a Fristle fifi who was eager to tell us where the captives were. Captives. I frowned.

We padded along on the carpets, past statuary of an erotic and convoluted kind, up stairways where candelabra branched, unlighted now, and tall mirrors reflected us as two stikitches, murderous with intent, stalking their prey. I fancied the mirrors did not entirely lie. . . .

This Lattice House contained a distinctive smell compounded of sweat and scent, of heavily perfumed flowers and that sharp aroma that Jilian would call armpit-smell. There were mirrors and statues, paintings and tapestries everywhere. I wondered if Seg had ever been here, and, if he had, why the place still stood.

The Fristle fifi hurried ahead. Her fur was of that sweet honeydew melon color so highly-prized by connoisseurs, most of whom deserve chains themselves. She led us along a purple velvet draped corridor toward a balass door. No guards stood there. Lol pushed on ahead, eagerly, and thrust the door open. The Fristle let out a little squeal of surprise, and half-turned to me. Lol yelped. He vanished. His yelp broke up in a startled bellow, and echoes caught it, twisting and magnifying it into a booming hollowness. I caught the Fristle by her upper arm and held her gently and so looked down into the pit.

The shaft was black and unpolished by a single shard of light save what few rays fell from the lamp over the door. No sound reached me from that ebon pit.

I said, "How far did he fall?"

The Fristle was sobbing and squirming, terrified. At last she got out, "There is straw below. He is not killed."

"You should, fifi, be very thankful for that." I saw that the pit extended from jamb to jamb. "How do we reach the bottom of the pit?"

"You cannot. It is guarded by werstings. The handlers will come later and—"

"Show me the way."

"I cannot! I cannot!"

The scene was not pretty. I said, "I think you can—I think you will, Fristle."

She wailed and sobbed but began to lead me back and along a side corridor covered in pink brocades. I carried the drexer naked in my right fist, and my left hand clamped the fifi's arm. She wore a copper bracelet there, and that should have warned, me, onker that I am.

The liklihood was that she was more terrified that I did not rave and shout, and my calmness in a situation she must know was one of frightful horror for me unnerved her. She led me along the corridors and I sheathed the blade only three times so as to avoid suspicion as we passed people. The girl Fristle made no attempt at raising the alarm at these times and, to my sorrow, I realized she imagined she would be the first to die.

At the next corner of the corridor, where an ivory statue of a talu swirled multiple arms in exotic frozen dance, she hung back. The tears glistered pearl-like on her face.

"Go on, girl."

"There are guards—"

I pushed her back, still holding her, and stuck my head around the corner. Four apim guards lounged outside a door. Clad like the others in ochre and silver, bearing swords and spears, they yet, for all their lounging, looked alert and a cut above the usual run. One revealed the glitter of a silver pakmort at his throat.

"The lady captive," I said to the Fristle fifi. "She is in there?"

"Yes. She and the child."

I pondered.

No harm seemed to have come so far to Thelda Polista and her child. The priority appeared to me to get Lol safely out of that black pit, then rescue his Thelda, and so make our break out. I did not wish to be lumbered with a woman and a baby going down against Werstings. So I hitched my left fist around the girl's arm, very friendly, and said to her a few home truths, whereat she trembled anew, and so started off with a confident swing, my story all ready for the guards.

Well, men grow corn for Zair to sickle.

Somewhere a harp was being played, long muted ripples of sound pouring through the close confines of the corridor where the lavender drapes and the pictures set an incongruous note against the harsh armor and weapons and the passions. For I was wronght up, and the Fristle was half-dead with fear, and the guards to relieve the tedium were mindful for a little fun.

We walked along as sedately as a pair of candidates for the Dunmow Flitch. But these idle-bored-half-witted guards! The antics of people attempting to relieve the tedium by teasing and taking pleasure from baiting others have always repelled me, and, by Krun, always will. These four started the usual nonsense and I walked on with a stony face which, in their ignorance, they failed to observe. The Fristle gasped. When the buffoonery became too coarse, for they halted us with a lazily dropped spear to bar the passage, and the Fristle, shivering with a paroxysm of terror, fell half-swooning, and the guards moved in with more intent purpose, there was nothing else left for that onker of onkers, Dray Prescot, to do but prevent them.

They went to sleep peacefully enough, all four of them.

"The devil take it!" I was wroth. Now, as there had been nothing for it when the guards started to have their idiot nasty fun, so now there was nothing for it but to go in and bring Thelda Polista and her son out. The guards' slumbering bodies would soon be noticed. If we dragged them in and locked the door their absence would soon be noticed. And if we simply left them they would recover and they would soon give notice.

So, in we went.

The revolting behavior of the guards outside should have given me some warning. Of the four, one had been a paktun. Their Hikdar inside the prison chambers was also a paktun, an apim and a damned handsome fellow in his own eyes with his curly brown hair and striking eyes and smooth easy swagger. The woman he held in his arms in an alcove struggled silently with him. He had begun his little antics early. I wondered if Layco Jhansi was aware, and realized instantly that he could not be. Or, he might—and not give a damn. Provided Lol's wife was still alive to act as a bargaining counter, Jhansi wouldn't care what tortures she went through. The two were in partial shadow. I let go of the Fristle, who swooned clean away, and crossed the rugs in half a dozen strides, knocking an ornamental table with spindly legs over on the way. The baby lay in a crib to the side and Thelda's dress was disarranged and I guessed she had been putting the infant to sleep after his morning feed. I felt inclined to put this rast of a Hikdar to sleep, also.

I hit him with a certain force under the ear.

He collapsed, face first, soundlessly, onto the carpets at the woman's feet. Her face blazed up. She swayed. Her hand went to her breast.

"Dray! Oh, Dray—it *is* you!"

I stared, appalled.

Chapter Fifteen

I Postpone a Problem

Sometimes a man will leap out of bed after a vile dream with a cry of horror on his lips, and his hand will reach out for the sword scabbarded conveniently on the bedpost.

Well, I could not stop the anguished cry from bursting past my lips. And I already held a sword in my fist.

But I knew I could not awake from this nightmare.

Seg!

"Dray, oh, Dray!" Thelda lurched toward me, her arms out and I could only take her into my arm, and hold her and feel how she trembled, like a hunted beast in a snare. She was trapped, horribly trapped, and she did not know it.

"Thelda," I said, stupidly. Then, "We'll get you out of this. Now, love, brace up."

Her face lifted and she looked at me. Tears spangled her cheeks. She was just as I remembered her, just as beautiful, just as plump and happy, just as self-oriented with all her outward devotion to her friends, like puppy-love. Yes, this was Thelda, whom I have mocked and laughed at, who was a good comrade to Delia and me, and who was Seg's wife and the mother of his children.

I moved a little back in a gentle attempt to free myself from her embrace and swung about a little; but she clung to me, her naked arms about my neck, her tear-stained face reaching up to mine. I did not kiss her. I do not think I ever had. Standing thus so closely-entwined I could feel the warmth of her, the perfume, and I saw the door open with a smash and a man burst in. I started to hurl Thelda away and then there was no need.

Lol Polisto stood there, dishevelled, the sword in his fist caked with blood to the hilt and blood splashed most horridly over that smart Chulik uniform. He saw us.

The instinctive and fierce flash of jealousy that burst up like flame into his face was instantly quelled as I spoke.

"Thank Opaz you got out of that pit, Lol. Here is Thelda and safe. The baby too. Now, for the sweet sake of all we hold dear, let us get out of here."

"Yes, yes," cried Thelda. There was no pretense in the way she freed herself from me and flung herself at Lol all blood-caked as he was. I stood there and the brains in my old vosk-skull felt as though they were frizzling. Didn't Thelda know Seg was still alive? And, if knowing, did she care? Then I remembered what Lol had said, off-handedly, that the Kov of Falinur was dead. Thelda must believe that, too. She *must*. . . .

"Now, my heart," said Lol, holding Thelda close, stroking her back, her hair, soothing her in an old familiar way that spoke eloquently of their intimate relationship. "The emperor and I will get you out of here, and our son, and then—"

Thelda drew back a little, her face flushed; but she still clasped Lol with a fierce and supplicating grasp. "Is the emperor here with an army, then? After all I have done for him and his family that is the least he could do for us."

And, I swear it, I laughed.

Wasn't that Thelda—to the life?

The puzzlement in Lol's tough face added to my amusement.

"Here is the emperor, Thelda, my heart, so do be—polite."

"I do not see him, Lol. What—?"

"Come on, you two," I broke in. "If you must gabble, gabble as we run."

Leaving the unconscious and unharmed Fristle where she lay a-swoon, and the Hikdar, of whose conduct I felt it best not to apprise Lol, draped across the carpets, we went out. Thelda carried the baby on her breast. Lol's protective instincts were now so fully aroused I had not the slightest query to make how he had got out of the pit. As we went quickly along the corridor he told me that he had chopped a couple of werstings, those ferocious hunting dogs of Kregen, and a couple of slave handlers, too, the cramphs. At this I lost my smile. He had arrived here from the other direction, the way the Fristle was leading me, and seeing the guards guessed at once he had arrived at where he needed to be. He had also, he said, breathed a quick prayer to Opaz before flinging the door open and bursting in.

At the first stairway we went up, for Thelda told us there was a small and private flier park on the roof of the Lattice House. This was the means by which she had been brought here. The next flight of stairs was guarded by two Fristles, lounging and yawning, and they yawned in a more ghastly way after Lol was through with them. The stairs were no longer carpeted with lushly decorative patterns, merely a plain ochre weave. Our footsteps remained soundless. Near the top an alcove held a silver lamp shaped in the form of an airboat, its tall single flame unwavering. The quietness struck oddly after the racket below. Thelda paused, and gasped, and half-laughing said: "Give me leave to rest awhile, my love."

At once full of contrition, Lol halted and Thelda sat down in the alcove and began to fuss with the baby. I stood with my back against the wall below and Lol above on the stairs.

Thelda wanted to talk and she asked again about the emperor and his army. I said, "You found yourself in Evir, Thelda. So what then?"

Being Thelda and being faced with something she found incomprehensible, she had simply blotted the incident out as though it had not happened. From the Sacred Pool of Baptism in far Aphrasöe she had been magically transported to her homeland of Evir. She had at once started for Falinur where she was the kovneva and her husband, Seg Segutorio, was the kov, however unwilling a kov he might be. She had arrived just in time to be caught up in the Troubles.

"Oh, it was terrible, Dray! The burning and the looting and—"

I could not help noticing how Lol kept jumping each time Thelda called me by name. Despite all my own views on the idiocy of protocol and suchlike fripperies, I do not accept into the circle of those who may call me by my given name everyone who may imagine he or she has the right. So—beware! And for Lol Polisto it was very clear I should be addressed as majister. So, to smooth one difficulty and to skirt another, I said: "Thelda and I are old friends, Lol. And, it is clear she does not know of Jak the Drang."

"Who?" said Thelda.

Lol started to say something; but I went on speaking, asking Thelda to tell us the rest before we pushed on. From below stairs no sounds reached us. And Thelda was still in a state of shock, too abruptly released. And, also, I wanted to scout the roof before we burst out.

She had been through a lot in her kovnate of Falinur, where she had been thoroughly detested. And, in the way of things, Lol Polisto had come along and rescued her from a particularly nasty scrape. And nature had taken its course. She firmly believed Seg was dead. She had been told so by taunting officers of Layco Jhansi before Lol took her away from them.

The inevitable had happened. For, as she said quite simply: "Seg wasn't there when I needed him."

By Zair, he wasn't! He was busy trying to escape the lash and the chains of slavery with a damned great wound in him, that had healed only to be broken again and again, and now this last breaking would be attended to, or my name wasn't Dray Prescot. The machinations of the Savanti nal Aphrasöe through their creature, Vanti of the Pool, ensured that Seg could not be in the same place as Thelda when she needed him, for he had been pitchforked back to his homeland of Erthyrdrin in Loh. Never had fate—and fate had been employed, this time, by the Savanti—played a much dirtier trick.

By the way in which these two looked at each other, the way they touched, by what they said, I could see with limpid clarity they were deeply in love. Well, that was all very fine. I knew that Seg and Thelda had lover each other very deeply, also. Some people aver that it is possible to love more than one person at the same time; love, I mean, in the intimate, sexual union properly belonging to man and wife. Monogamy was the fashion in Vallia, never mind what exotic goings-on occurred in other parts of Kregen. To love more than one person in sequence, that is understandable, else widows and widowers would never escape happily out of their state. But—at the same time? I was not sure. It is a knotty one, and demands scrutiny. Total love, well, by its very nature that cannot be given to more than one at a time. Can it?

Equally, although I had known Lol Polisto for a short time, a very short time, I fancied I had summed him up as a courageous, upright, honest man, who fought for what he loved and believed in. There was nothing here in this new union of the moist-mouthed contemptible underhand way of Quergey the Murgey, the arch-seducer. The obvious way out meant it was all down to Thelda. For the time being I would not, could not, tell her that her husband still lived.

Lol did not know, for he had been out on his fruitless bid

to break through the ring of besieging mercenaries when Seg and I had arrived in the fortress of the Stony Korf. So why destroy the happiness of these two now? Anyway, despite his immersion in that milky fluid that gave such tremendous recuperative powers, Seg might still die of that ghastly wound. And we were not out of the wood yet. Lol might die. Thelda might die. We might all die. I pushed away from the wall and, saying, "Bide a space here while I scout the roof," went on up the stairs.

What a situation! Maybe it is not new on two worlds, maybe it seems trite to the blasé, I could feel for my comrade Seg, and feel for Thelda, and, by Vox, I could feel for Lol, also. Emotions twist a fellow's guts up in a positively physical way, putting him off his food, making him lean and irritable. And I was feeling highly wrought up as I shoved the door open and stepped out onto the roof, the naked brand in my fist.

The roof was empty.

A single small flier stood chained down, and a tiny wind blew miasmic odors in from the niksuth.

I went back through the doorway and motioned to them to come up. Thelda carried the baby up first, and Lol guarded the rear. We stood on the roof and looked at the flier.

"That is a single place craft, . . ." Lol stated the obvious.

"Hum," I said, for I had nothing helpful to add.

"It is very clear you must go," said Lol, speaking with a tightness to his lips that, while it warmed me, made me angry, also. "As for us, we will—"

"Thelda and the baby will go, Lol, and you will ride the coaming. That voller will take you both, I know. I have built the things." I walked across, not prepared to have any further argument.

Lol wouldn't have it. "But—" he began.

I took Thelda's arm as she came up and swung around to face Lol. "In with you, Thelda. Careful of the baby. Now, Lol, stretch out here, on the coaming, and we will strap you tightly."

"But there is room for you—"

I shook my head. "The way they build these things is a disgrace. All Vallians know that. But this will be built by Hamalese for Hamalese and so should not fail. But she won't take us all. Now, Lol, get aboard!"

"But you! How will—?"

I lifted Thelda bodily and plumped her into the narrow cockpit of the flier among the flying silks and furs. She held the baby with a care that was completely genuine. I faced Lol.

"Do you wish to argue, Tyr Lol?"

His face betrayed the emotions of rebellion, fear for his wife—for the woman he believed was his wife—and loyalty to Vallia represented by me. I wanted to smile at his confusion; but time was running out. I jerked my head at the voller. "In with you."

"But it isn't right—"

"I am perfectly prepared to knock you over the head," I told him. "But would prefer to say, simply, that your emperor commands you. Would you disobey a lawful command of your emperor?"

"Emperor?" said Thelda, looking up from the child.

"I'd obey any damn command, lawful or unlawful," said Lol, feelingly, on a gust of expelled breath. "But—"

"Go!" I bellowed. "And buckle the straps tightly."

So, still loath but his conscience clear, Lol climbed onto the coaming. The straps were fastened, Thelda took the controls, the baby started crying, and the voller took off.

"Well," I said as the airboat lifted away. "Thank Zair that little nonsense is over. What a to-do!"

But what the to-do would be when Thelda discovered Seg still to be alive was past me. It was all down to her, it would have to be all down to her. No one else could dictate what she should do. I found all my feelings for Thelda rising and tormenting me, for she had been a good companion, as you know.

So, feeling treacherously free of the problem, for I had merely shuffled it off for a space, I went back to the stairs and started to think about getting myself out of this dolorous place.

Chapter Sixteen

The Carpeting of Ros the Claw

Before I could do that desired thing there was another task to my hand. I had not failed to ask about Dayra as well as Thelda on the way in; and had received no useful answers. At the time, with Lol along, Thelda had been our main concern, and rightly so, for Dayra was here not as a prisoner but as an embassy, bringing offers of alliance from that bastard Zankov.

It seemed to me perfectly proper to find another guard with a fancy uniform, a pakmort and the rank of Jiktar, take what I wanted from him, clean myself up, and then go looking for my wayward daughter. All this I did, and as a smartly-turned out Jiktar, with the silver mortil head on its silken cord at my throat, went through from the slave quarters to the inner recesses of Trakon's Pillars.

This stronghold within its encircling bogs was an open place covering a fair amount of ground. Much of it was on stilts, some on mats, and the hard ground was reserved for the highest of the high. The Pillars from which the place took its name were volcanic extrusions, tall separately trunked obelisks of naked tufa, pitted and worn, rising like unformed Easter Island statues in a clump at the center. They provided a pivot around which the busy stronghold revolved.

In lifting terraces below, the palaces had been buiit, each one more grand than the last. White columns, pavements and walls blinded in the suns as I climbed leaving the dank mists below. I was not stopped, was not even questioned. A Jiktar is a reasonably exalted rank, and the insignia told observers that I was an ord-Jiktar, having risen eight steps in the grade. The pakmort carried more weight, even, than that, here where gold still bought swords.

Now, just because a Jiktar is a pretty high rank, the holder usually commanding a regiment, the disguise took me through the lower ways up to the palaces. But once there I would have to find a swod's gear; for all Jiktars would be known and recognized. A party of men marched across and the dwa-Deldar in command saluted me. I returned the compliment. They were archers, and their bows were long and hefty, round staves of a certain length. They were Bowmen of Loh.

Finding one on his own was not easy; but eventually I was buckling up the leather gear of a Bowman of Loh and settling the bronze helmet on my head. I kept my own bow. Then I went boldly into the first palace, a sea-green confection profuse with satyrs and nymphs carved on the walls.

The quondam owner of the archer's gear had told me that the embassy from Zankov was housed in this place, the Palace of the Octopus. So, in I went. In for a zorca, in for a vove.

Layco Jhansi had been the old emperor's chief pallan and had run things in Vondium most tightly. He had subverted the allegiance of the Crimson Bowmen of Loh. So there were plenty of Lohvians with their red hair about, as well as dark-haired archers from Erthyrdrin. My brown hair, being Vallian, did not attract undue attention. Five-handed Eos-Bakchi, that mischievous Vallian spirit of luck and good fortune, favored me unduly. A Deldar spotted me and bellowed and soon I found myself marching in a three-deep column of Bowmen, en route to provide a guard. Well, the ploy got me in well enough.

Five-handed Eos-Bakchi, however, did not see fit to arrange for me actually to attend in the reception for Zankov's embassy. That would have been to ask too much. We were stationed at intervals along the corridors and the tessellated pavements, and I drew a billet at the head of some stairs that led down to what depths I did not know. I stood there, alert, looking the very personification of one of those guards I have detailed as being fancifully dressed, spear-bearing and ripe for knocking on the head.

Now it is perfectly true that most people inhabiting palaces staffed with a plethora of guards barely notice their guards at all. Old rogues like myself who have served their time do notice; but we are in a pitiful minority. No one noticed me. I'm damn sure they'd have noticed had I not been on duty, like a pickled gherkin at my post.

And so my daughter Dayra walked along the corridor and past the stairs, deep in conversation with that foresworn scoundrel, Tyr Malervo Norgoth, him who had once come with an embassy from Jhansi to me and set his sorcerer, Rovard the Murvish, on me. I just stood there, lumpen, my face shadowed by the ornate helmet. Malervo Norgoth with his gross body and spindly legs looked much as I remembered him. He wore loose robes of a sickly green color, with much gold and silver embroidery. But Dayra—Dayra looked magnificent.

She wore a long dress of the imperial style, all in sheerest sensil, that finer silk of Kregen, of a pale oyster color that shimmered as she walked. Her carriage was that of an empress. There were feathers in the golden circlet around her brown Vallian hair. Her face glowed with conviction and passion as she talked. Her figure was a knock-out. Yes, I well realize the dignity and impudence of that; but it fitted. Fitted perfectly. For I had seen this glowing girl when she had been clad in black leathers, with her long legs flashing, driving wicked steel with her right hand, and her left taloned in those vicious raking claws.

Her jewelry glistered and blinded. She wore far too much. I fancied the massed iridescence of gems was genuine. Just whose gems they were seemed to me—her father—as a matter of moment. But, not for the moment. Why she wore so much jewelry might have been puzzled out by an earthly psychologist, with a glib theory that it reflected rebellion against her mother's elegant and refined taste, which leant more to small and costly items of quality, rather than a massed and vulgar display. I did not think so. This was Kregen. Dayra flaunted the gems so as further to convey the power she represented as embassy from Zankov.

Malervo Norgoth was saying as they walked along: " . . . doesn't mean a single damn thing, my dear, and it would be best if you did not forget it."

The reply Ros the Claw would make to that insulting comment intrigued me; but she simply said: "Yet Zankov's new allies do mean a damn thing. They mean very much. No one is going to stand before them, you may believe me."

"There are many dwaburs between the east and Vennar."

"They can be crossed. Zankov would cross them in friendship."

"A friendship which he values highly in terms of what he asks in the way of gold..."

They walked on, wrangling, and a few personal guards followed them, whereat I drew up even straighter and angled the helmet to shadow my face even more. Rovard the Murvish trailed along at the rear, emitting his unmistakable effluvium of dead rats and sewers, and shaking his morntarch with a reflective gesture. His furs and bangles and shaggy hair lent him a wild and grotesque appearance. The party moved on and I breathed out and glanced back along the line of guards.

The Deldar was nowhere in sight. Not one of those ramrod guards would move if I walked off. That was a racing certainty. So, shouldering the spear I had taken from the archer, an ornate and highly-polished piece with tufts of white and ochre ribbons, I marched off after Malervo Norgoth, Dayra and the rest.

The search for the two madmen who had broken into Trakon's Pillars from the bogs continued and so I assumed no one had yet discovered the absence of that single-place voller. That pleased me, for it meant no pursuit would take off after Lol and Thelda. So, feeling ready for what might come, I followed the embassy into a cross-corridor where tall windows threw diamonds of brilliance across the carpets and where Norgoth led Dayra into a room through an ochre and silver doorway.

The thought occurred to me that both Zankov and Jhansi were avid for an alliance. Both felt their own weakness and needed additional strength. And both, it was clear, would seek to dominate their partnership. It seemed to me clear cut that I should do all I could to upset that understanding between them and prevent the alliance. That fitted in with my plans for Dayra. I fancied it was high time that minx answered to her mother and father. That her answers might make the sweetest of sense I have already indicated, and I was fully prepared to take her side in all things, if it came to it, bar, perhaps, a coherent understanding of the man who had slain her grandfather. And, even there, reasons impelled him that were sound, even honorable, to him. I owed him that much. Zankov might not be the black-hearted scoundrel everyone said he was. The odds were against it; but the chance remained.

And, as I walked up with a swagger toward the two Bowmen who guarded the ochre and silver door, I recognized in my thoughts the bias I owed to, the condemnation of Zankov that stood in my brain like a lighthouse in stormy seas. I was prejudiced against him—for good reason—and must attempt in justice to take that into account in my dealings with him.

"Lahal, dom," I sang out to the first guard, scraping up a frozen grimace that might pass muster for a smile, and nodding to his companion. "You're in luck, by the Seven and Two."

"Oh?" spoke up the first worthy, flicking a glance to his comrade. "And, dom, how are we so fortunate?"

"Why, to be sure. Here am I come to stand your watch while you have fun chasing after these madmen who have broken in. I wish you well of it, although I could do with loosing at fair game rather than the butts."

The guard favored me with a hard look. But I had slipped the longsword on its strap down my back so that the checkered cloak covered it, and although the sword of the Bowmen of Loh was usually the Walfargian lynxter many of them preferred other weapons picked up in their mercenary trade, so that my drexer passed muster. The second guard let a broad and happy smile part his whiskers.

"That is good news. Come, Nath, let us go and feather a few rasts and earn our hire."

"Gladly, Naghan. I am with you."

And, with that jaunty mercenary swing, they marched off with a perfunctory: "Rember!" and a laugh. I stood by the door and breathed out and considered.

To break in would be easy. To slay a few of the cramphs in there probably also not too difficult. But Ros the Claw would fight. She had fought before, although sparing me in the end. I did not wish once more to face my daughter with naked steel between us.

A subterfuge of the simple-minded kind was called for.

No food had passed my lips for far too long, a most unhealthy and anti-social attitude that for Kregen, by Krun, and I had not slept much lately, either. But one must accept the needle. I pushed the door open and slanted my head so that the helmet brim shadowed my face. The small chamber beyond was an anteroom, with doors in three walls, fast closed, and a rumble of voices reached me from the door with a strigicaw head in half-relief above the architrave. I put my ear to the wood and listened.

A rumble of voices in which no words were clear left me,

as ever, it seemed of late, no alternative. My hand reached out for the latch fashioned after a pair of entwined totrixes and then I halted, dumbstruck at my own stupidity. My hand withdrew and I looked about swiftly. The next door along, the one with the chavonth head above it. Yes—another alternative had presented itself, and the simple-minded stratagem had become positively imbecile.

The door opened soundlessly. Two young fops, all lace and embroidery, playing Jikaida looked up with guilt stamped all over their asinine faces. They went to sleep peacefully and I pressed my ear against a grille in the wall adjoining the strigicaw room. The voices spurted, not particularly clear; but I heard enough to make me feel that my daughter was a scheming minx and a half, a worthy daughter to her mother.

". . . voves! Nothing will stand before them."

"So you say, Lady Ros. But the distances and the gold speak against you."

"The clans are with us in this. Their hatred of Vovedeer Prescot is as the prairie fire. It rages up fiercely and is all-consuming. Beware lest you and your master are broiled in the blaze."

"Threats?"

Dayra laughed, that ringing, silvery, contemptuous laugh of Ros the Claw. "You have put these chambers at my disposal, good Norgoth. How sits a threat against you here?"

"I am glad you remember this."

Then another voice broke in, a more distant rumble, and scraping sounds indicated the movement of chairs so I took it the conversation was ended. A few strides took me back to the door and I peered through the crack. Norgoth and Rovard and their retinue sailed out like galleons of Vallia, proud and puffed and supremely conscious of their superiority. I waited.

When they had gone I eased across to the door of the strigicaw and tried the totrix-latch. The door was locked. I rapped my knuckles on the wood. How formal one becomes in these moments! The door made clicking sounds of sliding metal and opened a fraction and a young, handsome, boy's face showed, slightly puzzled, perhaps a trifle apprehensive. I pushed up and spoke in a swod's metallic bark.

"Message to be delivered personal to the Lady Ros."

"She does not wish to be disturbed. She will not see anyone save the lord—"

"I think," I said, "she will see me."

The boy jumped, and his face twitched, and he closed the door and went away, whereat I smiled. Presently he returned, the door was opened, and I went in. My right hand rested at my side. The hilt of the drexer angled across most conveniently. If Ros came at me with a rapier of her damned steel claw I'd have to skip and dance a measure, and no mistake. . . .

The room led onto another chamber of some refinement and luxury, with rugs and hangings and golden lamps on chains. A zhantil-skin pelt was strewn artfully across a couch whose strigicaw-head legs rested on ochre and white rugs. Long curtains at the far end parted and Ros walked in. She was in the process of buckling up a war-harness over her black leathers, and her face was tight with annoyance.

"Who demands to see me so intemperately?" She struggled with a bronze buckle which refused to close. "There can be no more messages to which I will listen unless they bring firm promises of gold." She looked up, breathing hard, and saw the Bowman of Loh who stood ramrod straight but submissively before her, as she must have seen so many in her time.

"Voves," I said. "So you bring voves into Vallia."

She jumped as though I had struck her.

Her naked left hand struck up before her face. The fingers extended. She wore no rings. Her nails were trimmed and polished, unpainted, neat. That left hand clawed at the air in reflex so automatic it left her gasping.

"Yes, Ros," I said.

To give her credit she did not gasp: "You!" like some ignoramus of a heroine from one of the operettas of the flea-pits of Vondium. I enjoy operetta. She lowered that lethal left hand, naked of its lethal weapon, and gazed on me and her look passed from astonishment through anger to a brooding puzzlement. Then:

"What am I to do with you?"

"Nothing. It is what I am to do with you. Boy!" I turned to the lad, who was not yet full grown, a dimpled handsome boy wearing a rose-colored tunic and with a pretty little dagger swinging from silver chains at his waist. His brown Vallian hair tumbled in locks about his ears. "Boy! Pull out that carpet—that long wide one with the silken tassels and spread it out on the floor."

She knew at once.

"You would not dare!"

"How much do you hate me, Ros?" I kept to this name of hers, instead of Dayra, out of an instinctive feeling for the moment, where Ros the Claw was at home and Dayra not.

"Hate you? More than you can imagine—more than the whole world can encompass!" She had not moved since that first instinctive gesture. Her face—beautiful, ah, yes, beautiful and passionate, willful, stubborn, marked with a pride I could sigh over, and marked, also, with a vicious sadness I found desolating—her face bore now the high flush of a controlled anger. "Are you not deserving of all the hate and all the contempt of the whole wide world?"

"Yes."

Her hand went to her throat, above the rim of the black leathers. She was surprised. "But—"

"Turn around, Ros the Claw, and I will fasten up your wrists. Stand, boy!" For the lad made to draw his toy dagger.

The footfall at my back was soft. It was not soundless. I should not speak to you had that footstep been soundless. I ducked and turned and the drexer was out and the giant who slashed a giant sword at me staggered on with the violence of his blow. He was quick. Off balance, before I could get back and the drexer into him he swung around, the giant sword sweeping. I hurdled it and landed cat-footed and so faced him.

Well, he was big. He was broad and wide and bulky and he went up and up and up, his thatch of straw-yellow hair overtopping me by seven good inches. He wore a bronze-studded leather kax, and arm-bands of beaten gold, and a war-kilt of ochre and bronze, pteruges which swung to his knees. His sandals would have carried a landing party from ship to shore. And his sword—massive, thick through and wide, with a solid pommel shaped like a zhantil-head—that sword was like no other I had seen on Kregen. I rather fancied it would be slow, even for him, even with his enormous muscles.

Dayra laughed her silver tinkle.

"You have not met Brun before. I think the meeting opportune." She was enjoying this. "Do not slay him Hyr Brun. His mangy hide has a certain value in certain quarters. We will grow fat on his profit."

Despite the gross proportions of that sword, Brun carried it one-handed and the hilt was close, not fashioned for two-handed work, not even for hand-and-a-half. I took three quick backward steps. Brun's cheerful face, open, mellow, clean-shaven and with a few spots on one cheek, broke into a delighted smile. His reactions were those of a cat stalking a mouse. The drexer snapped away into the scabbard. I reached around.

"So, master, you give in?" Brun's voice carried a clarity of sound amazing, until you realized the enormous cathedral-cavity of his lungs. "That is wise of you. The mistress is to be obeyed in all things."

"I don't know where you got him, Ros," I said, as I put my hand on the hilt of the Krozairbrand. "But I'd like to make friends with a thousand or so. What a bonny regiment they would make for Vallia!"

"For my Vallia!" she spat at me. "Never yours!"

"Well, my girl, you are going into that carpet, and this Hyr Brun is going to carry you out. You had best reconcile yourself to that." I whipped the longsword out and it sparked a shard of light into that chamber as it swung out into line. "As for you, friend Brun. I shall not slay you, as you would not me. But carry your mistress in the carpet you will."

He boomed a gigantic laugh and rushed.

The fight was not pretty—or extraordinarily pretty—depending on your personal viewpoint.

He had a knack of swinging the huge sword around in his fist as though it was a length of rope so that it wove a circle of light. The trick was effective. Besides demonstrating his strength it confused his opponent. Inch had a similar trick with his long Saxon-pattern axe. Again I do not wish to dwell on the fight. It was interesting. Brun wore a leather strap around his head which confined his thatch of yellow hair. The Krozair brand met the gigantic sword and the metal rang and the jolt belted up my arms and across my shoulders. But the Krozair Disciplines held and the blows slanted and glanced, and, like a striking risslaca, the longsword licked out and sliced neatly through the leather fillet. Not a drop of blood was drawn, the skin was not marked. But the leather fell away and Brun's yellow hair dropped down before his face.

Before he had time to brush it away I stepped in and clouted him over the head with the flat.

He dropped. I do not think there can be many men born

of women who will not drop when struck by a Krozair brand.

Before he hit the carpet I had leaped aside and swung the flat around horizontally and the boy was swept away, his toy dagger spinning up like a comet of diamonds in the lights.

Ros leaped for me and she wore her talons.

I ducked, put my shoulder into her stomach, clapped my left arm about her back and hugged her. Horizontally she thrashed her legs wildly. I felt the kiss of the talons against the back of my thighs, and so banged her—gently, gently!—on her bottom with the hilt.

"Stay still, daughter, or I shall tan you, but good."

"You—!"

"Yes."

Presently we were sorted out. Ros, with wrists and ankles fastened with the silken cords from the curtains, lay rolled in the ochre and silver carpet with the silk tassels. Brun said to me: "You would not really slay the boy?" I stood with a dagger at the boy's throat, the rest of my armory scabbarded.

I said, "Do you wish to find out? Pick up your mistress and we will walk out of here, all friendly and nice. Boy, do you walk quietly and not wriggle." I took the dagger from his throat and flapping a corner of the cloak over it, pressed it into the small of his back. "You walk before death."

Well, it was detestable; but he believed me. And, believing, said, "You may kill me, master, if you desire. But I will not betray my mistress."

"Well spoken lad. Your name?"

"I am called Vaxnik."

I was astonished. Vax was the name used by Jaidur in the Eye of the World. And Jaidur was Dayra's twin. I would ask the boy his history when we were safely away. Now, I said, "You have my word as a koter that no harm will befall your mistress. Despite her seeming hatred of me, I love her more deeply than you can understand. I would be cut down before harm should come to her. Now, lead on."

Brun rumbled: "Do you speak sooth, master?"

"Aye, Hyr Brun, I do."

"You are a jikai, master, that is plain. And we do not do well in this evil place. But—"

"Carry your mistress out of here. All will be revealed."

Cheap and easy words; but they were true, by Vox.

A serving man—for Brun was clearly no slave—carrying an expensive carpet, and an important boy to strut his office, and a dour professional mercenary to guard them, excited no attention in the busy warren. We saw parties of guards searching for those who had broken in. We walked solemnly on and were not challenged all the way down from the Pillars to the beginning of the mists rising and stinking from the niksuth.

Besides the carpet in which was rolled Ros the Claw, Brun carried a leather sack hastily stuffed with portable food, a few bottles of wine, and a curtain stuffed down on the top. He could, I thought, have carried a whole wagon-load of supplies without visible effort. So we walked on and passed parties of guards still searching and began to discern a pattern in the search for the intruders. I fancied we might run into serious trouble at the gates, and Vaxnik led on with an eager step.

Now it appeared to me improbable that the outpost guards would have an expensive carpet delivered to their blockhouse. So we would have to re-arrange ourselves for the next step. I halted us in the shadows of a half-ruined building fronting the open space before the gate Vaxnik had chosen, and stared out as Bowmen and churgur guards moved about, parties coming and going, with Deldars yelling and a group of totrixmen spurring across in a swirl of dust and blown leaves. H'mm. . . .

There was a double enceinture here, where Vaxnik had led us, and I chalked a mark up to him, the cunning little devil.

Waiting until the open space was completely free of guards would take too long. Time pressed. Norgoth as Jhansi's lieutenant would be raging with impatience that the intruders had not been found, and I suspected that some, at least, of those unfortunates who had been knocked on the head had recovered to add further to the alarm. So, once more, there was nothing for it. I settled the longsword more conveniently to hand. The shadows lay blue and bright. The suns shone. And then tendrils of oily mist wafted and the whole scene dulled to a dun mange, and a chill descended.

"March straight, Hyr Brun. And you, too, boy. I have a story for those guards yonder."

A party of diffs wearing the gray slave breechclouts passed in a straggling line. They carried obese pots on their shoulders, no doubt water for the baths of those up in the palaces, if they'd run out of milk. I made a face, and we stepped out.

Two parties of guards approached. That to our right rear was composed mainly of Rapas, with a few apims and Brokelsh. They carried their spears all at the regulation slope and were mercenaries, skilled fighting men. The party advancing through the gate wore the ochre and white, and were armed with a medley of weapons which spoke again of mercenaries, although not the regimented and disciplined kind. I frowned.

Walking along a couple of paces in rear of Brun I readied myself. We attracted no attention from the guards with the spears. They were commanded by their Deldar and would do as he directed. We made a picture that held no menace for him.

A movement caught the corner of my eye and I looked forward again. The open end of the carpet was moving like the trunk of an elephant. How she had done it I do not know. Dayra's head appeared, and an arm ripped free of the binding silks. Her face was flushed and her eyes looked murderous. She saw the guards. She yelled. She yelled good and loud.

"Guards! Guards! Here is the man you seek! Guards, ho!"

Her triumphant face bore on me, bright, vindictive, filled with passion.

Vaxnik squeaked. Brun dropped the carpet.

I saw the guards running on. Their Deldar bellowed and they turned toward us. The other party of guards, attracted by the shouts, also turned toward us. We were trapped between them.

"You're done for, now, you villainous rast!" shouted my daughter at her father.

I ripped the longsword free. Two-handed I gripped the Krozair blade.

"Done for!" shrieked Dayra. "They will not kill you. But you may wish they had."

"I do not hate you," I said, stupidly, spreading my fists along the hilt of the longsword.

"Throw down your sword, cramph! Oh that I could get free and sink my talons in you!" And her left hand at last broke free from the swathing carpet and the suns shone through the drifting mist and glittered most vilely upon that curved and cruel claw.

I saw the spearmen charging toward me. I half-turned and

A Life for Kregen

saw the guards from the gate pressing swiftly on, their weapons drawn.

And I said, very gently: "I do not think your guards will take me, Dayra. But it was a nice try."

Chapter Seventeen

Disaster

The spearmen ran yelling on their doom.

For a short space only I fronted them with the deadly Krozair longsword singing, and then Targon and Naghan and Dorgo and Korero were there, with the others of my choice band clad in their stolen ochre and white uniforms, and the blades clanged and rang. The spearmen were either cut down or ran. The fight was brief and bloody, swift and savage.

"Well met!" I bellowed. "Now back through the gate and into the swamps before they gather their wits."

"You are safe?" demanded Korero, and blood dripped from his tail hand and the blade he bore.

"Aye! Now—move!"

So we ran.

Brun lifted the carpet and I stuffed Dayra back, whereat she squealed and tried to slash me. I looped the silk around her wrists and drew it tight, tight, and said: "Daughter. Bide you still or earn a father's wrath."

"And what else have I ever had?"

There was nothing I could say to that. Filled with a sudden and blinding sense of infamy, I ran with my comrades out through the gate and past the dead guards sprawled there, and along the causeway and through the other gate where the guards lay naked, and so out and into the bog of Trakon's niksuth.

Well into the slimy stinking labyrinth we slowed down and caught our breaths, and I let them tell me the story as we pressed on. Inky the Chops had vanished when the risslacas attacked. My men had gone on, finding their own way through the boggy maze, half-blinded, choked with the miasmic stinks, but coming at last to this gate and so making their way through determined to rescue Lol and me or burn the place down. I said: "I regret we had no time to do that. It would have been—useful."

"Useful," growled Targon. "Aye, majister, and overdue."

The riding animals were gone and so we must walk. So we did. I reflected that the reasons that had impelled my fellows to choose a double-walled entrance, so that they might obtain uniforms without arousing suspicions inside, and the reasons impelling Vaxnik, that we would have a double chance of being caught, had coincided nicely. My band would have wrought fearful havoc looking for me; chance only had decreed we should meet when we did. Now chance, or fate, decreed we should walk.

We reached an area somewhat less boggy than most and opened the leather bag carried by Brun. Its provender gave us all a slender meal, and then it was done. Ros the Claw was brought out. I told her that she would walk, seeing she was so limber and lithe a lass, and that Hyr Brun would carry Vaxnik. She was amenable to this, having an affection for the boy.

No one knew a certain way out of the bog, and so we walked in as straight a line as we could contrive. We knocked over a few risslacas on the way, and Brun smashed in the head of one ugly monster with a single swipe of that giant sword. We kept alert for sounds of pursuit on the backtrail. We heard none and so got clean away. At last we emerged from the miasmic labyrinths of Trakon's niksuth and breathed in air that tasted like best Jholaix.

"However," said Targon, hitching his belt. "We are as like to be out of the frying pan and into the fire. All this country would as lief chop us as say a cheery Llahal."

"They would find us a prickly mouthful," I said.

That night we made a cheerless camp; but were able to catch up on our sleep. Our sentries reported all's well during the hours of darkness and by dawn we sat up, hungry and thirsty, and contemplated the labors of the day.

I do not propose to give a blow by blow account of the shifts we were forced to in the ensuing days. We headed south and we foraged for food and we picked up a few riding animals here and there; but of fliers we saw no sign. During this period I was obsessed with what was going on in Vondium, and cursing myself that I should have been so blind or foolhardy as to leave the center at this moment. That no other invasion armies had been reported now, in retrospect, appeared to me, tortured by guilt, to be totally irrelevant. Dayra, quite naturally, would say nothing about her plans or the voves. I am a zorca and a vove man, each superb animal supreme in the tasks nature has intended for each. The vove—well, yes, there is the supreme riding animal of Paz, as I understood then. Powerfully built, large, with eight muscle-packed legs, the vove boasts both fangs and horns through his mingled ancestry, and a coat of a glorious russet color. He is exceptionally ferocious to those he does not know. And he will run and run until his heart bursts asunder, for his strength and his loyalty are well-matched; but his devotion is the stronger.

The obvious answer to the problem was an ugly one. Zankov must have gone to Segesthes, the large sprawling eastern continent of the Paz grouping, and there contracted an alliance at best, or a mercenary undertaking as the more probable, with clans hostile to the clans owing allegiance to me as their Zorcander and Vovedeer. Hap Loder, my old blade comrade and the man who stood in my stead with the clans of Felschraung and Longuelm and Viktrik—and any others he had taken over lately—had been with us to the Sacred Pool. He must have been pitchforked back to the Great Plains of Segesthes. Well, I could send a flier to him—when we got back to Vondium, Drig take it—but the logistical problems involved in shipping an army of the massive voves staggered. Phu-Si-Yantong could have done it. The galleons of Vallia could do it. The skyships of Hamal could do it. And, by the disgusting diseased entrails of Makki Grodno, so could the ships of the great enclave city of Zenicce.

That was the answer. And here was I, traipsing about like a loon in the backwoods of Vallia instead of being in Vondium.

It was enough to make a man swear off strong drink for life.

No, I will not go into that journey or into my state of mind.

The occasion is worth a mention when, during the night of storms when the wind blew streamers of screaming fury across the sky and the moons remained hidden so that the world became bathed in darkness like a night of Notor Zan, Hyr Brun, Vaxnik and Dayra escaped. They hardly escaped. They simply staggered off into the darkness, holding on to one another and with Brun like a massive anchor to hold

A Life for Kregen

them to the earth. They vanished within a couple of arms' lengths and we did not see them again, or for a very long time thereafter.

In order to bolster my failing sense of direction and to give some semblance of rationality to what I was doing, to counter the absolute loss and waste of my efforts with Dayra, I told myself that this journey had been worthwhile for the rescue of Thelda and my discovery of the misery in store for Seg and Thelda, and for Lol Polisto, too. So I told myself.

In the fullness of time we trailed into Vondium.

We had obtained vollers for the last part of the trip and when I vaulted out on the high landing platform of the palace and searched the faces of those who waited to greet us for just the one, and failed to see her, I felt another and more treacherous feeling of loss. I needed Delia near me now.

And then—well, I looked again at the faces of the crowd.

Glum. Drawn. Haggard. Cast down as though sent reeling by some ghastly catastrophe. Many of the women wore mourning. A chill gripped me. And, of course, I already knew. But I did not know the full horror of what had befallen the pride of Vondium, capital of the Empire of Vallia.

Kyr Nath Nazabhan, a good comrade, a fine fighting man, commander of the Phalanx, Kapt, was so cast down in his pride that at first he would not look at me, merely cast himself down in the full incline, trembling, clad in black, contrite, ashamed, grief-stricken—and guilty.

"For the sweet sake of Opaz, Nath! Stand up straight and tell me. Openly and honestly, as we are comrades."

"Majister—majister—the army. My Phalanx ... ."

"Voves, was it?"

His gray-carved face looked up. "Majister? How could you know that?"

"You forget, the Emperor of Vallia has eyeballs everywhere."

Well, how can one remain unamused and not essay a feeble jest in the face of disaster?

So the story came out, brokenly, the grim, ugly, cold story.

I sat at my desk in that book-lined room with the maps and the weapons, and presently Nath was persuaded to sit across from me. He stabbed the map as he spoke. Lines, arrows, routes of penetration, ambush and surprise, and, at the end, the battle. News had reached Vondium that an army had at last been sighted, an army marching southwest from Vazkardrin on the east coast. I nodded. Vazkardrin lay between the coast and the Kwan Hills which demarcated the borders of Hawkwa country thereabouts. Zankov clearly had inserted his tendrils of power into the vadvarate of Vazkardrin, which had been run by canny old Vad Rhenchon, a numim, who had always kept himself unaligned in the struggles of power politics. Zankov had taken over with his cronies and his renegade Hawkwas and provided a secure base for the arrival of the clans carried in Zeniccean ships from Segesthes. It had to be.

Southward of Vazkardrin lay the imperial province of Jevuldrin. That was flat country, ideal, as Nath said, for the maneuvers of the Phalanx. It was also ideal cavalry country. And there is no cavalry in all of Paz, so I thought, to compare with vove chivalry. The only animal and human thing to stand against a vove charge was another vove charge. . . .

"We shipped out," said Nath. Then he caught himself, and paled, and ground his fists together. "No, majister. *I* shipped them out. Me. I did it. Every sailing skyship we had. Every last one. We—I—took the First and Second Phalanxes, leaving the Third here. The churgur infantry, the axemen, the spearmen, three quarters of the cavalry of all kinds. And the artillery. We were a brave sight." He swallowed. "A brave sight."

"Yes."

"We landed and formed. And then came a storm, a monstrous storm. The sailing ships of the sky could not stand before it but had to run."

In the skirts of that storm Dayra and her friends had run, too. . . .

"So," I said. "Farris could do nothing with his air?"

"Nothing. The army formed on the second day. Magnificent, magnificent. You should have seen them, majister—"

"I wish," I said, with a note of dryness in my voice I could not withhold. "I wish I had."

Nath understood and he bowed his head.

"We stood as we had been trained. The Phalanx resplendent in crimson and bronze. The paean was chanted and the songs sung. And we advanced. And they rode like an avalanche, like the wind, like the irresistible tides of the ocean. The voves. . . ." For a space he could not go on.

Well, in Vallia they ride the nikvove, the half vove, and

A Life for Kregen

that is indeed a fine animal. But he does not have the fangs and the horns, does not have the sheer crushing battering bulk. A vove, it is half believed, could knock down a church steeple. I have ridden in many a vove charge, coursing knee to knee with my clansmen, charging headlong into the massed ranks of the enemy clan. Terrible, a whirlwind of destruction, the vove charge. I did not want to think what had happened to my Phalanxes. But I had to. I was responsible. Not Nath. I had warned him, oft and oft, against fighting unsupported against sword and shield men, the churgur infantry. But he had believed implicitly that the Phalanx could defeat any cavalry charge, any cavalry charge at all.

"There were many casualties?"

He could only nod.

"And the army?" I riffled out well-thumbed papers. "Here are the lists. Take up this pen and strike through the formations that no longer exist."

He did as he was bid. As the pen scratched with a vicious stab across the paper, time after time, I felt the cold clench around my heart. Most of the fine Army of Vondium had been swept away.

People talk of an army being decimated, not knowing what the word means, intending to imply wholesale destruction. We had been far worse than decimated. We had lost far more men than a mere one in ten. The units had been drastically thinned, the ranks devastated. That army had to be written off.

That campaign had been lost. This was not Jikaida. Those men had not been swept up in the cupped hand to be placed back in the velvet-lined box, to be brought out again all fresh for the next game. They were gone forever. They were dead.

"The Third is still here," I said. "With its Hakkodin and three regiments of archers and spearmen. There are two regiments of zorcamen, four of totrixmen and one of nikvovemen. Artillery is thin, but can cover." I looked at Nath. "This army of clansmen from Segesthes was not brought against us by that Opaz-forsaken Wizard of Loh. His ruse is still hanging. We still have him to contend with. This cramph Zankov—he brings the clans against us."

"Nothing has happened in the southwest. Fat Lango's army stagnates. The man you saw, Kov Colun Mogper of Mursham, has disappeared. Had he assumed the command—"

"Thank Opaz he did not. But, Nath, mayhap he has gone to command the real army from Yantong against us."

Nath spread his hands. "We are doomed, it seems."

"No." I rubbed my nose. "No. I do not think so. I remember a man called Filbarrka. He is a great zorca man, the Filbarrka na Filbarrka. He and I have talked about zorcas and voves and his theory is overripe for the testing." I stood up. "You and Farris, and everyone else, must rebuild the army. Work hard and work fast and work well. I am for the Blue Mountains."

"The Blue Mountains? But—"

"Yes. But I fancy Filbarrka has not taken kindly to a damned invasion from anyone. Build up the army. And stay close. If I am wanted, ask in the Blue Mountains."

Chapter Eighteen

We Gamble on Filbarrka's Zorcamen

Certain important tasks had to be completed before I could leave. I went to see Barty, who was up and pacing about, rotating his arm and bristling to get back into action. I told him to see about raising fresh regiments. We had lost a doleful number of good men; but there were others, and the spirit of the people, with that stoical and yet fierce Vallian integrity, rose to the crisis. New armies would be formed. He wanted to go off adventuring with me until I convinced him he was more valuable in Vondium. As to Dayra, I told him what had happened, and he blamed the storm again, this time not for wafting away an air fleet leading to the destruction of an army. I wondered. Perhaps I had secretly wanted my daughter to run off again. Perhaps I could not face the meeting between her mother and me and her. . . . Had I wanted to keep her close I could have hobbled her feet and tied up Hyr Brun and Vaxnik.

Then, with a mere continuation of my feelings, I went to see Seg. He mended. That cheered me. Very soon, he told me, he would be back fighting fit. He, too, wanted to come with me. I told him, sternly, to get well first. I could not speak of Thelda. How could I? He did not know. The hateful thought occurred to me that perhaps Lol and Thelda were dead already. They had not flown to Vondium, and had no reason to, since they resisted the occupation of Falinur.

All of life during this period was a pickle. Delia was away, Seg's problems and Barty's problems weighed on me. Jilian cheered me up a little; but she was busy doing just what she had said she would, and I stole a half-bur to watch her Jikai Vuvushis at practice.

"By Vox, Jilian. They frighten me. Opaz knows what they will do to the enemy."

"Not a one of them has been through Lancival and so none wears the—wears the claw. But they come on apace." She looked ravishing, seductive in her black leathers. I thought of Dayra and I could not find a smile. She went on to talk of the disaster to the Army of Vondium, which had taken place near a little village called, ominously, Sicce's Gates, from the eons-old cracks in the earth nearby which led down so deeply into the crust of the planet none had ever ventured to the bottom. The Battle of Sicce's Gates would be recorded in agony and lamenting in the records of those times kept by Enevon Ob-Eye. I bid Jilian farewell and took myself off to the landing platform.

Farris, with a pinched look, had spared me a fast single-place airboat. My mission demanded urgency. I missed the fond preparations made by Delia on these occasions, and shifted for myself in the matter of provisions. Be sure I took many wicker hampers. My armory remained as it had been, it had served me well so far.

Observing the fantamyrrh with care as I went aboard I called down the remberees. Barty had come up to wish me all speed with Opaz. I had a hell of a game with Korero and the others. But the voller was a single-place job and that, it seemed to me, was that.

"I will send for you when the Lord Farris can place a sizable voller at our disposal. But the defense of Vondium is vital and our air fleet—well—" I did not go on.

That dratted storm had not only blown the sailing fliers away from Sicce's Gates, it had destroyed the majority of them. Farris was busily rebuilding. And we had cut down forests to build those ships. . . .

It would be infantile and pompously stupid of me to suggest that my brief reappearance in Vondium had made a vastly impressive increase in the recuperation of the people from the debacle. But more than one old sweat had said that, by Vox, now I was back and safe they could get on with drilling the coys and look forward to knocking the daylights out of those zigging vovemen. Off on my travels again, I prayed that Farris and Nath and Barty and all the others—including Seg when he had recovered—would, indeed, recreate the Army of Vondium.

For much of the journey the River of Shining Spears paralleled my course. Once I had taken a roundabout way to the Blue Mountains, by way of Delphond, riding a hired zorca. I felt that Korf Aighos would have dealt very harshly with the invaders of Delia's country. Filbarrka ran the wide plains country at the foot of the Blue Mountains in the fork of the two rivers, and that country, I believed, was the best zorca country in Paz. Now I was going to put to the test the theories Filbarrka held. Despite all the long series of misfortunes, despite what had happened, despite my intense sensation of loneliness, despite the foreboding dread with which I viewed the future in spite of my brave words, I still experienced a profound excitement at what was proposed.

Vallia swirled past below and I ate roast vosk sandwiches and drank superb Kregen tea brewed on the little spirit stove packed within a sturm-wood box. I looked up. Yes, there he was, the Gdoinye, the giant raptor of the Star Lords. A beautiful scarlet and golden bird, glistening in the mingled rays of the Suns of Scorpio, he flew lazily above me, looking down with one beady eye from his sideways cocked head. The Star Lords wanted to know my doings. Well, I felt the uplifting sense that I was far more involved with what I was doing in the here and now, attempting to hold Vallia together, than in the machinations of the Everoinye, who could hurl me back to Earth, four hundred light years away, at a whim.

There appeared to be no sign of the white Savanti dove.

More out of habit than with a positive feeling of enmity, I shook my fist at the Gdoinye. He slanted a wing, and flew away. I went back to my food, and scooped a fistful of palines.

There was a squish pie in the hamper and I thought of Inch, and sighed, and so prepared to finish the long flight and bring the flier to earth. I did not anticipate too much trouble in finding Filbarrka. He would be leading the resistance and, I felt sure, the local people would be solidly on his side, the Vallian side, against the mercenaries and flutsmen and aragorn who had flooded in on the misery of Vallia. A few careful inquiries in out of the way places, and I would be directed to him. I just had to steer clear of the occupation forces.

These things worked out to plan and I caught up with Filbarrka as, big, bluff, red-faced, happily twitching his fingers together, he watched his zorcamen run rings around a hapless party of totrixmen. I landed the flier and walked across, aware of the bows bent against me. But Filbarrka recognized me and bellowed a cheerful greeting.

"Lahal, majister! I am glad to welcome you to the fun. See how the rasts run!"

The totrixmen were remorselessly cut down. I did not particularly relish the sight; but it had to be done if you concede that the freedom and happiness, not to say health, of a country matters more than the lives of its harsh invaders.

The amusing thing here was that Filbarrka did not seem in the least surprised to see me. He talked away, filled with his news, as we jogged along together. In a predominantly grass land I would have thought that guerila tactics would prove particularly difficult; but Filbarrka would have none of that.

"We ride rings around 'em, majister! And there are the foothills of the Blue Mountains if things get tough."

My flier was stashed away in a wood and the locals would keep an eye on it. The country was pastureland, lush and lovely, well watered and wooded, and zorcas could live here as though grazing in a zorca heaven. I told Filbarrka that as I was the emperor now, and the Blue Mountains and this plains section of it called Filbarrka, the same name for man and country, was the empress's, he, Filbarrka na Filbarrka, was now an imperial Justicar and might style himself Nazab. He was pleased. But titles, I felt, meant little to him beside the thrill of simply riding a zorca.

I told him the problem.

He fired up at once. Eager, alive, filled with a fretting spirit, he tore into the problem.

"Voves. Ah, yes, voves. . . ."

He had seen voves in action, having visited my clans in Segesthes at the invitation of Hap Loder. Now he began to talk in his quick, bubbling way, red-faced, twitching, full of cunning and guile and sound common sense.

"As San Blarnoi says," he observed. "Preparation is improved by digestion. Ha! We have a snug little camp in a fold of the hills—pimples to a Blue Mountain Boy, to be sure—where we can eat and drink—and think. But the tactical situation vis-a-vis a zorca and a vove is fascinating, fascinating. And I have had thoughts, by Vox, yes!

"No clansman would dream of riding against voves with zorcas."

He did not say: "But they are only shaggy clansmen," as many a wight would have done in Vallia. For, was not I, Dray Prescot, taken for just such a shaggy graint of a clansman?

He did say with bluff politeness: "We do not have voves to go up against voves with, majister, as they do on the Great Plains."

"Discard all notions that I can magically produce an army of vove cavalry. The damned Hamalese burned most of the galleons. I'd hazard a guess that the shipping from Zenicce has been engaged to transport these voves we're up against. And our own sailing skyships were dispersed and smashed up by the storm at Sicce's Gates. We're on our own, Nazab Filbarrka. It is zorcas for us—"

"What could be better?" He rubbed his hands as we stepped away from the steeds where handlers were already leading them off, talking to them, cajoling them, for every Filbarrkian loves a zorca. We entered the camp area, tents under the trees in a fold in the hills. The weather remained bright; but I fancied it would rain before morning. The food was good, straight from a looted caravan. Filbarrka ate and drank as hugely as he talked. "The zorca is close-coupled, we know that. A good animal can turn on a copper ob. So we can run rings around voves—"

"They charge in an unbroken knee-to-knee mass."

"Naturally. They aim to crush anything in their way."

"They do."

"So, majister, we are not in the way."

I quaffed good Vallian wine and hid my smile.

The problem spread out for Filbarrka spurred him on as he would never spur on a zorca. I had my own ideas which I intended should meld in with his, so as to maintain the pleasant harmony. He shared my view that if an army was really serious about fighting to win and to stay alive, or as many swods as might be who would stay alive, the discipline must be instant and automatic. That demanded high-quality officers, and these, too, must instantly obey the orders of their generals. As to these latter, if Filbarrka himself was to be a Kapt, I fancied I'd take his recommendation on the others to be appointed. He drank his wine and then looked at me, his face large and happy in the lamplight.

"How long do I have, majister? And—numbers?"

"As to numbers, the reports I have indicate the clans brought over at least six divisions."

He nodded, for the calculation was easy. A division consisted of a thousand warriors. The clansmen stuck to the old ways of ranking, so that their Jiktars who commanded the divisions did, in fact, command a thousand.

"By their colors, weapons and harness, it seems, there is more than one clan involved. From what I have been told I have identified the Clan of Rudimwy. The others are unknown to me and must come from north and east of the parts I know."

"Six thousand vove-mounted cavalry, clansmen, renowned and feared." He brisked up. "Life is going to be interesting."

"As to time—yesterday. The army or armies that menace us from the southwest cannot be discounted. The lice that infest Vallia daily suck more blood. And Vondium's army is not yet rebuilt, not ready." A nasty thought occurred to me. "Anyway, it will be interesting to see who can train and provide their force first; the army in Vondium or you here."

That got to him. As I say—nasty.

He drank again and one of his lieutenants—a raffish bunch, these, liberally bedecked with the ritualistic trappings of zorcamen—leaned across and passed the opinion that any zorcaman of Filbarrka, of the Blue Mountains, which was the blessed Delia's province, could do what ten of those fat and callous-arsed citizens of Vondium could do, and in half the time, by Vox!

That made it my turn to hide my face in the wine cup.

Presently I asked about Korf Aighos of the Blue Mountain Boys.

Filbarrka roared out a belly-laugh.

"The old Korf! Why, he's strung up so many damned flutsmen he could build a hedge with them. No mercenary ventures into the Blue Mountains these days."

"Does he send men to assist you down here on the plain?"

"Aye, oh, aye. We strap everything down, then, and chain and padlock it all triple-tight."

Great reivers, the Blue Mountain Boys. Only because they shared a common fealty to Delia prevented the Blue Mountain Boys and the Filbarrkians of the plains from being at each other's throats as once they had to their mutual loss and benefit.

"And the Black Mountains? Kov Inch—?"

"Not a word. The Black Mountains remain as impregnable to the invaders as the Blue. But they are hard-pressed by that rast up north of them, Kov Layco Jhansi."

"And east, too," I said. "In Falinur."

A Life for Kregen

"And, over the river, the black and whites, may their eyeballs fall out."

"Amen," I said, companionably, and drank, and we chatted in this polite way a little longer.

At last, judging the moment ripe, I proposed to Nazab Filbarrka that the Blue Mountain Boys be invited to contribute a component of the zorca force he would form. They might be infantry, archers, axemen, to fight in the intervals—anything, in my view, just so long as I could get their ferocious fighting ability put to use in the coming struggle.

"And if we can get word to the Black Mountain Men, them too."

The threat posed by raids by the Racters over the border into the Black Mountains was serious; but the greater menace drew swiftly on us with those infernal Pypor-worshiping cramphs of clansmen and their voves from Segesthes. The Black Mountains must strip much of their own strength away, if we could reach them, to face Zankov. These are the hateful decisions emperors have to make every day before breakfast.

For a brief treacherous moment my thoughts dwelled on Drak and his fortunes in Faol among the Manhounds.

Filbarrka nodded in his enthusiastic fashion. "The great two-handed Sword of War of the Blue Mountains will serve excellently once I have broken up the main mass. I know they regained their pride in the weapon." He cocked an eye at me, a knowing eye. "There was this business of you and the shorgortz, majister, as I recall."

"Aye," I said. "And the Sword of War was blunt."

"Against the Racters and Jhansi, and now these vovemen, the great Swords of War will be sharp."

"By Zim-Zair!" I said. "Yes!"

Filbarrka began to expatiate on the methods and equipment he would use and need. "I am prejudiced toward comfort in the shape of a four-legged animal, and am convinced that in spite of apparent lessons to the contrary, zorca cavalry can successfully fight those mounted on heavier animals." He rubbed his fingers together, happily planning cunning tactics and stratagems. "Weapons will be a slender lance, twelve feet long, for a start, until we see how the men behave and the weapons serve. A number of lead-weighted and feathered throwing darts with broad barbed heads will be kept in a case at the saddle."

"And a striking weapon, Nazab?"

"From a nimble zorca curvetting about against an oaf astride a lumbering vove? Oh, a mace. A heavy, flanged head mace. Hit the fellow anywhere with that, and one of the flanges will bite in and do his business for him."

"Very pretty. These weapons can be built for you in Vondium, together with such harness as you require."

"Excellent, excellent!"

"And you will leave sufficient forces here to contain the confounded mercenaries."

"I will. But it will be a task to choose who is to go and who is to stay."

"That's why you are a Nazab."

"And you, majister, an emperor."

Just because of that it was possible for me to introduce the subject of shields. Some of Filbarrka's people emitted loud snorting noises of derision at this; but I noticed others who, sitting forward intently, marked what was said.

"Shields?" said Filbarrka. He entwined his fingers and bounced up and down on his seat. "Well, now. . . . Yes. Yes, I have seen shields in action and, if we are to have them, I would favor a long triangular convex-section shield."

Well, argument ensued. In the end we agreed that the suggestions put forward by Filbarrka would be acted on to the best of our ability. The arsenals in Vondium had been instructed in the best way of manufacturing shields, and I guaranteed to supply the articles requested.

As for armor, Filbarrka wanted a light quilted knee and elbow length coat with a steel bar sewn to the outside of the sleeve, steel right forearm guard and shoulder plates. These latter, being the trademark of the Vondium soldier, fitted in perfectly. In all probability what the arsenals produced would be high-quality iron; but we tended to call it steel, as one does. Steel is usually reserved for weapons.

For helmets of the force, it was proposed that a small, round helmet rather like an acorn in shape, be fitted with a mail hood fastening up to the nasal. Mail was not easily come by in Vallia, as you know. The mail of the Eye of the World was effective but crudely heavy in comparison with the superb mesh of the Dawn Lands of Havilfar. The arsenals in Vondium could produce a mesh link that would serve. I had the sneaky suspicion that many a man of Filbarrka's zorca force would ride into action without this mail hood.

"And, in the rear ranks," said Filbarrka with anticipatory satisfaction, "we substitute bows for the lance and darts. The shields must be different, too. Smaller round parrying shields fastened to the lower arm. They should serve capitally."

So it was settled. Settled, that was, in conference. The hard slog of bringing theory into practice must begin now. One supreme advantage Filbarrka did have. He could call on the services of superb zorcamen. That gave him a flying start.

Although pressed to stay and see some more fun—they had a raid against a caravan of whose route they had been apprised planned for the next day—I expressed my regrets. Vondium and the raising of a great city to renewed effort called. Satisfied that the mercenaries and aragorn in this part of Vallia were paying dearly for their plunder, I bid the zorcamen of the plains of the Blue Mountains remberee, and flew fast back to the capital city.

The news that met me, conveyed by Enevon Ob-Eye with an appearance of studied calm, was that Barty Vessler the Strom of Calimbrev, wounded though he was, had stolen an airboat and flown from Vondium in the devil of a hurry and the devil of a state. My chief stylor contrived to appear matter-of-fact, but he was enraged, amused, and downright admiring about the stir.

"Hardly stole, Enevon," said Seg, stretching his arms, as he kept doing to explore the pains in his mending back. "It was his to start with, you know."

"It is gone now, and the Lord Farris is shorter still of air for surveillance."

No message had been left. I could only assume that Barty could contain himself no longer and had gone to carry on the overdue talk with Dayra interrupted by the storm and their escape from us. I did not know how long it had been since he had last seen her. I'd wager a king's treasury against a copper ob that she was never the girl he remembered.

Nothing could be done about that situation. Every effort must be bent to building up the warlike capacity of the city. Seg said: "I have scoured around, Dray, in the taverns and dopa dens and stewpots. I've dug up three hundred men who claim to have been Bowmen of Loh. Some may never have been within a hundred dwaburs of Loh; but I have them sweating over their drills now, under command of Treg Tregutorio, a right old devil but a man with a bow, by Vox. You will find they will stand come the day."

"Good," I said, cheered in a way Seg could not hope to understand. "But, come the day, I shall need you to command the vanguard, as ever. I rely on you, you know."

"That is where Treg will want his men if I know him."

Despite his shortages, Farris kept up observations of the country and the day did come, sooner than we expected. Farris burst into my room without ceremony, looking wild-eyed, a most unusual state for him to be in.

"Majister! That cramph Kov Colun! He is found—aye, and an army with him. A great army of mercenaries from Pandahem and Hamal, marching from the south on Vondium. There is little time left."

So, with what we had, we marched.

We marched to the south.

The host of clansmen mounted on their terrible and terrifying voves pressed in on us from the north. If we were to be the nut in the nutcracker, then we would make sure we broke off one of the jaws, broke and splintered and sent it shattered back before we turned—with what we had—to strike at the other.

In those dark days for Vondium and for Vallia there were few, and fewer with every day that passed, who believed any more that we would win through. But, still, we would fight. We would fight on, although doomed, fight on without surrendering. For that was the way of it, in those days. Surrender would bring our utter annihilation. Everyone knew that from bitter example. So we would fight on and if we were doomed, why, then, we would go down before Fate and put as brave a set of faces on it as we could muster.

That was the way of the new Vallians.

Chapter Ninteen

Suprises in the Delphondian Campaign

I had been wrong about Delphond.

Delphond, the Garden of Vallia, a sweet, languorous, easy-going place where the fruit hung heavy on the tree and the fat kine filled lush pasturelands, where men and women laughed easily and ate well and quaffed good Delphondian ale, where life flowed in smooth mellow rhythms and it was good to be alive and rest awhile—Delphond, Delphond —the sword and fire and destruction came to Delphond. And the good people arose in their wrath. Calling on the name of Delia of Delphond, they rose and smote the invaders.

Always I had considered the Delphondi would be too lazy, too good-natured, too easy-going, to resist, even though I had seen evidence of a new awareness and a growing suspicion during that time I had sought news of the mystery of the Black Feathers of the Great Chyyan.*

The distance from Vondium to Delphond is not great. That was the paramount reason why the invasion army under command of Kov Colun Mogper of Mursham had chosen to land there, on the south coast. He might have sailed his fleet up the wide mouth of the Great River; but then he would have faced crippling odds as all the small craft we could muster would have assailed him. He was confident, I'll give the cramph that. Straight across Delphond he marched, in a straight line, through the orchards and the cornfields, over the pastureland, and in his wake he left a broad swathe of destruction.

Also, he left many a man of his regiments hacked to pieces in a ditch where the enraged Delphondi had thrown him.

We marched southwest to get around that curve of the

*see Dray Prescott 15, *Secret Scorpio*

Great River, crossing the imperial province of Vond. We cut well south of the route of that earlier quick and improvised march against the mock army of Fat Lango. The comparative failure of that ruse had not deterred Kov Colun from setting forth on the balance of the ploy. If we did not stop him, he would be in Vondium, and Yantong would have won another round.

Although I had long ago come to the conclusion that bricks and mortar were not worth human lives, there were other considerations in the decision to defend Vondium. The arsenals being there constituted one obvious reason. But for that, by Zair, I'd have let Kov Colun and Zankov fight it out between them.

"By the Veiled Froyvil, my old dom," exclaimed Seg, reining up and shading his eyes. We looked up into the high blue of a Kregen day. "That looks a trifle likely."

Up there, swirling away from the advance guard of our little army, black dots pirouetted across the blue. They appeared to frolic between puffball clouds; but we knew they were not of the frolicsome kind, being aerial cavalry of the army we challenged.

"Mirvols," I said. "So Colun has brought aerial forces with him."

"We've seen them off before, Dray! D'you mind the times in the Hostile Territories—and that scheming woman, Queen Lilah of Hiclantung?"

"Aye, I mind me, Seg. But we have no air to speak of."

"Your Djangs from Valka—"

"If they get here in time."

"Erthyr the Bow will see to it that they do."

Ahead of us stretched the open park-like landscape of Delphond. We had marched fast and light, having information from our spies that Colun tarried for his rearguard to come up. If all went as we planned, we would harass the invaders as far as we were able until we were all formed. That was a grim note—all. There were pitifully few of us left. And the new regiments were not ready.

Karidge's regiment of zorcamen—the First—went cantering past. Because Nath Karidge had caught a small punitive excursion mounted by Farris against a fortress of the aragorn over our borders, he had missed that fight at Sicce's Gates. At the time he had raved. Now he said that Opaz had saved him and the best zorca regiment in the army for greater things—for victory. I had agreed with him. His men were raging to get at the invaders and a deal of the gloom and doom so rampant elsewhere was missing in their ranks. Karidge's wife had recently had twins, and Seg made some remark as to his good fortune, and mentioned Thelda.

Again and again I had struggled with myself, quite unable to decide the best course. In all mercy I ought to tell Seg that Thelda was still alive. That would lead to questions. I could simply say that I had had a report that she had been seen, alive and well. I knew what that would mean. Instantly, Seg would be off hot foot on the trail. And I knew he dared not go with that wound in his back. Now the wound was almost healed, and the doctors of Vondium had expressed their amazement at his recuperative powers. Now, if I spun him some cock and bull story, he would have no reason not to go off. The plight of Vondium ought not to move him. It wouldn't me, if it had been Delia I was chasing. So. . . .

Up until now I could with justice claim I had not told him Thelda was alive so as to save him from killing himself by searching for her with that damned great wound. Now that he was well again—could I in conscience keep the news from him? The half of the news? Sink me! I couldn't tell him about Lol Polisto. And yet, for him to discover the story in some hole-in-the-corner way would be even more frightful.

By the disgusting diseased tripes of Makki-Grodno!

And then a trumpet pealed sweet and silver, hurling notes through the air and sending birds scurrying from the nearby wood as though the notes took wing. A zorca rider burst up over the ridge and bore on toward us, riding hard and low in the saddle.

He was from the forward advance guard and so I knew one of our patrols had come in with news. We might have no aerial scouts; but we kept our patrols probing well ahead. He brought the news for which I had hoped, scarcely thinking such good fortune would fall our way. But Five-Handed Eos-Bakchi had smiled and his knuckle-bones had turned dexter.

"Ha!" said Seg when the rider had finished speaking. "We have the cramph now."

"We have the opportunity," I said, mildly. "We have but to execute the design."

"Execute! Aye, we'll execute Colun and all his villains."

Waiting for his rearguard to come up Colun was separated

from them by a good forty miles. If we could strike into the gap and turn on one force before they linked, we would stand a chance. The forces were ill-balanced. Which should it be?

"Hit Kov Colun," counseled Nath Nazabhan, sturdily. He had left his devoted Phalanx, being infantry, to be with us in the vanguard. Our vanguard was all cavalry or mounted infantry.

"His main body outnumbers us five to one, Nath."

"Maybe," said Seg, screwing up his eyes and with all the shrewd practicality of his race showing through the fey recklessness in him in these matters of operational policy. "Maybe it would be better to chop his tail off first. They are two to one. I'd say he was waiting for stores and equipment. Then he'll be isolated, and if your Phalanx gets here in time, Nath—"

"If? If!"

"Well—when. We will crush him sweetly, like a rotten gregarian."

I said: "I would like to hit Colun immediately. He has at least fifty thousand or so with him, with twenty thousand in the rearguard. We have almost four of cavalry and six of mounted infantry. And, in the rearguard, I fancy as Seg says, will be artillery, stores, battering equipment." I looked at these men with me, loyal, shrewd, experienced. "The rearguard it is!"

Nath sniffed and nodded. "Very well, by Vox. I am with you, majister. But when my Third come up—why, then we hit Colun—"

"We do, Nath. We hit him most severely."

The orders being given, the vanguard stirred into motion again, ten thousand jutmen riding in a jingling, turf-thumping stream of zorcas and totrixes and nikvoves. To the regiments left after the debacle at Sicce's Gates we had added a further regiment each of the three main saddle animals. Seg's Bowmen of Loh rode zorcas and acted as mounted infantry. They wore dark crimson uniform with light bronze-studded leathers and I had great hopes for them, a mere three hundred though they might be. So we rode on through the mingled streaming lights of Antares. As Jiktar Nath Karidge said, breathing hard with his beard all a-tufting: "By the Spurs of Lasal the Vakka, majister! We will tweak this rast's tail for him—aye, yank it out by the roots!"

He then went on to make some disparging comments about our mounted infantry, typical jutman's talk, and he made great play with his pelisse as he spoke. Some of the mounted men riding in the group of messengers and aides-de-camp with him started to wrangle at this, and a merry little professional ding-dong ensued as we trotted along in the suns shine. We had twelve regiments of infantry mounted up on an amazing assortment of saddle animals, preysanys, hirvels, totrixes, marlques and urvivels among them. We also had, would you believe, a regiment of spearmen mounted on sleeths. Sleeths!

This last regiment had been formed by Tarek Roper Ferdin, a passionate sleeth-racer who still, to the despair of us zorca men, refused to concede the superiority of the zorca. The regiment, being a private one, was clad in a bright bottle green outfit with a quantity of bronze studding. But, troops as green as their uniforms though they were, I had inspected them and fancied they would stand firm on the day of the battle. They were representative of what Vondium had put forth, again, and if they failed then all might fail.

By a series of forced marches we covered the ground and, choosing our time and place well, were able to strike at Colun's rear guard just as they had begun preparations for pitching camp for the night. Give them their due, they were not like Fat Lango's apology for an army. They were tough and hardened. But, all the same, caught with tents half-erected and men out collecting firewood and fetching water and leading the animals to the picket lines, they folded. Pockets fought madly and well; but the cavalry swamped them and the infantry raced in with a whoop and dismounted and finished the job.

It was all over as the last of Zim and Genodras flushed ruby and emerald fires over the land, painting everything in an eerie sea of flame and verdigris.

There were many prisoners and the local Delphondi promised not to slay them all but to keep them penned until they might be ransomed or exchanged. We counted the cost and felt the satisfaction of relief from dire foreboding that our casualties were so few. We were still an army in being, and, into the bargain, an army crowned with success.

"Now," said Nath. "For the main body?"

"We must chivvy them a space, yet. Hit them here and run. Ambush there—and run. We run rings around them and no man will take shame that he runs. When we have them nicely molded to the certainty of their defeat—then we will deal with them."

Certain information reached me that this Kov Colun had been badly shaken by the defeat of a part of his army. He continued his advance; but he advanced cautiously instead of, as we all felt would be the wiser course, making an all-out effort to race through to the capital. His air component, mainly mirvols although he had some fluttrells, would prove uncomfortable in the day of the battle. During this period as we prepared his army for destruction they were chiefly an irritant. They scouted us with insolent ease and at times we were forced to pretty shifts to deceive them.

Seg's contingent of Bowmen set themselves the task of driving off the mirvols, and succeeded remarkably well at most times. But there were many pretty little skirmishes as Bowman and flyer clashed.

In the end Farris spared us a couple of small four-place airboats and these did sterling work. Colun's air was almost all flyer-mounted; of fliers he had a few he kept close and I, with a cynicism born of being an emperor, had no need to be told what those particular vollers were intended to do.

As each day passed and Colun struggled nearer and nearer Vondium, we chipped away at his forces. And, each day, messengers reached me with the latest news. Much of it concerned the preparations we made. The most ominous told me that the clansmen led by Zankov were now moving steadily down toward the city. As a defensible city, Vondium stood in much the same league as a holiday camp. The walls and fortresses had suffered so severely in the Time of Troubles that, even Yantong had seen when he had been in control there, it would take many seasons to rebuild them. Mind you, by Zair, Vondium would be defended at the end. There was no doubt on that in anybody's mind. None whatsoever.

This discrepancy in the defensive power of the city between the time when we Vallian Freedom Fighters had taken it back, and now when we sought to defend it, lay in the nature of the forces involved. Now the attackers would be clansmen from the Great Plains of Segesthes. The very thought of them sent cold shivers down the backs of civilized men.

The determination to fight on to the end and, if it came to it, die well, carried the men on during this period. They just did not think too far ahead. When the day came to meet the clansmen in battle, well, they'd call on Opaz and go forward and fight. And when it was over and they lay in their windrows of death, what would it matter then?

Seg remained amazingly cheerful, fully occupied, a fiery spirit of defiance and resistance. I could guess at the hurt he thus hid, the agony in him, and still I could not allay that hurt or intensify it by a single word.

Every day the sense of pressure increased. We chivvied and chopped Kov Colun's army, and ran. The clansmen drew nearer the city. The recruits drilled and sweated in Vondium and the adjoining areas. The arsenals worked all day and night producing the new arms and armor we required. Each day twisted another circle in the spiral of the press that closed on us. But we soldiered on.

The progress of Colun's army slowed. It faltered to a stop, clustered about a bend in a tiny river, a mere stream, where once it would have boldly pushed on. Provender had been scarce for that invading army of late. We hemmed them in, and still they substantially outnumbered us.

Nath walked over to where I stood in the shade of a group of missals and his face bore a wide and beaming smile. Seg looked up, and said, "So your Third have come up, then, Nath?"

"Aye, Kov Seg. They have. And a magnificent sight they are, fined down, lean and hard. By Vox! Let me at this rast of a Colun and his cramphs."

The Third with the accompanying churgurs and spearmen and archers had had to march. You could account the Third Phalanx a veteran body, now, after their victory at Yervismot where, thanks be to Opaz, we had found Seg Segutorio again. But most of the infantry were green troops, churgurs and spearmen. As for the archers, Seg pulled a face, and took himself off to make a most careful and intolerant inspection.

Now that the chance for bringing Colun's invading army to battle had come, and the opportunity must be taken on the wing, I was plagued by all those old and hateful doubts. The idea of splendidly attired regiments hurling into the clamor and horror of battle is bad enough. But you must never forget that those bright blocks of moving color beneath the banners and the glitter of weapons are men. Living men. To hurl them into battle must, inevitably, mean that many will be dead men.

So, for the next few days as Colun sought to move his men away from the stream, we chipped away at him. Then, when he did move, it was a question of maneuver and countermaneuver. The army appeared to have abandoned all ideas of marching on Vondium. They began to move south again, trying to keep in a single compact body and reaching strong places for each night. Patrols reported in regularly. I took a flier and went ahead and scouted the terrain most carefully, at last selecting a likely looking ridge bisecting the expected path of the enemy. The ground sloped just enough to make the Phalanx into a tiered and impregnable wall of steel. The level ground would give the cavalry a capital chance of putting in some real charges. With a heavy heart I gave my orders and the Army of Vondium moved out to secure the ridge and the surrounds.

Many deserters fled the ranks of Colun's army. They were mercenaries, and told us much of conditions; but they were astonished that we refused to hire them. We rounded them up and let the locals escort them to the coast and their ships. The invaders had swept up most of the occupying forces in their march, and, now that our tactics had dragged them to a standstill and then a reversal, the country was just about clean. Once we had disposed of these invading cramphs we could claim this southern section of Vallia back.

A Rapa veteran, his beaked face filled with outrage, was brought to my tent. My men stood looking on. This Rapa wore hard-worn harness, and his weapons were bright.

"You are the emperor?"

"Aye."

"I am told, majister, that you will not hire my men. We relinquished our allegiance to Kov Colun to join you. We are honorable men, paktuns, whose living is by the sword. Tell me, majister, why you do not hire us to fight for you?"

I told him. He either didn't understand or didn't want to understand. He could see that my new policy meant there would be no employment in Vallia for mercenaries in the future.

As he turned to leave, much cast down, he said: "Well majister, at least Colun will not be there to see the defeat of his army."

I quivered alert. I looked at the Rapa, and his vulture-face twitched and he went on quickly: "Kov Colun left the army by voller when we were encamped by that muddy little stream."

I sagged back, both elated and dejected. The army was doomed. Colun had seen that, despite its apparent strength. So, that meant—where had the rast gone to stir up more trouble?

The Rapa did not know. Diligent inquiries elicited no further information. Colun had flown away and left them to their destruction. The question now was: Would the new army commander, Kapt Hangreal, fight? Or would he agree to terms? You may imagine the tenterhooks we were dancing on as we awaited his reply to our message. The reply was short and brutal. Kapt Hangreal was confident that his army could whip us and make a clean escape to the coast. So, to my chagrin, we were committed to a fight.

That was the Battle of Irginian.

Kapt Hangreal completely misjudged the strength of the Phalanx, as the aragorn had done. Formed, compact, a solid mass of crimson and bronze, glittering with steel, the Third Phalanx took the foam-crested shocks of the cavalry charges. When Hangreal flung in his infantry our own churgurs swept in from the flanks. And, all the time, the deadly arrows crisscrossed. His aerial cavalry played a small part, until Seg's Bowmen rode up, dismounted, and shot them out of the sky as they tried to attack in flank. Well, it was a battle. It was not a particularly bad battle. Long before it could develop into a slogging match the Phalanx moved. Surrounded by clouds of churgurs and archers, the Phalanx charged.

The Battle of Irginian was over.

The local people, many of whom were sending their strongest sons to join the new armies of Vallia, cleared up. There was no time to waste. With a single day for recuperation the Army of Vondium started in motion, heading back for the capital. Forces of observation were left to ensure no flare-up occurred as the lines of prisoners marched for the coast. I left Seg and Nath in command and took voller and flew for Vondium. Now it was Zankov's turn. Now, perhaps, we would reach the beginning of the end.

Chapter Twenty

The Battle of Kochwold

Drak had not returned so far from Faol. Jaidur had not been released by the Sisters of the Rose from whatever deviltry they were egging him on to. And Zeg had not as yet responded to the call to leave Zandikar where he was king. As for the distaff side of the family, the babies, Velia, and Didi—the daughter of Gafard, the King's Striker, and our daughter Velia—were growing apace but not yet old enough to cause us the kind of pangs their elders were so good at. Lela, presumably with Jaidur, was off adventuring. And Dayra —ah, well! No word had come from Barty telling me how he fared in his renewed search for Dayra, and I fancied that Ros the Claw would lead him a merry dance, by Zair, yes!

And, as you will instantly perceive, Delia had not returned home.

I mumped about the city, and in between brooding over the unkind cuts of Fate got on with rebuilding the army.

There were a few burs to spare for lighter moments and Jilian proved a tough and cunning opponent at Jikaida. She had a most devilish way of cutting in from a flank when you were sure everything on that side was battened down tight. Also, of course, her person was such as to distract the most hardened old misogynist from the board and the marching ranks of model men.

"By Vox, Jak! As Dee-Sheon is my witness something addles your brains. You've let my left-flank Cuktar in—and, see—" and here Jilian did the most diabolical things to my model men. "Do you bare the throat?"

"Aye. Aye, I bare the throat."

We sat on a snug balcony bowered in moon-blooms and with a table handy loaded with silver flagons of wine. The night was cool and refreshing, and She of the Veils smiled down serenely, her fuzz of pink and golden light shedding a mellow roseate glow over the rooftops and battlements of the palace spread out below. Jilian yawned and covered her face with her hand, and then stretched.

"You had your girls hard at it today."

"And every day. But I wish I had been able to lay that cramph Colun by the heels."

"He'll turn up again," I said, comfortably. "That sort of villain always does. The only trouble is—"

"He'll turn up when it's most damned inconvenient, I know!"

Jilian wore one of Delia's loose lounging robes all of white sensil and she shimmered like an ivory flame in the moonlight. During the day she strode about among her girls and although she did not crack and snap her whip, she carried the ugly thing looped up around her arm.

The Enevon walked onto the balcony from the room beyond, rubbing his eyes, bringing fresh problems to be sorted out.

The exact spot at which we would like to meet Zankov and his wild clansmen had been chosen. If Opaz smiled, then the enemy would choose that route. In order to encourage Opaz to make up his mind I'd sent high-speed forces out to cut the bridges of alternative routes and to harass Zankov enough to make him swing, like a bull, to face the fancied threats. If he was prepared to follow the guidelines I had set for him, he would—Opaz willing—pass across the stretch of land known as the Kochwold. If he did, as we prayed, we would be waiting for him. And this waiting came as a vast and unexpected reprieve. Mind you, as a wild and hairy clansman myself I should have anticipated what was occurring up there in Jevuldrin. Clansmen are clansmen, accustomed to the airy sweeps of the Great Plains. When they ride through hamlets and villages, seeing the spires of cities rising before them, they feel all the itchy-fingered avarice of your true reiver. Plunder was retarding the onward march of Zankov's hired army. And, that very plunder was the hire money. I raged and fumed and could not, in all conscience, following the sad example of King Harold, allow the enemy to devastate the country. A policy of scorched earth would have served, perhaps; but the country up there was generally in the hands of that rast Ranjal Yasi, Stromich of Morcray, the twin brother to the strom,

Rosil Yasi. Zankov was having either to fight or come to terms with his old ally.

So the Kochwold it was to be. Zankov was clearly aiming to march to the east around the mountains, known as the Mountains of Thirda to some folk, rather than the west of them. That way would force him to make too many river crossings. East about he would have fewer major rivers to bar him. Kochwold extended its sweep of moorland on the southern borders of Jevuldrin and the northern borders of Forli. The last I had heard of Lykon Crimahan, the Kov of Forli, was that he was fighting desperate guerilla actions, with the help of us Valkans as promised, and slowly, painfully slowly, regaining some of his province, the Blessed Forli. All that was now, if not irrelevant, then of far less importance than the rampaging invasion of ten thousand wild clansmen.

Oh, yes, ten thousand. A further four thousand had been disembarked. And, again, that explained the disembarkation point still further. The ships from Zenicce were engaged in ferrying men and voves across, and the passage between Zamra to the south and the islands below Vellin to the north afforded relatively sheltered waters. No doubt they were making a third trip even now. So that, starkly, was a most potent reason why our waiting, useful as it was, must be curtailed.

"Come on, Jak! For the sake of Vox's Arm! You look as though your zorca's run off and you've found a dead calsany."

"I was wishing Delia was here."

Jilian smiled. "So do I. From all I know of the empress she would have my girls trimmed up in no time at all."

"Oh, aye. Mind you, I don't think she ever went through Lancival. Although, everything is possible with that lady."

"Everything, Jak. Everything."

She spoke in so knowing a way that my old head snapped up. But Jilian just smiled her smile, her dark hair low over that broad white forehead, and her red mouth arched, so that I knew I was beaten. Jilian was not prepared to let me into her secrets—not just yet, anyway.

While we awaited certain news that Zankov and the clansmen had chosen the route we wanted we labored hard and long. The army was built up again. The remnants of the force almost destroyed at Sicce's Gates had come in and formed cadres. Nath was fiercely determined on having three full Phalanxes, and the veterans of the First and Second were slogging away teaching the newcomers to the files. The brumbytes worked willingly, with the triumphs of the Third to guide them.

Spearmen, archers and churgurs filled the regiments of the infantry, along with axemen and double-handed swordsmen and the rest. The cavalry was not, to their baffled fury, unduly expanded. But they worked hard, damned hard, and I concentrated strength on the armored nikvove regiments. This was obvious sense to anyone who knew what was going on in Filbarrka.

A message had been sent to Filbarrka telling him that instead of six there were now ten Divisions to be dealt with. His reply was typical. I could imagine him entangling his fingers and bouncing up and down as he dictated it to his stylor. "A better target for the dartmen and archers, majister! They'll be so confused, being so many, they won't know which way to run or what is hitting them."

Well, it was comforting to know *someone* was so confident.

Enevon sought assistance from the army in gathering the third mergem harvest and this was done. Mergem, a capital all-purpose foodstuff, would be vital in the campaigns.

Farris reported that the new ship-construction proceeded well, although: "Ships!" He pulled his lip. "Mere rafts."

"Exactly, Farris. And functional."

The production of silver boxes which would lift the new ships was well advanced. So I had said we would simply construct huge raft-like structures, open-sided, railed in and five or six storied. Each one would be propelled by a rig of the utmost simplicity: foresail, mainsail and mizzen. With the silver boxes exerting their lifting power and extending their invisible keels into the lines of force, we could sail and tack and steer a course. When it rained, well, we'd get wet.

But, with these flying chicken-coops we could transport the army.

I may add that there were very few forests left for dwaburs around Vondium.

On three separate occasions I saw the gold and scarlet hunting bird of the Star Lords circling above me. I took no notice. If the Everoinye switched me away to some other part of Kregen now—or, horribly, banished me back to Earth—there would be a struggle and I might win or lose. As of now, as they say, the defense of Vondium and the uniting of all Vallia obsessed me. Every day we heard fresh stories of atrocities committed in those areas occupied by any of the various invaders. We all felt, unshakably, that we had to ensure that the new flag of Vallia floated over a free country.

Trite, chauvinistic, opportunistic—maybe. But it was not me, not Dray Prescot, not even Jak the Drang, who alone held this point of view. Nothing could have been done if the people were not every one fully dedicated and committed.

So, mentally committing the Gdoinye and its masters to the Ice Floes of Sicce, I stuck doggedly to the task at hand.

A regiment of my Valkans flying the superb flutduins eventually reached us, and they were greeted with roars of pleasure. Everyone regarded these splendid flyers with great affection and treated their riders right royally, a very different situation from even a few seasons ago when most Vallians regarded saddle flyers as birds of the devils of Cottmer's Caverns.

Came the day.

At last.

Zankov was reported as definitely taking the route that would lead through to the Kochwold.

Imagine a miles wide area smothered in men and animals all loading aboard vast and creaking five-story rafts, like a bedlam of the Ark in monstrous proportions. Dust, yelling, smells, the neighs and whinnyings of animals, the choleric bellows of Deldars, the snapping of whips, the creaking of wheels. And, over all, the forest of masts and yards. Well, somehow or other the mass was loaded and the ships—the flying chicken-coops—lifted into the air.

Wearing the blazing golden and scarlet Mask of Recognition specially made for me, I stood in the bows of a small voller and watched the departure. The ships rose and spread their wings. The wind zephyred them along. One by one, three by three, squadron by squadron, they took up their stations. Sailing orange boxes flying through thin air. Railed rafts loaded down with men and animals, with artillery and weapons, stores and fodder. They excited enormous sensations of disbelief, and wonder, and sheer jumping excitement.

This excitement thrilled through the air, leaping from man to man, bringing the color up, lending a sparkle to the eye, making every conversation bright and meaningful. Off they sailed, off to war, off to fight the Kregen-renowned and ferocious clansmen of Segesthes—off to find their destinies.

When the voller landed back at the palace, for there was

still work to be done before I could leave—always there was work—Jilian waited for me to wish me remberee.

She looked stunning. Her black leathers clung to her, molding her figure, and her long legs seemed to go on and on for ever. She carried her bronze-mounted balass box under her left arm, and rapier and main-gauche were scabbarded to her narrow waist. Also, she carried a drexer at my wish. Her hair was covered by a helmet in which crimson feathers tufted bravely. She smiled.

"So it is remberee, Jak the Drang."

"Aye, Jilian. Remberee."

Her voller was waiting. The mingled streaming lights of the Suns of Scorpio fell about us, drenching us and the landing platform in ruby and emerald fires. The air smelled sweet with that pungent, unique, glorious Kregen sweetness.

And then she surprised me. Still smiling she leaned forward and kissed me. I was stunned. She stepped back, observed the fantamyrrh of her voller and climbed aboard. She lifted her arm in final salute.

"Remberee, Jak. I do not forget what help you have given a poor girl from a Banje shop."

"You mean a wild tiger-girl, do you not? Remberee, Jilian the Claw."

The voller lifted away. I wondered if I would ever see her again.

Work—well, there is always work. The army was commanded by men of whom you have met in my narrative, and others I have not so far mentioned. But all, I felt, were competent, brave and loyal. To be anything less in those dark days for Vallia was a species of crime. Nath had taken his three Phalanxes. Farris commanded the air. He would have nothing of remaining in Vondium to be the imperial Crebent-Justicar. The Presidio would run things in Vondium. If we failed, of course, there would be nothing for them to run, except—to run themselves. Seg stood by me and we would fly up together, he to command the vanguard as ever.

Most of my choice band had gone; but about fifty of them remained to escort Seg and me, enough to fill the voller we would use. And, in these last days I had discovered what their secret was. Many a time, when one or the other of them should have been off duty I had stumbled across them on duty at my door or the flap of my tent on campaign. Slowly I realized that after the assassins' attempts on me they had, privately, formed a kind of purely personal bodyguard. This was something I had never encouraged, for palace intrigues can breed in this kind of Praetorian Guard, this Imperial Guard, this Life Guard syndrome. But they insisted, and, to be truthful, I knew every one of them and fancied every one a true comrade.

They called this new bodyguard the Emperor's Sword Watch.

They all wore a yellow scarf tucked in around the corselet rim. Also, I noticed that their crimson trappings tended more to the scarlet. . . .

Left in Vondium were a few regiments so new the armory grease still clung to their weapons and their uniforms were not marked by a spot, and a convalescent regiment of men recovering from sickness or wounds. All the rest flew northeast. We followed and I, at the least, had thoughts of Armageddon plaguing my mind.

The armada was blessed with favoring winds and we lost only two of the sailing chicken-coops, the vast rafts crashing in splinters but not harming the men in them. These last, I know, raved frantically and then set about repairing their ungainly craft. The rest of the army set down safely.

The details of the campaign need not be gone into at length, suffice it to say that by luck and planning we contrived that the army should be drawn up in proper array on the ridge we had chosen, with the Kochwold about us, in good time. Zankov's scouts had reported our presence. The enemy host drew in and concentrated. They possessed such sublime confidence in their own invulnerability that we anticipated a wild and reckless clansman's charge which, they supposed, would settle the issue once and for all.

Filbarrka, brought by a flying collection of rafts and chicken-coops, landed his zorcamen. At once I rode out to inspect them. I rode Snowy, that coal-black zorca, and I was dressed in my usual fashion. The brave old scarlet glowed under the suns. I carried a longbow, a quiver of arrows fletched with the rose-red feathers of the zim-korf of Valka, a Krozair longsword, a drexer and a rapier and main-gauche. Also, strapped to the saddle swung an axe. Not overdressed, not carrying a ridiculous overamount of weaponry, I fancied. This was the Kregen way. Not as many weapons as a man can carry—no. As may weapons as are needed for the job in hand—yes. That is the Kregen way.

Accompanied by aides-de-camp and escorted by the chiefs of the Emperor's Sword Watch, we cantered out to the place where Filbarrka, radiant, immense in armor, had drawn up his brand new zorca force for inspection.

And, indeed, they looked splendid.

"Let 'em bring on their ten thousand," said Filbarrka, twitching his fingers. "We'll dart 'em and feather 'em and then you lot can have a go."

Our sailing rafts had taken the equipment asked for out to the Blue Mountains and so the zorca force was accoutered as I expected and as Filbarrka had suggested. Also, a contingent of the Blue Mountain Boys was present, extraordinarily ferocious and many of them armed with the great Sword of War. Korf Aighos was there and I greeted him as an old friend and kept a wary eye on my own equipment.

"Although," said the Korf. "What is going on in the Blue Mountains now I do not like to think."

"Why, Korf! I'm surprised anything remains for anyone to want to take away."

"You would, majister, be surprised. And we have some Black Mountain Men with us, although not many. They are hard pressed up north."

"All in good time."

He did not mention Delia and so I knew she had not been to her province of the Blue Mountains. She hadn't been in Delphona, either. I remember I said to myself something like where the hell can the pesky woman be? and immediately felt aghast at the thought. What the Sisters of the Rose got up to would make even Korf Aighos scratch his head.

The ground over which the coming battle would be fought was surveyed again most thoroughly. Hundreds of lads were out spreading their caltrops, and the chevaux-de-frise were stacked ready and waiting to be run out onto the flanks as required. That night the sky glowed with the reflections of camp fires.

As a general rule I do not believe in Councils of War and I saw no need to make an exception now. We gathered, the Kapts and the chiefs, and there was little talk of what to do on the morrow. Every one knew his task. So we drank in moderation and cracked a few silly jokes and sang and then sought our beds. If they slept I did not inquire. I made the rounds of the campfires and was aware of the hovering shadows of the men of the Sword Watch. One of the songs that was currently popular kept breaking out from this group or that clustered about their fire. "She lived by the Lily Canal" the song was, a sickly sentimental ditty of very little musical worth; but somehow it got to the men, and they warbled it over and over, almost obsessively. Yes, I can never hear that old song now without a powerful pang of remembrance of that night before the Battle of Kochwold, among the campfires of the army, the sizzle of the flames, the smells of animals and dust, the tang of leather and sweat and oil. Well, a battle is a battle, as I have said, and they are all the same and all different—as I have said. . . .

Well before dawn the host was astir and breakfasting mightily. Then we moved forward from the camp area and took up our battle positions. Patrols reported that the clansmen were doing exactly as we anticipated and were moving forward for the confrontation that daylight would bring. Nothing would stop them from putting spurs in and charging. It was our job to stop that charge.

Perhaps one day a full and detailed account of the Battle of Kochwold will be given to you by me, for it was a fascinating battle and deserves commemoration. Enevon committed all the salient facts to paper; but it needs a military historian to sort them out and make sense of them. Very many fine poems were written and there are countless songs marking this or that incident. At the time and to most of us engaged, it was a huge sprawling untidy mess.

And, to be sure, the message I received half way through did not make understanding any easier. The initial stages went as we had planned—almost.

The sprawling untidy mess occurred, as in many fights, after the initial movements of each side, being completed, had achieved or failed to achieve their objectives. Our first requirement was to stop that charge. That objective had been required by many a fighting host before us, and most of them were long a-mouldering.

But the clansmen of the Great Plains of Segesthes, among whom I am proud to be numbered as a member, although not in my own eyes skilled enough to be dubbed a clanner, are not your stupid brainless illiterate barbarians. They are not like the Iron Riders, the radvakkas whom the Phalanx had so signally overthrown.

"By Vox!" said Seg, at my side just before he left to take over his position with the vanguard. "The cramphs!"

"Aye, Seg," I said. "Clansmen are clansmen. It will be a bonny fight."

For the tremendous dark mass of the vove cavalry halted, a plains-filling concentration of men and animals, silent, awe-inspiring, totally menacing in their appearance. And forward trotted the archers. These were men who were the occupiers of the land hereabouts, Ranjal Yasi's men, and so I knew the Kataki stromich had come to terms with his old friend Zankov. Perhaps the sight and sound and stink of ten thousand clansmen and their voves had had a deal to do with that. . . .

Also, of course, in these nation-wide struggles for power, the double-dealing would always go on. No doubt Phu-Si-Yantong kept a close observation on what went on and had advised his lieutenant, Ranjal Yasi, to appear to acquiesce in the rebellious plans of Zankov, who had been disowned by the Wizard of Loh. That, at least, would be in keeping with the character of the participants.

Whatever accommodations had been reached, we faced in addition to the ten divisions of vovemen a host of other cavalry and infantry. They were mercenaries, hired by Yasi to keep the country in subjection, and they had been earning their hire. We men of Vallia vowed to make them rue their wages this day of battle.

"Better clear them away with your cavalry, Seg. But I shall keep the nikvove regiments under my hand for a space."

"Yes, my old dom, and make damned sure they nip in quick when they're needed. By the Veiled Froyvil! I really think this is going to be a battle that will be remembered to the end of time." He walked with me toward the four-place voller he required as a commander and which he would quit for a zorca or nikvove when he reached his battle line. "This is going to be a big one, Dray!"

"Aye. Would to Zair it was not necessary."

In the voller waited his pilot, his trumpeter and his standard bearer, all old friends to whom I spoke a few words. Then Seg Segutorio took off, flying forward into battle. Would I ever clap eyes on my blade comrade again? That kind of thought always occurs to me, always tortures me, and is always a stupid nonsense. When Zair crooks his finger, then up you go, my friend, and nothing will detain you on Kregen. . . .

It was time for me to perform what later generations

would call the Public Relations Stunt. Mind you, I do not denigrate the value of thus showing myself, as the commander, and the flags. Mounted on as large a nikvove as we could find, a superb charger called Balassmane, and clad in a brilliant golden armor, emblazoned with scarlet, I rode along the forward face of the army. The blazing Mask of Recognition glittered in the light of the Suns or Scorpio. Scarlet feathers fluttered. I lifted the drexer high in salute.

Following me trotted Cleitar the Standard bearing the flag with the yellow cross on the scarlet field, Old Superb. With him rode Ortyg the Tresh proudly lifting the new red and yellow flag of Vallia. Volodu the Lungs rode to hand and his silver trumpet, much dented, gleamed like a leaping salmon. At my back and on the side nearest the enemy rode Korero the Shield. It would take a very great deal to shift him from that devoted position. Others of my Sword Watch trotted in that imperial cavalcade, glittering with light, colorful with uniforms, proud, eager, nerved to the occasion, men you have met in this my narrative, men I am proud to call comrades.

As we passed down the lines the roar of approbation swelled and the men in the ranks lifted their weapons, a swirling forest of blades, and cheered. The answering shouts from our foes drifted in, thin and attenuated. But, then, all our bellowing would reach them as a mere whisper beside their own war chants.

"By Aduim's Belly!" said Dorgo the Clis.

"I never thought to see a day like this," said Targon the Tapster.

"Nor me," said Naghan ti Lodkwara.

Their words were lost and blown away in the swelling cheers from the army.

By the time that morale-boosting and flag identification exercise was over and we had returned to our positions, the first clashes had taken place. The archers had been sent forward by Zankov to prepare our mass. He must, then, have a great deal of control over the unruly clansmen. But Seg would have none of that and he would not sit on his hands when there was shooting in the wind. His advance guard cavalry swept out, screeching, long lines of glittering figures bounding over the moorland. They tumbled the enemy archers over and Seg's mounted Bowmen roared forward. He had so few Bowmen of Loh to hand that he reserved them for the special occasion, the *point d'appui*. But the compound reflex bows of our men spat. The range to the enormous mass of clansmen was far too far; but the confused fighting between the two ranked armies slowly sorted itself out, and then the recalls were blown and our men, triumphant, rode back.

Of course, the discomfiture of that ploy of Zankov's would merely make the grim Chuktars of the clansmen say in their savage way that he should not have bothered with all this fancy strategy and tactics. Let the clansmen charge. That would be the end of it.

Our position on that little ridge must have worried Zankov. I had not formed any great opinion of his qualities as a military captain; but something must have alarmed him at the sight of those massed ranks and files of men, silent and motionless in their crimson and bronze. Perhaps he had heard of the fate of the radvakkas against the Phalanx.

Looking about, I'll admit I missed the warm and eager presence of Barty Vessler. Nath Nazabhan cantered over and instantly wanted me to order the advance. I looked at him and he said: "Well, majister, by Vox!"

"Once Filbarrka has been at work for a space, then you may advance, Nath. But you will not move until you have my personal word. Is that clear?"

"It is clear and it makes sense, as we planned. But it is damned hard standing still with a pike in your fist at a time like this."

"Agreed. You saw their bowmen?"

He ducked his head, eager, alive, vehement. "I did. I may have spoken harsh words against the Kov of Falinur in the past, when I did not know him. No one could have cleared our front as well as he has just done."

That, I may say, pleased me enormously.

The clansmen with the failure of their missile men were not as foolish as the knights at Crecy. There was no Comte d'Alençon in their ranks to bay out: "Kill me this rabble! Kill! Kill!" and go spurring down on his mercenary allies. They waited calmly for the outcome of this first encounter and when it went against them they waited for the ground to clear. Again, that made sense, for even a vove in the midst of a charge may stumble over a wounded man flying on a wounded and terrified zorca or totrix. So we watched them and the ranks held and the suns crawled across the sky and I knew Filbarrka was bringing his torrent of zorcamen up on flanks and rear.

Whether the clansmen charged before or after he hit them, I knew, made little difference to Filbarrka. Except that if they attempted to charge afterwards their onslaught would be a little dinted....

For myself, I would prefer the vove charge to begin and then for Filbarrka to hit them, as they rode bunched, knee to knee.

A certain amount of aerial activity took place. Our flutduin regiment had done splendid work in scouting; but there were too few of them to affect in any greatly material way the outcome of the main battle. But, at least, it was better they fought for us than against us. I saw them swooping down and shooting into the ranks of the vovemen, and presently a mirvol-mounted force of aerial cavalry flew up and tried to chase them off. The aerial evolutions were pretty to watch. But my Valkan flutduinim had been well-trained by Djangs who are past-masters at the art of aerial combat, and they both held off the mirvols and continued to attack the army below.

Those mirvols—they wore gaudy trappings and their riders no less gaudy uniforms. Uniforms, I fancied, I had last seen in Fat Lango's army.

Abruptly, Nath rapped out an oath. "I am for the Phalanx, majister. They move! See! The clansmen move!"

And, indeed, the front ranks of the vovemen were in motion, leading out, beginning to stretch forward into the charge.

So—the moment everyone waited for, hoped for and dreaded, had at last arrived.

"Stand like a rock, Nath!" I bellowed after him, and he half-turned in the saddle and flung up his hand in parting salute.

I could tell to the mur when Nath arrived with the three Phalanxes. From every Jodhri the battle flags unfurled and broke free, thirty-six Old Superbs, to add a special luster to the display of heraldry and defiance flaunting in the breeze.

Cleitar the Standard grunted and shook his own flag, Old Superb, making it ripple and glisten.

"It is a right they have earned, Cleitar."

"Aye, majister. And, anyway, the Jodhri banners are smaller than your own personal standard. As they should be."

And I had to smile.

Where one caltrop will bring a four-legged animal crashing to the ground, a vove with his eight legs will carry on until he

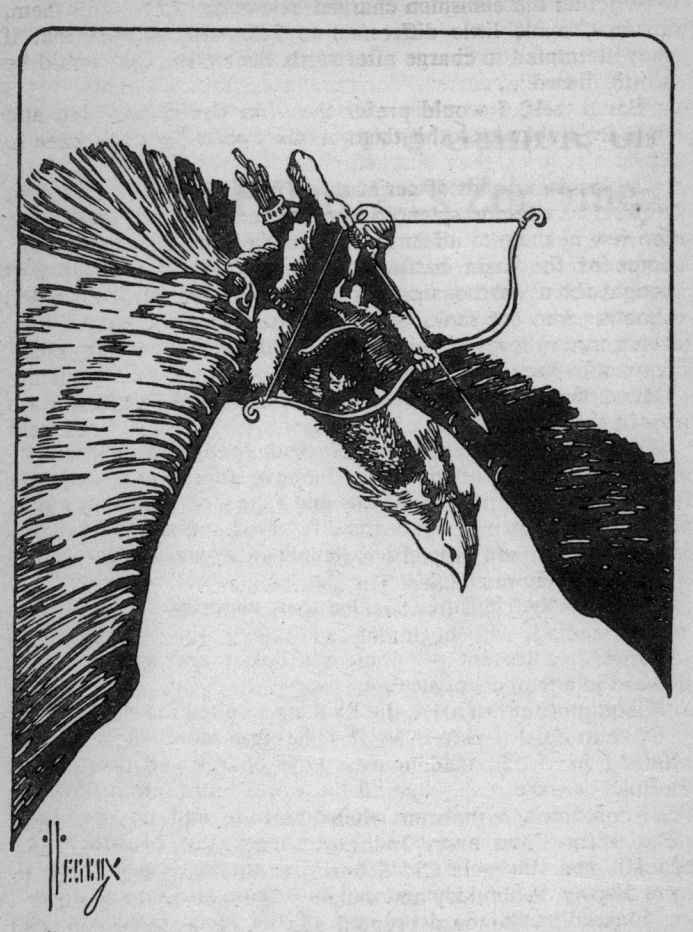

"I saw the bowmen swooping down and shooting into the ranks."

is a veritable pincushion with the vile things tangling him. I do not like caltrops or chevaux-de-frise as a cavalryman; as an infantryman they are gifts from the gods. The vovemen moved. They advanced. Their banners fluttered. Their pace increased. Like the irresistible ocean, like the Tides of Kregen themselves, like—like a charge of vovemen!—like nothing else in Creation, they charged.

The drumming hoofbeats battered the ground. The ground shook. The onward surge consumed the senses. On trampled the vovemen. On thundered the sea of steel. Forward they came. Six thousand in that first charge. Six thousand monstrous beasts. Six thousand ferocious warriors. On they rode, onward, ever onward, cantering into a gallop, racing full stretch, pouring resistlessly on, on, roaring down on the grim compact masses of the Phalanx.

How they rode! How they rode, those wild shaggy clansmen of the Great Plains!

Timing their attack to coincide with that great charge the enemy's vollers crested forward above that sea of tossing heads and flaring pelts, of horns and fangs, of clansmen gone wild. But our own airboats rose, reserved for this stratagem, and soared up and forward to tangle in a wild melee above the onrush below.

And now the clansmen shrilled their warcries. Onward they rushed.

Onward, a torrent of monstrous beasts and savage men, onward in a tempest of steel.

Silent, motionless, solid, the Phalanx awaited the shock.

By Zim-Zair! I admit to it. The fire scorched into my blood. I have ridden in many a vove charge and thrilled to the mad onward rush when all the world blurs into a flowing frieze of color. When you know nothing and no one can stand before you and live. The sheer bulk of the vove beneath you, the solidity of him, the square impact of his eight hooves beating the ground in unison, the smooth flowing onward rush, the steadiness of the lance couched and pointed, its steel head sharp and glittering, bearing on, bearing on!

These vovemen had shattered and destroyed two Phalanxes already. We had rebuilt, and there was the Third. But, but . . . Oh, yes, by Vox, I sweated apprehension, tension—and fear.

Six thousand in that first wild charge. And the other four

thousand? The spyglass confirmed it. They were circling out on the flanks, two Divisions each, like horns, like pincers, raking forward to encircle and crush us.

But a stir was visible in that onrushing riding horde on either flank. The vovemen were in disorder there. And, at the rear of the great main charge a further disturbance attracted the attention of my men.

Filbarrka was in action.

His zorcamen, light-armored, swift, deadly like wasps, darted in and out, maddening, pirouetting, curvetting, slaying. In orderly groups they fought with intelligence and cunning and high courage. Their archery shot coolly and methodically. Their dartmen raced in, flung their barbed weapons, and withdrew. The darts were poor at penetrating armor; but against unarmored parts of men and animals were highly effective and unpleasant. They penetrated deeply and were hard to remove. They caused constant pain as they flopped about in the convulsive movement of the voves, maddening the animals and causing them to disorder the formations still further.

The long slender twelve-foot lance was employed against man or animal. Then the mace—the vicious, heavy-headed mace, unerring—crunched with bone-smashing power. The zorcamen were nearer the ground than the vovemen. Many a clansman felt that stunning smash against his thigh or pelvis, toppling, his armory of weaponry flailing the air over the aggressive zorcaman, falling, being hit again as he fell. Oh, yes, Filbarrka's Lancers and Filbarrka's Archers wreaked enormous havoc and confusion as the vove charge poured across the plain and narrowed the gap.

And that gap itself proved a deadly obstacle to the voves. Liberally we had strewn the ground with caltrops and chevaux-de-frise, with narrow, wedge-shaped ditches. Many voves pitched to the ground, all their eight legs unable to cope with the obstacles. And our own dustrectium flayed them. Shaft after shaft sailed across the narrowing gap. Our archers shot well on that day, thanks be to Opaz. The steel-tipped birds of war thinned the onrushing mass. But still they came on, upborne with pride, with knowledge of their own invincibility, and, by Krun, my heart rode with them, for they were clansmen.

Following them rode the mass of totrix and zorca cavalry put into the field by Zankov and Stromich Ranjal. Their infantry waited in dense masses for the outcome. But the charge, the charge of the voves—that was the battle winner!

Watching, lifting in my stirrups, I saw the way the leading masses roared up the first of the slope to the ridge. Would nothing stop them? On and on they raged, beating on and up, and the pikes all came down as one, and the trumpets pealed, and the crimson and bronze stretched out, taut and thin to my eye, firm and like a rock in a raging sea.

The three Phalanxes had been arranged with the First on the right of the line and the Second on their left and half of the Third, the Fifth Kerchuri, on the left of the line. The Sixth Kerchuri stood fast in reserve to the rear. All the emotion of two worlds concentrated down for me in that impact. I was aware of the flanks surging on and of churgur infantry and spearmen clashing on the wings. I was aware of the ceaseless flights of arrows. I was aware of the cavalry fights taking place all over the plain. But the impact, nearer and nearer, took my attention and I could not tear my eyes away from that enormous collision.

Irresistible and immovable objects? No, by Krun, not quite. For the Phalanx had been bested before by the clansmen, and the clansmen knew nothing of defeat. The impact, when it came, racketed such noise, such clamor, such soul-searing horror, that I felt the salt taste of blood on my lips.

That was where I should be, down there, in the front rank of the files with the faxuls, down there, wielding my pike against that onrushing host. And I sat my nikvove and watched and could only judge the time to send forward the Sixth Kerchuri and order in the churgurs and the spearmen. The Hakkodin were slashing and slicing away, the front swayed, locked, striking in insane fury. Incredible, the ferocity of the charge and sublime, insane, the solidity it met.

The Second swayed.

The Second Phalanx swayed and its front crumbled.

I saw the yellow and red flags go down.

Voves began to pour through a narrow gap that rapidly widened. At my instant order Volodu blew Sixth Kerchuri; but Nath was before me and I saw the Sixth moving up, solid and dense in their masses, the crimson and bronze shouldering forward to plug the gap. The Second recovered. The officers down there were raging and bellowing and the files reformed and the pikes came down again, all in line. But the lines were thinner, now.

The confusion down there tantalized me. The voves recoiled and came on again. The Phalanx held. I saw the rear markers going up, the Bratchlins urging the men on. I saw the swaying movement as though the very sea itself sought to pour on and over a line of rocks. And the zorcamen were in among the voves now, prancing around on their nimble steeds, striking and sliding return blows. The state of flux might continue, or it might break on an instant.

Zankov flung his infantry in, before they had time to decide if the day was lost or won, hurling them on intemperately to support the charge, to get in among the Phalanx. Our own infantry moved to mask the flanks, channeling the attack onto the melee. The Hakkodin now had fresh targets for their axes and halberds and two-handed swords.

This was the crucial moment.

Even when he fights in the melee a clansman is an opponent greatly to be feared. Even when he does not hurl forward in the charge, he is a fighting man of enormous power. The slogging match had begun.

At that instant a troop of zorca riders flew up the long slope to my left side, riding hard, and I saw they were girls, Jikai Vuvushis.

Some of the Emperor's Sword Watch angled out to halt them; but I saw the leader, drooping in the saddle, saw the arrow in her shoulder.

"Let her through!" I bellowed.

Jilian hauled her lathered zorca up before me. Her pale face was so white I fancied she had no blood left at all, and knew that was not so, as the blood stained around the ugly shaft in her shoulder. She tried to smile and the pain gripped her.

"I am sorry to see you in such case, Jilian." I spoke with anger. "I had thought you in the reserve where—"

"Where you ordered my girls, aye, Jak, I know. But I have had another zhantil to saddle. My regiment is in the reserve and will go forward with the victory." She swayed and I leaned down from the nikvove and got a hand under her armpit. "But there is no time. You must fly—" Her gaze flicked to the reserve troop of flutdiuns who waited beside Karidge's Brigade, in the reserve, under my hand. Her girls were there, brilliant and chattering, and every eye fixed on that titanic fight going on along the face of the ridge. I looked there, alert for any change; but the slogging match continued and the Phalanx had not moved and the clansmen had not retired. Men were dying down there, dying by the hundred.

"The empress . . ." Jilian swayed and I was off the nikvove and hauled her off her zorca, and held her, looking down, and my face must have appeared like a chunk of granite.

"What of the empress?"

Jilian caught her breath. And I saw she bore an axe wound in her side, gashing and horrible, exposing pink and white ribs.

"That is nothing, Jak. The empress needs assistance—the Sakkora Stones—"

"I know it." I placed her down, gently, for she was a great spirit, and bellowed at my company of brilliant aides. "Send to Seg Segutorio, the Kov of Falinur, commanding the vaward. My compliments. He is now commanding the army." I was running toward the flutduins as I shouted, and each one of the great birds ruffled his feathers, as though asking me to pick him. "Tell the Kov to send in the reserve the moment the line wavers. Not before, not afterwards. He will know."

Then I was hauling the flutduin Jiktar off his bird and mounting up, disdaining the straps of the clerketer. Everyone was yelling. Shouts of consternation broke from the Emperor's Sword Watch. The flutduin troop gaped. I cracked the bird and he rose at once, his wings wide and gorgeous and of immense power. Together we rose into the air.

Below us a tremendous battle raged. Thousands of men were locked in hand-to-hand combat. I barely saw the red horror of it, barely heard the screeching din.

Over the clangor, over the blood, over the agony and death below I flew. I left the battle in the culminating moments of victory and defeat. Headlong, caring for one person and one person only in all of Kregen, I flew like a maniac across the gory battlefield of Kochwold.

Delia. . . .

Chapter Twenty-One

A Life for Vallia

Desertion. Infamous conduct. Lack of moral fibre in the face of the enemy. Lack of judgment of issues. Nothing of that mattered. Vallia did not matter, nor Kregen itself.

Only Delia mattered.

I knew the Sakkora Stones.

Like the Kharoi Stones of my island of Hyr Khor in distant Djanduin, it had been raised by the Sunset People who had lived on Kregen before the Star Lords had brought diffs to that beautiful planet to make it the wild and terrible world it is today. Ruined, tumbled into mouldering stones, mysterious, unforgettable, the buildings of the Sunset People yet lived in legend and song.

Over the battlefield I flew and mirvols attacked me and I shot and slew them and their riders, and with the long whippy aerial sword strapped to the saddle fought off those who would have stopped me. In a straight line across the front I flew. The Sakkora Stones had been figured into our calculations in picking this site for the battle, and had been reckoned as not having any influence, one way or the other. They stood some ulm or so in rear of the position taken up by Zankov and we expected them to be used as a field hospital or supply dump. They lifted from the moorland, quite plainly, fallen columns, walls and roofs marking a once-vast star-shaped structure whose function remained obscure. As on Earth today when an archaeologist is faced with an artifact whose manner of use he does not know will say it is a cult object or a ritual object, so we said the Sakkora Stones were a cult object.

Over the rear echelons of Zankov's army I flew and alighted in the grove of drooping trees gaining nourishment from some underground stream in this desolate moorland country. The flutduin immediately lifted off with a massive beat of his pinions and a wicked toss of his head. Magnificent saddle birds, flutduins. He was off back to his master.

I looked about, sternly and yet filled with terror. What in blue blazes Delia had been up to, how Jilian was involved, I did not know. But, by Vox, I would find out!

All the detritus, human, animal and material, in rear of a great army in conflict lay scattered about. The trees afforded a slight amount of cover and men and animals moved to and fro, with a steady stream of wounded coming back. A party of spearmen, second-line troops no doubt assigned to guard the baggage train, approached the wood to question me. It were better—and more decent—not to relate what happened to them. I did not deign to don one of their uniforms as a disguise. I ran toward the nearest abutment of the Stones.

Anything could be happening in there. Jilian had been in no case to be specific. If she did not die I would be in her debt—if Delia lived. Whether or not I lived seemed to me of scant importance then, which is a strange attitude for me, Dray Prescot, to take, by Zair!

As I ran on with the blood thumping around my body it felt as though that very blood fought against constrictions in my veins. I'd been living very high and mighty, just lately, very high on the vosk, and, now. . . ! This was more like the old Dray Prescot, rushing headlong into danger with a naked sword in his fist. Rushing, like the veritable onker I am, headlong into danger that forethought would avoid. But, then, that is me, Dray Prescot, prince of onkers.

The clansmen started up from their fire on which grilling ponsho smelled sweet. There were four of them and they were not skulkers, each being wounded. They saw my scarlet and gold flummery of dress and they did not hesitate. Out whipped their broadswords and they charged.

Well, it was a merry little ding-dong; but I was frantic with worry and in no mood for a long exchange of handstrokes. The drexer snapped back into the scabbard. The next instant the Krozair longsword flamed. They were skilled clansmen, enormously powerful warriors; but they were not fighting for the life of Delia of Delphond, Delia of the Blue Mountains.

As the last of them sank down, he gasped out: "You fight like a clansman, Vallian."

"Believe it, clanner," I said, hurdling him and rushing on

into the gloom of the stones. "By the Black Chunkrah, believe it!"

Something caught in his eyes as he died.

Headstrong, headlong, and utterly foolish, Dray Prescot. I should have paused to snatch up a clansman's russets and cover my insolent scarlet and gold. But there was no time, no time. . . . Through the gloomy aisles of the leaning columns I raced. And I began to catch a glimpse of the truth. This place had been used as a headquarters. That would have made no difference to us. And what had been wrought here had been wrought with cunning and stealth and high courage. Running on I passed dead clansmen, dead mercenaries of various races of diffs. And, also, I passed dead bodies of Jikai Vuvushis, Battle Maidens. They looked pitiful and twisted in their fighting leathers of russet or black. And on their supple bodies, so lax and ghastly now in the final sleep, the badges of the Sisters of the Rose glowed in mockery.

This was the kind of operation I, the stupid, proud, so inordinately presumptuous Emperor of Vallia, should have mounted. I had not. I had staked all on the impregnability of the Phalanx, the prowess of the warriors of the army and the new Filbarrka zorcamen. I prowled on, understanding what had passed here, and knowing that I would find the answers I sought when I came at last to the operations room of this headquarters and discovered what had chanced between Delia and her Battle Maidens, and Zankov, the slayer of her father.

Entwined clumps of purple-flowered Blooms depended from the shattered columns. Here and there the orange cones of Hyr-flicks congealed spots of deadly color. Their green tendrils snaked this way and that, seeking prey, snatching up the tikos of the cracked masonry, snaring any animal of reasonable size unwary enough to venture here. A Rapa had been caught and engulfed; only his beaked face glared sightlessly from a distended orange cone, and soon that would be gone, digested along with the rest of him.

Many of the Hyr-flicks, gigantic cousins of the flick-flicks that graced the windowsills of Kregen homes, had been slashed through. And yet still their tendrils writhed.

"Sink me!" I burst out as I ran on. "That Delia has put her head into a mighty unsavory pest hole, by Zair!"

The Krozair brand carved me a slimy way through and I understood this way was what could be called the rear entrance. Those four clansmen, hunkering wounded over their roasting ponsho, had been all unwitting of the drama enacted here. They had been of a clan I did not know. But I would know them hereafter, and Hap Loder would be advised.

Thinking sour thoughts like that led me on, as I ran, to a single scarlet speculation of the fate of the battle. The front would still be in flux, for the sounds of combat reached here as a muted hum, as of bees on a sunny summer afternoon, without the devil-boom of gunnery. The Hakkodin would be fully in action, the sword and shield men attempting to smash forward, the reserves being used—I must trust Seg. He must judge the time when to send in the reserves, when to commit our nikvove cavalry. But I pushed on without a pause, for ahead of me in the half-light of the aisled and gloomy Stones a radiance like the eye of the setting Zim, the red sun of Antares, drew me on.

There were diffs there, I remember, men in armor and brandishing weapons, and the manner of their going is something I do not clearly recall. I can still feel the hot wet drops of blood falling from my longsword onto my fists.

I must, I realize, have looked a monstrous sight. I had fathomed out, or thought I had, what had passed here. Delia and her Battle Maidens had struck, and kept their doings close, and somewhere up past that blood-red radiance which vanished from sight ever and anon as I twisted through the labyrinth of columns, up there—yes—Delia? Where was she, what was she doing now? Where her Jikai Vuvushis?

The Sakkora Stones spread over an extensive area, more than I realized; but through smothering vegetation I neared the operations room at the forward edge of the Stones—and Zankov. The battle raged apace, and knowledge of what reserves he could muster would have mightily interested me only a very short time earlier. Now—only reaching Delia obsessed me.

Soon I reached a part of the Stones where recent work had provided roof coverings, imported wooden beams with straw laid across making impromptu roofs. In one chamber a pile of dead lay sprawled in the attitudes of frozen battle. Diffs of various races including Katakis, Jikai Vuvushis at whom I looked with a mingling of quick and useless sympathy and a live and vibrant dread, and clansmen. I passed on and now the sounds of voices raised in anger reached me from beyond a curtaining wall of vegetation. I quickened my steps. I realized with a shock my hands were trembling on the hilt of the Krozair longsword.

The half-lit gloom of the place and the bone-aching sensation of its unfathomable age lent mystery and terror to the Sakkora Stones. I slashed away a tendril that sought to encircle my neck and drag me into an orange gullet, and so put my ear to the green and living wall.

"Keep out of it, mother! It is no concern of yours!"

"You are my daughter and therefore my concern—"

"If Ros pleads for your life, I may grant it."

I knew those three voices. I knew them!

With a vicious and intemperate slash with the longsword I ripped the curtained hangings across. Samphron oil lamps beyond splashed mellow light into a lurid scene. I stepped across the threshold and checked, struggling to focus on what lay beyond.

A further hanging partially obscured my view and, in turn, hid me from those who wrangled so bitterly. Delia—Delia stood there, pale-faced, wrought-up as I could see, unutterably lovely in her russet leathers, bereft of weapons, chained to one of the millennia-old columns of the Sakkora Stones. Facing her—Zankov stood, thin and brittle, alert and alive, his head jutting forward and the sneer of his face like the blow from a whip. At his side, Dayra—Dayra, Delia's daughter and my daughter, Dayra, who would be called Ros the Claw. She wore the wicket stell set of talons now and they glittered in the lampglow. She looked almost bereft of reason, high-colored, frantic, beside herself with a fury she could neither understand nor control.

Delia, Dayra, and Zankov. I stood for perhaps a heart beat, for I saw they did not intend to kill Delia just yet. And the reason for that lay in Delia's spirit, in her refusal to beg or to cringe. She spoke to Dayra as she must have spoken to her in the long ago, when I was banished to Earth.

"Do you know, daughter, who and what this man is? Do you know what he has done?"

"Whatever he has done—he belongs to me!"

"No man and no woman ever belong one to the other, Dayra."

Those words struck through to me with the pain of a white hot iron. I knew Delia spoke the truth; but I could not accept that truth. Perhaps the word "belong" was the wrong word. I could accept another, less final, word. . . .

"My army is now winning a great victory over that onkerish cramph of a husband of yours, majestrix."

So Zankov still spoke to Delia as majestrix. I listened on for a space, wanting the words I hungered for to be spoken.

But Delia just said: "I do not think you will beat him. He is very proud of his new army. He is a man with a stiff neck. I know."

"He is a clansman, is he not? A hairy barbarian savage?" Zankov laughed in his bright, brittle way, most puffed up with his own pride and cleverness. "Then he knows full well the ferocity of the clansmen. They obey me, me! And I am Zankov."

"You call yourself Zankov. But that is not your name. I know who you are, now—"

"Mother!" cried Dayra. She started around, and I saw she trembled.

"Aye, daughter. This man who calls himself Zankov is the son of Nankwi Wellon, the High Kov of Sakwara. And Kov Nankwi has sworn allegiance to the Emperor of Vallia—"

"Son!" shrieked Zankov. "Aye, son. Illegitimate son!"

"So you seek to gain all by slaying all—"

"That is the way of the Hawkwas."

"And if you murder me before the eyes of my daughter, as you murdered her—"

"Enough of this nonsense!" bellowed Zankov and I saw he thus shouted in anger because Dayra did not know he had killed her grandfather. "You will say the words required to pass Ros—Dayra—into my keeping. You will say them, majestrix, if I have to—" Then he paused, and shifted his gaze to Dayra, who stood taut and lovely at his side.

"You had best leave us for a space, Ros. There are things of the bokkertu I must discuss with your mother."

So that was the way of it, then. The mother's agreement and her full acceptance of the bokkertu must be obtained. Even in this, the people of Vallia would not be hoodwinked. So Delia's life was safe for a space yet.

This knowledge did not make me relax as much as the point of a Lohvian arrow. But I did become aware of other people in the partially roofed chamber between the Stones. They stood under a straw-thatched roof supported by twisted beams of raw wood, in a shadowy space, and they watched Zankov and his doings with the bright blood-lusting avidity of a crowd in the Jikhorkdun watching the death-sports of the arena. As I looked at them the whole brilliantly attired group wavered and rippled as though I peered drunkenly at them through a ghostly waterfall. I blinked my eyes. The images slowly refocused and I put my hand up to my neck, just above the rim of the kax, and, lo! an arrow, embedded in the flesh, all unknown to me. I must have got this beauty in one of the fights astride the flutduin.

With a pettish snap I broke it off.

There was no time, now, for shilly-shallying; but my warrior instincts recognized why I had not rushed headlong out into the cleared area. Those cramphs watching so avidly would take a deal of beating. But, beat they had to be, because Dayra was at last leaving the chamber, with a long hungry look back at Zankov and I knew what lay in store for Delia.

"Do not be long, my love," she said.

"Not so long as the time between an axe and death."

I felt a fist constrict around my heart, and then Dayra, looking back, her eyes brilliant, her form tensed, lifted that vicious steel claw. "I shall do as you ask of me, and my Jikai Vuvishis call. But, Zankov, as you love me. I wish to speak with my mother when I return."

His laugh was high, brittle and, at least to me, artificial. But, I could be wrong. "Of course, Ros. She is, after all, your mother whom you love. It is not your father we ask this bokkertu in all legal formality."

"Him!" spat Dayra. "The betraying rast—I would it was him. Then I would stroke him with my claw."

The scene wavered again before my eyes. For a desperate moment ghastly phantasms of the time I had ridden after my daughter Velia rose to rend and torture me. I shut my eyes, pressed down hard, hard, and struggled to regain my senses. When I looked again, Dayra had gone. Now I saw under that partial roofing there were Battle Maidens there, twisted lesten-hide thongs cruelly constricting their limbs. There were four Katakis in the front rank, arrogant, lofty men, with their bladed whiptails flaunted menacingly. Them first, then. . . .

Next to them the two clansmen. . . . They were Zorcanders. No doubt they were witnesses to this bokkertu, the Vovedeers out conducting the battle. And, the sight of Katakis, here, involved in legalities of Vallia gave eloquent testimony to the kind of country Vallia would be if Zankov had his way.

Very carefully I placed the Krozair longsword hilt-up on the stone flagging, leaning against the column. Next to it went six Lohvian arrows. I bent the great Lohvian longbow. Seg believes I can shoot as well as he, although I am not sure; I think even he might nod a tight approval of that six-shot group.

The four Katakis and the two clansmen were flung back by the smashing power of that tremendous bow. The longsword was in my fists and I was leaping forward and, as though the uproar in the chamber was the signal, other men boiled in from the far side, men and Jikai Vuvushis.

Leaping for Zankov, who sprang away with a high screech of sudden fear, I saw Barty Vessler there, splendid, splendid, hacking his way through the ranks of diffs who sought to drag him down. His personal guard fought at his side. He made for Zankov who, attempting to escape me, scrambled into Barty's path.

Men reared before me and there were handstrokes aplenty. Then I was through them or their remains and the Krozair blade bit cleanly through the iron links of the lapping chain. I took Delia into my arms.

She said: "Dayra—"

"I know. Hush."

"There is no time to hush. Give me a weapon, and—"

"Perhaps she truly loves this Zankov, as he her. Perhaps—"

"No, my heart. It is not like that." She pushed me away and bent to retrieve a fallen rapier. As she straightened, her face, incredibly lovely, tautened, and I whirled, sword up.

Barty was in the act of bringing his drexer down on Zankov. Zankov's rapier angled, the light runnelled along the blade, and then the drexer bit into his face. With a demoniac screech he leaped away and the blood poured down that thin and bitter face, painting him like a devil of Cottmer's Caverns.

His face as red with passion as Zankov's was red with blood, Barty bellowed. "Cramph! Seducer! Pray to all your evil gods, for, by Opaz, your time has come!"

I saw it.

Colun Mogper, the Kov of Mursham, sprang up, tall at Barty's back. The dagger in his fist did not glitter, for it was dulled a deep and ominous green. High, Kov Colun raised

A Life for Kregen

the poisoned dagger. With a convulsive effort he brought it down and plunged it deeply into Barty's neck.

His life saved by his ally, Zankov did not hesitate. He ran under the roofing and vanished in shadows. I started after him, and found I was barely moving. The stones of the floor surged up and down under me like a swifter in a gale. I was sitting down. I was the Emperor of Vallia. I could not sit down when the country depended on me. Delia bent to me.

"Stay still, my love. The arrow is deep."

"Zankov . . . Dayra . . . *Barty!*"

She pointed.

Through the ferocious hand-to-hand struggle as Barty's men and the Battle Maidens sought to overthrow Zankov's people a man moved with a purpose I recognized. Clad like a Krozair of Zy, he wielded a great Krozair longsword, and he cut down all those opposed to him as the reaper cuts corn. He carved a path to the far side and ran into the shadows after Zankov.

"There goes our son, Jaidur. He has worked well for Vallia!"

"But—Barty!"

She put her hand on my forehead and it felt like ice against my skin. "Barty Vessler is dead."

I could say nothing. Nothing I could say was of any use.

With a roar as of a volcano exploding the roof broke into a thousand shards, dragged up by hooks hauled up by airboats. Men smashed down, sliding on ropes, men wearing scarlet and yellow, their weapons aflame. I recognized them. The Emperor's Sword Watch. Devoted to the Emperor of Vallia, each one would give his life. They were here to ensure the emperor's safety. And this they would do. But they had come too late for another life. . . .

A life for Vallia had been given, given willingly, but that life was gone, snuffed out, and Barty Vessler would never rush eagerly, honorably and joyously headlong into adventure at my side, not ever again.

"Barty," I said. I just felt stupid. Delia held me.

Korero bellowed at me. "The battle is won! They flee!"

"That," I said. "Is very good, by Zair."

And, as I spoke in a strange stupefied whisper, I saw a glistening red scorpion waddle out contemptuously from under the ancient stones.

ALAN BURT AKERS—the first five great novels of Dray Prescot is The Delian Cycle:

☐ **TRANSIT TO SCORPIO.** The thrilling saga of Prescot of Antares among the wizards and nomads of Kregen. Book I.
(#UY1169—$1.25)

☐ **THE SUNS OF SCORPIO.** Among the colossus-builders and sea raiders of Kregen. Book II. (#UY1191—$1.25)

☐ **WARRIOR OF SCORPIO.** Across the forbidden lands and the cities of madmen and fierce beasts. Book III.
(#UY1212—$1.25)

☐ **SWORDSHIPS OF SCORPIO.** Prescot allies himself with a pirate queen to rescue Vallia's traditional foes! Book IV.
(#UY1231—$1.25)

☐ **PRINCE OF SCORPIO.** Outlaw or crown prince—which was to be the fate of Prescot in the Empire of Vallia? Book V.
(#UY1251—$1.25)

DAW BOOKS are represented by the publishers of Signet and Mentor Books, THE NEW AMERICAN LIBRARY, INC.

THE NEW AMERICAN LIBRARY, INC.,
P.O. Box 999, Bergenfield, New Jersey 07621

Please send me the DAW BOOKS I have checked above. I am enclosing
$_____ (check or money order—no currency or C.O.D.'s).
Please include the list price plus 35¢ per copy to cover handling costs.

Name _____

Address _____

City _____ State _____ Zip Code _____
Please allow at least 4 weeks for delivery